D1539044

TALES FROM THE GUNPOWDER CHRONICLES

A collection of Opium War steampunk novellas

JEANNIE LIN

TALES FROM THE GUNPOWDER CHRONICLES

Print: ISBN: 978-0-9909462-6-7

Copyright © 2019 by Jeannie Lin

All rights reserved.

Cover design by Deranged Doctor Design (www.derangeddoctordesign.com).

No part of this book may be reproduced in any form or by any electronic or mechanical means, including information storage and retrieval systems, without written permission from the author, except for the use of brief quotations in a book review.

For inquiries, please contact Jeannie Lin via the e-mail contact form at www. jeannielin.com.

PART I

Big Trouble in Old Shanghai

Chapter 1

QING DYNASTY CHINA, 1853 A.D.

I startled awake from my slumber, surrounded by cold and darkness. Every muscle within me coiled with fear. *Fight or flight.*

Someone's hand was on my shoulder.

"Ming-fen."

At the sound of my brother's voice, I slumped back down onto my pallet, breathing deep. "Ren. Wh—why are you up?"

"I'm going early to the docks. Perhaps I can find work today."

His voice sounded strained. Work had been scarce over the last month, but there had been nothing for the last three days.

I fumbled around in the dark, feeling for the oil lamp. Our hands collided as he reached the lamp key before me. With a click, the burner ignited and the room was filled with a muted glow.

We lived in a small room large enough to fit two sleeping pallets and little else. There was a single door which also served as our window. We'd kept it propped open last night in hopes of a breeze. In the late summer in Shanghai we were faced with either punishing heat or drenching rain—and often both.

Ren was crouched at the edge of my sleeping pallet, already

dressed. He wore a tunic with sleeves cut away, revealing arms and shoulders tanned dark by endless hours in the sun. His hair was braided into a single, long queue which he coiled loosely around his neck to keep out of the way.

At twenty-five years, Ren had seen and experienced more trials than men twice his age. Though my brother was only four years older than me, the lines of his face spoke of a much harsher life. He'd traveled from one end of the empire to the other, or rather he'd been dragged there at the whim of Manchu administrators.

His face wasn't gaunt, but it was weathered like worn leather. There was no softness in it. What was left was the hard contours of his cheekbones, the jutting point of his chin. My skin was ivory pale by comparison. Sheltered and coddled while my brother had been subjected to forced labor.

His jaw clenched tight now. "There's something I must ask you. I need red cloth."

I rubbed at my eyes. "I'll go to the clothier's shop today," I said, still groggy from sleep. I'd only returned to our dwelling a few hours earlier. My employment kept me up until the late hours of the night faded into morning.

"There's none there. None at the market either. Do they have shops in the foreigner's settlement?"

I was starting to doze off again but jerked awake at the question. My brother waited intently for my response.

"Yes, of course they have shops."

Like most of the inhabitants of Old Shanghai, Ren had never been to the foreign concession. The city had been designated a treaty port after the war with part of the prosperous riverfront handed over to the foreign invaders. Now a wall separated the Northern City from Chinese Shanghai, and the *Yangguizi* controlled who could enter. I had been issued papers due to my job at one of their nightclubs.

"Can you go this morning as early as possible? Buy some red cloth and bring it to me at the docks."

I opened my mouth to tell him it was impossible. We barely had any money and even if we did, the merchants weren't there to sell to Chinese.

"Is this something to do with that lot from Canton?" I asked instead.

He paused before answering. "Yes, the crew from Canton."

With a sigh, I asked him how much he needed, told him I would try. There was no logic to what he was asking for, but I'd try. Shanghai was a fractured city, broken into old and new, Chinese and foreign. All people like Ren and I could do was avoid the jagged edges and find a way to survive.

He slipped out of the compartment shortly after and I could see the sky was already brightening behind him. I sank back onto my pallet and tried to sleep. I could hear the surrounding tenants stirring to begin their day. The East Gate neighborhood where we lived was packed wall to wall with migrants and laborers. On a typical day, I would rest until midday, oblivious to the noise around me as a crowd of men, like Ren, rose to go and seek out jobs early in the morning.

There had always been plenty of work in Shanghai, but lately competition for employment had grown fierce. No matter how hard Ren searched, he came back at the end of the day empty-handed.

I rose after most of the dwellings had emptied and dressed in my day clothes, a faded gray jacket fastened with cloth frogs and a pair of trousers. In the corner hung my green evening dress, woven from silk and embellished with gold thread. That dress was for the Ming-fen of the evening, a hostess who was paid to pour whiskey and light cigars for the foreign merchants and businessmen who frequented the foreign concession. Easier work than loading and unloading cargo from sunup until sundown, and one of the benefits of having been taught *Yingyu* —the English language spoken by the *Yangguizi*.

Out in the courtyard, the communal pump was broken again. Our resident *zágong* was tinkering with the network of pipes. Liu wasn't a municipal worker; he was just someone with a set of tools and a passing knowledge of how to get things to work. If we waited for the city to send someone, we'd all be smelling like pigs and dying of thirst.

Liu was tightening a bolt with his old battered wrench as I approached. He was small in stature and balding on top. It seemed to take all the strength in his arms to tighten the bolt. A collection of copper and iron pipes lay scattered before him on the ground.

"Should be fixed now, Miss Wei," Liu assured. "There was another blockage somewhere. I redirected the flow of water."

The tangled assembly of pipes he'd pieced together over the last two years stood taller than he did.

"Good work, *Zágong*."

I placed the basin beneath the pump and pushed down on the lever. Water started flowing from the spout as well as from the newly added section of pipe. The thin spray hit Liu in the eye and I pressed my lips together to keep from laughing.

"Need to tighten that a little more," Liu muttered, lifting his wrench again.

Out of the corner of my eye I spied two men sauntering into the courtyard. Men who didn't belong.

Liu had seen them as well. He ducked his head a fraction lower, focusing intently on the pipe joint. I straightened to face the two interlopers, keeping my expression blank as they approached. The taller of the two had a small scar below his eye. I immediately marked him as the leader. His partner had a thicker build and a darting gaze that made a point of targeting each inhabitant who remained in the courtyard.

"Where's Ren?" the scarred one asked.

"Ren isn't here," I said evenly, keeping my gaze fixed on them.

I didn't recognize their faces, but I knew who they were aligned with. In Old Shanghai, every bridge and tunnel had a gang. We'd been hearing much lately about the Canton faction.

The magistrate's office had arrested fourteen of them for banditry several weeks ago only to have *Taotai* Wu release them the next day.

Beside me, Liu kept on working, giving the bolt more attention than any bolt in Shanghai. I made note of where he held the wrench as I conversed with the two strangers. I'd left my daggers in the apartment, not that I should need them. If they knew of my brother, they would know of me as well. And Ren would have told me if he was in any trouble. If there was anyone I needed to be wary of.

"Another time, then." The two lingered in the courtyard just to make sure their presence was known before sauntering out.

"All done, Miss Wei." Sweat beaded on Liu's forehead and his hands trembled as he bent to gather his pipes.

"Thank you, *Zǎgong.*"

I meant it in more ways than one. Liu may have remained quiet, but he hadn't left me. As I returned to our stoop with the basin of water, Auntie Ma held out a rice cake from her basket. She didn't live in our compound, but she diligently made rounds through the quarter with her food basket every morning.

"It's a good thing they respect you and your brother," she said.

I accepted the rice cake, tucking it into my pocket, and thanked her humbly.

When I reached our dwelling, I immediately set the basin down on the stool outside and went to retrieve my daggers. Numerous factions and gangs had formed in Old Shanghai to support and protect their own. It was often their influence that determined whether someone was given work or not at the docks or on other projects throughout the city. Usually the gangs avoided fighting amongst themselves, but over the last month, it seemed several large factions were consolidating power. I only knew of this from the bits of gossip Ren had fed me.

The gangs were known to train in martial arts. It was part of their mystique and identity. For Ren and me, our training was part of a long tradition that had started with our parents. We maintained our skills now for defense, but also to keep Mother and Father's memory with us. Unfortunately, our skills had given us a reputation in this small corner of Old Shanghai.

The daggers I wielded were not the kind used by workmen. The weapons were fashioned from two steel plates and had been shaped with curved indentations on either side to serve as hand-holds. The tips were sharpened to a point for the purpose of stabbing or piercing. What made the weapon unique was how the daggers were linked together by a length of silk cord, turning the two blades into a rope dart. The cord allowed me to shoot the daggers out as projectiles, trap an opponent, or strike from a distance.

I tucked the rope dart with the two daggers into the waist of my trousers, hiding the weapons beneath my jacket so they remained within easy reach. This strange business with the red cloth and the unexpected visit by the Canton faction made me think our reputation alone was not going to keep us safe for long.

Ren and I preferred to stay out of trouble. We had refused membership in the gangs, which could be the reason Ren had been barricaded from jobs at the dock. I needed to confront him about this. Ren was keeping something from me.

After washing up, I coiled and pinned my hair before heading out through the streets. Auntie Ma's rice cake was still in my pocket. I bit into it, tasting the red bean paste filling. It was gone in two bites.

A crowd was already gathering in the East Gate market-place. Vendors squatted over baskets of fish cakes and turtles, arguing prices down to the last *wen*.

There was a series of posters in red and black pasted on the side of a walkway. It was the same design, posted one after another.

Shanghai will be as secure as the Great Wall.

The posters stood as tall as a man and the city had plastered them all over the market.

The slogan was referring to the official proclamation that Shanghai would raise a militia to protect the city against rebels. Though *Taotai* Wu was offering a generous salary to all who enlisted, Ren never considered it.

The street gangs and sects battled for influence in Shanghai, but they all had a common foe. It was the Manchu government that conscripted our people into labor camps, not any short-haired rebels. People disappeared into the Emperor's factories and mines, never to return. Anyone who dared to question the practice tended to disappear as well.

It was very easy to have a person declared a traitor and sent away. I knew this all too well. In Old Shanghai, it was our group loyalties that kept us from disappearing.

I had to walk through the North Gate in order to reach the foreign concession. A bridge led from Old Shanghai to the settlement checkpoint, which was a heavy iron gate guarded by *Yangguizi*. The guards had changed shifts since I'd left the concession earlier that morning.

I handed my work permit to the new guard on duty. I didn't recognize him. Lately there were many new faces among the guardsmen. This one's hair was brown with a reddish tint and his face freckled with spots. He looked at the papers for a long time.

"A bit early for work here, aren't you Miss?"

I blinked at him. "I work at the Dragon's Den."

"Yes, but it's a bit early for that." He spoke slower and louder.

"I work at the Dragon's Den," I repeated, keeping my expression blank. "Sing-song girl."

I opened my eyes wide and smiled prettily. The ladies of the missionary school would go into a fit if they knew this was how I was using their lessons. I was capable of arguing at length with the guardsmen, but this approach was usually easier.

The brown-haired guardsman surrendered and decided I was harmless enough to let through the gate.

The concession was an entirely different place during the day. In the nighttime, under the glow of gas lamps, Nanking Road could pass for any other bustling Shanghai corridor with its drinking houses and gentleman's clubs. In the morning light, the streets were unquestionably foreign. The storefronts were too quiet, for one. The wealthy foreign businessmen appeared to still be asleep. They would start to stir when the great clock sounded the eighth hour. The days at the missionary school had been like that; set by the chime of a clock.

The only activity here this early was along the river, with men loading and unloading cargo. An airship spouted steam as it lifted off from the dock on the far bank, the white sails unfurling like the clouds. Western airships were only allowed to dock at this treaty port as well as a few other designated ones along our coast. It was an uneasy agreement. If an airship were to stray inland, the Emperor's army had the authority to shoot it down, but it was authority on paper only. The Emperor's cannons had failed to keep the airships and steam destroyers from invading our ports ten years ago.

These docks were worked by both Chinese and foreign laborers. I'd considered trying to get Ren a job here, but it would harm his chances of ever getting work in Old Shanghai again. It really was a fractured city, broken and then broken again.

I turned away from the docks to seek out the Grand Hotel, which was the tallest building in the concession. The shop I was looking for would be nearby. The owner was a frequent patron of the Dragon's Den.

It was easy to find. The place was large, twice as large as the shops in our marketplace. It was built in the Western style with a large glass window out front to show off the wares. Burton's Mercantile was painted in bold letters on a sign over the door.

A pale-looking young man stood beside the counter, broom

in hand. He looked up as I entered and immediately the corners of his mouth turned downward. "We don't sell to Chinese," he said in English.

I ignored him and moved into the shop. "Mister Burton, please."

"No...sell to Chinese...here."

He made some undecipherable gestures that were meant to illustrate his intent. I took a deep breath, gathering patience. No need for direct conflict if conflict could be avoided. Better to deflect.

"Mister Burton, please," I said again.

A large man dressed in a dark suit emerged through a beaded curtain at the back of the shop. I'd become accustomed to the yellow-haired, blue-eyed strangers from the nights at the club so the sight of them no longer startled me, but they were still a curiosity. Eyes like the sky.

I'd only seen Dean Burton at the club and had served as hostess for his parties more than once. Though we had always been cordial to one another, I wondered how he would behave outside those boundaries.

He appeared more formal outside of the club, wearing a stiff-looking suit jacket that fit tightly over his arms and shoulders with a tidy row of buttons at the front. It must be suffocating—all those layers of cloth and fastenings. Men dressed that way even when they were said to be relaxing with drinks in hand.

"Miss Wei, what a pleasant surprise." He looked puzzled to see me.

He gave my plain clothing a quick glance, then looked away. He was accustomed to seeing me in silk and pearls. Sing-song girls were like paper lanterns. Lit up at night to please the eye. Invisible during the day.

The clerk was immediately at his boss's elbow. "The woman doesn't seem to understand we don't sell to Chinese here."

"Percy, you should know Miss Wei speaks English as well as

you and I." Burton turned to me, smiling. "Six years at the missionary school, right?"

I gave him a nod. "You have a good memory, Mister Burton."

Six years of learning proper English behind a school desk, followed by a more practical education gained by observing foreigners at the Dragon's Den. Much of my secondary education wouldn't be considered proper.

"There will be talk," Percy muttered.

Burton took hold of the man's elbow and steered him to the back of the shop. Though they spoke in lowered tones, I could hear the sharpness of Burton's rebuke.

Out of politeness, I let my gaze wander to the shelves. There was a stack of red tins on one shelf with white lettering. *COFFEE.* The shelf was filled with other intriguing and exotic items. Biscuit tins and jars of oils and ointments. At the school, I'd learned the *Yangguizi* had come on ships from an island nation in the West. They were ruled by a queen and for centuries had drunk tea from our plantations.

Burton claimed to trade in tea and silk, purchasing the goods here in Shanghai and transporting them back to his country to sell. It seemed he did the reverse here, selling Western goods to the foreigners in the settlement. I turned my attention back to him.

"There's certainly no law against her being here," he was saying, smiling at me in a white flash of teeth.

The clerk, or Percy as he was called, ducked to the far corner of the shop and made a show of rearranging cans. Burton came to me and I was stricken by his height and the broadness of his shoulders. Burton appeared much larger when he wasn't seated.

"How can I help you, Miss Wei?"

"I am looking for red cloth."

"Red symbolizes good luck for the Chinese, doesn't it?" He moved to the far wall, stretching up to reach the top shelf.

"Yes, a very lucky color." I didn't smile at him as I might at the club. I was hoping to make this purchase quickly and return to the city. Ren would be waiting for me.

Burton set two bolts onto the counter and I let out a sigh in relief.

"I don't have much in red," he apologized. "Perhaps one of these."

I ran my hands across both, sliding the material between my fingertips.

"Fifteen *wen* a meter for the linen. Twenty per meter for the silk."

"So expensive."

This was one's immediate response in Shanghai upon being told a price. *Any* price. But it really was expensive. I could get it in the city for half that amount.

"It's very high-quality material. Purchased from a highly respected factory in Shanghai."

"To sell it back at twice the price? It is as if you English came here to steal from us."

Burton looked taken aback and Percy grunted from his spot by the shelves. I did give him my smile now.

"Eight for the linen," I proposed. "Which is still too much."

"Ten. And you can have the silk." His grin was back. "You did come all the way here for it, after all."

He had me on that point. I'd asked at the marketplace and Ren was right. There wasn't any red cloth left in the Chinese city, not a scrap.

"Mister Burton is most generous," I conceded.

I watched his hands as he smoothed out the cloth, measuring out exactly one meter. He produced a pair of metal shears and began cutting.

"You bargain like Chinese," I remarked.

His head remained down, focused on the work. "I'll take that as a compliment."

When he was done, he folded the cloth neatly and set it

before me while I placed the coins onto the counter beside it. It was strange for me to be exchanging money directly with Burton. At the club, we carried on with the pretense our interaction was purely social.

"I'm American, by the way," Burton corrected. "Not English."

I frowned, making a face. "You all look the same."

He started to reply but stopped when the ground lurched forward. I stumbled, grabbing onto the counter as the shelves around us began to shake with a violence that set my pulse racing.

"Earthquake," Burton breathed. There was one loud clang after another as the tins on the shelf toppled onto the floor. I could hear the crash of pottery in the back room.

When the rumbling finally quieted, I was still clutching onto the counter. Percy stood in the corner, eyes wide as a fallen can rolled by his feet. It was the only movement in the tense stillness.

Burton whistled. "That was stronger than the last one."

My breath rattled in my throat. I glanced around warily, waiting for the shaking to resume. Burton reached out to place a steadying hand against my arm. "Are you all right, Miss Wei?"

His touch startled me. I nodded and let go of the counter, letting my arm slip away from the contact. My heart pounded, and my knees trembled when I tried to take a step. Most of the goods had toppled from the shelves to cover the floor.

"That's three in two days," Percy noted.

"Earthquakes tend to happen close together, one tremor setting off another. I read a paper about it," Burton replied absently. "Is this area known for earthquakes?"

The last part must have been intended for me. I shook my head, admitting I didn't know. Before this year, I'd never felt the ground move before. In the last few months, it seemed the earth couldn't remain still.

"I should go," I said, voice shaking.

It wasn't just the earthquake, which was frightening enough. There was a sick feeling growing in the pit of my stomach.

Stepping past biscuit tins and broken glass, I reached out and fumbled with the door before it would let me out onto the street. I hurried back toward the bridge.

"Miss Wei," Burton called down the street to me. I turned to see he'd come out of his shop. "Are you certain you don't need an escort?"

I stared at him in disbelief. A foreigner like him was less welcome in Old Shanghai than I was welcome here. "It's not necessary. Thank you."

He remained standing in the doorway, a commanding presence in his dark suit with one hand braced against the frame. His mouth opened as if he meant to say something, but he decided against it.

"Be careful, Miss Wei," he said finally.

I nodded, raising my hand to wave. It was a Western gesture of farewell that seemed misplaced in the moment.

Burton frowned and returned the wave stiffly.

It was past time to go. As I hurried toward the bridge, another tremor rippled through the ground beneath my feet. This tremor was a mild one but served as a warning nonetheless.

Shanghai was like a pot ready to boil over. Something was happening to the city.

Chapter 2

The bridge between Old Shanghai and the foreign concession was now crowded with foot traffic. Laborers were making their daily trek into the settlement while I walked in the opposite direction back toward the city.

I had just cleared the bridge when the earth tilted again and I stumbled to the ground. A sound like the roar of thunder filled the air. I could hear startled screams around me and I realized the rattling sound was coming from the buildings. Wooden beams strained and cracked. Stone fell away from the walls in chunks.

I threw my arms over my head as brick and dust rained down around me. My pulse pounded and my ears rang with it. The shaking continued, longer and more violent than any of the other ones we'd experienced. There was something different about this quake and I sent a silent prayer to the Eternal Mother.

After the ground stilled, I gradually pulled myself to my feet. Others around me also rose from crouched positions and looked about, surveying the damage. Confusion and fear reigned over the crowd.

I forced myself to take a deep breath and then another. Years of training prevailed and a veil of calm finally wrapped itself around me.

Ren would be waiting by the docks for the red cloth he'd asked for. He hadn't explained what it was for other than it had something to do with the Canton faction. I suspected they were the ones keeping him out of work.

I passed by another poster plastered onto the entrance of an alleyway. *Shanghai needs your service! All recruits will be generously paid!* the poster claimed.

The earthquake had turned the familiar streets into a maze. Walls had been ripped apart into piles of rubble. Carts were overturned. I watched the inhabitants of Old Shanghai wandering through the lanes like ants, frenzied and at a loss for what to do next.

I'd heard rumors about the earthquakes that had plagued our countryside this year, but I didn't know what to believe. The first tremors were enough to start people talking. Then the tremors had become more intense. Two days ago, several families had packed up their belongings and left abruptly. I had dismissed it as superstition—it was common folk belief earthquakes were a sign of ill omen.

A brigade of the newly-formed Shanghai militia marched down the street and I stepped aside to avoid being trampled. "Get inside," the men shouted. "Go to your homes and stay off the streets."

I watched in a daze as the building before me suddenly ignited. A curtain of flame spread over the side of the building. The roar of it sounded like a gust of wind as the fire sucked oxygen into its depths. An overwhelming scent of sulfur clogged my nose and throat. When I tried to breathe, smoke coated my tongue.

Suddenly a large shadow passed overhead. The airship centered itself over the burning building and poured a torrent of water onto the flames. The fire crew had dispatched their airship though it might have been too late. The flames continued to climb. Right before the building was entirely engulfed, I read the characters on the signboard.

It was a gunpowder depot. Gunpowder was heavily regulated and taxed. There were several stores throughout Old Shanghai responsible for the distribution of the fuel. Gunpowder depots were all made of stone to reduce the risk of fire, yet this one was engulfed in flame.

I started running faster, pushing hard toward the East Gate. As I passed the magistrate's office, I saw two guards stationed outside. What happened next, I couldn't explain. The two guards reached into the front of their tunics. Each of them pulled out a blood-red sash.

They tied the sashes to their waists before pulling long knives from their sleeves and disappearing inside the building. What had I just witnessed? Should I scream for help? Report to the *taotai's* offices? I stared at the red silk clutched in my hands.

The red cloth was some sort of sign, but a sign of what?

There was no one stationed at the East Gate. I passed through and was met with a view of the river. The dock was teaming with laborers who were still at work unloading cargo from the ships. I searched through the crowd for Ren.

I found my brother standing by one of the weigh stations. He hadn't joined a work crew. Instead he was looking out over the water.

"Ren," I called out, running to him. "Something is happening. We need to get back—"

He turned to face me. "Ming-fen." His response was quiet. Too quiet. "Did you find it?"

Ren stood a head taller than me, his body broad and muscled from years of labor.

I held out the silk to him. "I found cloth in the foreign concession, just as you said."

He stared at the length of silk for a long moment before unsheathing a dagger from his belt. Taking the silk in hand, he slid the sharp blade into the center of it and used his hands to rend the cloth in two. He thrust one half back into my hands.

"Keep this," he said grimly. His eyes were dark and distant.

People said we looked alike, my brother and me. Maybe we had, as children, but after we'd been separated I could no longer see the resemblance. I'd gone to an orphanage and then the missionary school. Ren had been sent to the factories deep in the southern provinces. When he'd returned to find me, I'd barely recognized him. His face was the same but he appeared different—the light in his eyes had changed. We'd spent the last decade rediscovering one another.

What I saw in him at the moment frightened me. It was times like this when he was a stranger to me and not the brother who shared my flesh and blood.

The shadow of the fire crew's airship passed over us as it returned to the river. It positioned itself over the deepest part before lowering a siphon and pump.

"What's happening, Ren?"

He turned away from me to stare at the airship. Suddenly, I felt a shift, a ripple of will and intention that resonated throughout the waterfront from one man to the next. I'd felt the same sense of unease and anticipation in the streets. This energy had been building throughout the city for days, I just hadn't realized it until now.

"Keep that cloth with you, *Mèimei*."

Little Sister. It had been years since he'd called me that.

The boom of a cannon shattered the air. I ducked down instinctively, throwing myself onto the ground. Another shot exploded above us, making my ears ring. I clamped my hands over my ears and peered up to see smoke billowing from the hull of the airship. It tottered precariously over the river before the bow dipped downward.

With my heart in my throat, I watched the vessel plummet into the river. The impact sent waves crashing onto the dock.

Someone had gunned down a municipal airship.

My brother remained standing beside me. He hadn't flinched.

"Shanghai is under attack," I said in disbelief.

Ren nodded slowly as he lifted the torn strip of cloth. He reached up to tie it around his forehead, securing the knot in back. Then he unsheathed the dagger once more. He took hold of his queue and wrapped the long braid around his hand once, twice.

"No, Ren—"

With one motion Ren cut through his queue, the sign of loyalty to the Emperor. Tears stung in my eyes.

"Go home," he commanded. He let the queue fall to the ground and drew his second dagger.

Wielding the blades openly in Shanghai was outlawed, but that's what Ren was, now and forever—an outlaw.

I shook my head. Words had left me, even the simple ones. When? Why?

We'd vowed to be loyal to no one but each other. To stay out of the trouble stirring around us.

"Go home immediately, Ming-fen," he repeated. "Block the door and stay inside. We don't want any more bloodshed than necessary."

Ren stood like a wall before me, brandishing his daggers with shoulders squared to challenge the world. I knew he was skilled with the blades. We'd trained together as children and resumed after being reunited. For the first time, Ren held the daggers as if he was ready to kill. Behind him, the wreckage of the airship lay half sunken in the river, consumed by fire. I took one final look at my brother. Then I slowly backed away from the man who was lost to me, the one I no longer knew.

Chapter 3

I slid the rope dart into my hand to have it ready. The blades were easy to hide in my palm, as small as they were. The strip of red silk was still clutched in my other hand. I couldn't bring myself to tie the cloth around my arm. It was the symbol for a rebellion I wanted no part of.

Gongs sounded as I wove through the streets. More buildings had collapsed, scourged by fire. Another brigade rushed by me, each equipped with black powder rifles. My stomach sickened thinking of Ren and his twin daggers facing off against such firepower.

The recruitment posters proclaiming *Shanghai would be as secure as the Great Wall* had been torn into shreds. Someone had scrawled a symbol over the scraps that remained. It was a crude drawing of two crossed blades—the Small Swords Society. It was a newer group rumored to be made of the lot from Canton as well as several other gangs. When had Ren decided to join with them? Why hadn't he told me?

The next brigade I passed all had red bands tied around their arms. There was no way to know who was loyal to what. I just needed to get home and stay away from the streets. Maybe Ren would come home when this was all over.

A lump formed in my throat. Why was I being so naive? Rebellion only ended in bloodshed.

We had lost our parents to another uprising many years ago against the Emperor and the Manchu government. Mother and Father hadn't been directly involved, but they'd been marked as enemies of the state and marched off to the labor camps. That was the last time I'd ever seen them: heads bowed, hands and feet clamped in chains.

By the time I reached the marketplace, the vendors had scattered. Empty carts were left abandoned in the streets and produce had been trampled into the dirt. It had become a market for ghosts.

I was crossing the center when another explosion shook the ground. The force of it knocked me back and I crawled behind one of the empty stalls, crouching low to try to find cover.

This time, the tremors were not caused by any earthquake. The blast was coming from just below the marketplace. Another explosion split the air and a shower of dust and gravel rained down.

When I peered over the stall, the shops on the other side of the lane lay in splinters. Something stirred beneath the debris and I started forward, thinking someone was trapped beneath. Before I could reach the wreckage, there was more movement from underneath. The entire heap shifted as hands emerged to push away the broken wood and beams.

One by one, the figures climbed up through the debris to assemble in the abandoned market. Each one of them held weapons in their hands, from firearms to pikes and clubs. I lost count of them—there were nearly a hundred by my guess. And every person had a jagged strip of red cloth tied onto them.

These were the infamous Heaven and Earth rebels who were ravaging the countryside. They were a part of the rebellion along with the Small Swords sect. I crouched low, waiting for the invaders to move on, but as their numbers continued to grow, fear took over. I had to get as far away as possible.

I retreated toward an alleyway, crawling from stall to stall to remain hidden. As I crept through the marketplace, I heard the heavy clang of metal against the stone street. It was followed by another clang, then another. There was a familiar cadence to the sounds—they were footsteps.

"The scouts missed someone," came a man's voice.

I froze, sending a silent prayer to the Eternal Mother. My hand tightened over the blades. I could strike first, take out one or two, but in the end, it would do me no good. I was one against a hundred. Two daggers wouldn't save me.

"Come out." This time it was a woman's voice, ringing with command.

I took a deep breath and rose to find a sea of faces looking at me. There were men and women, young and old.

The crowd parted and the metal footsteps rang out once more. A woman emerged dressed in battle armor. She towered over the rest of them and, on first glance, I assumed she was wearing an armored pair of boots that made her unnaturally tall. As the woman came closer, I could see the lattice of metal-work and wire coiled around her lower legs and feet. The contraption moved with her, a set of springs absorbing the weight of each step.

Within the intricate metalwork, I could see a pair of tiny shoes embroidered with red flowers. She walked on lotus feet bound since childhood. It was a sign of status and refinement among more distinguished families.

"What should we do with her, Lady Su?"

It was another woman who spoke. She raised her rifle to aim squarely at my chest and my heart all but stopped. I struggled to find the words to explain myself, but my throat had constricted with fear.

"Leave her." The armored lady continued forward and glanced down at the red cloth twined around my fingers. "She's sympathetic to our cause. You won't tell anyone we're here, will you, *Mèimei?*"

I closed my eyes, the hitch in my chest like a wound. The way she called me "Little Sister" reminded me too much of Ren. What would we do if my brother were still here by my side?

We could have fought and died together. How useless was that?

I opened my eyes and looked up at the Commander. Lady Su's lips curved into a slow smile as her black eyes pierced into me. I shook my head, no. Who would I tell? The city authority had been crippled from inside. The docks had already fallen, taken over by the laborers who worked them day in and day out. Even my own brother had joined the rebels.

"I won't tell anyone," I echoed tonelessly. "The city is yours."

Lady Su searched my face with a steady, unreadable expression. "Do you wish to join us?"

From what I knew of the Heaven and Earth Society, they'd started as a band of dissidents in the south made up of miners and laborers who were conscripted into the Emperor's factories. The rebel army would sweep through village after village, conscripting new recruits with each victory. They forced men and women into their service. Other rebellions joined their cause. Soon, what had started as a scattering of rain became a raging storm.

It was said the Heaven and Earth rebels had raised an army of hundreds of thousands of men and women. That was what we'd heard from the comfort of Shanghai, behind our stone walls and cannons. Then the rebels took one city after another. Cities with walls and with cannons. With armed brigades.

We'd heard whisperings all summer about a potential attack, but Shanghai, for all its glory, was a broken city threaded together by a string of coalitions and co-agreements. The *taotai* did not have complete control of the city in order to mount a proper defense. How could he when the devil *Yangguizi* had carved out the northern part of the city and moved in their own armed forces?

If Ren had told me what he was planning, what would I have done? Would I have joined these rebels as well? I had no love for the Emperor, but I had no wish to fight him. The machines of war left everyone hungry except gravediggers. I knew this lesson, in my flesh and bone.

"I just want to go home," I told the Commander.

I could feel Lady Su's gaze on me, assessing whether I was a threat if they released me.

"She is free to go," Lady Su declared before turning to address her soldiers. The gears in her mechanized boots whirred as she moved. "Find *Taotai* Wu. See if the others have detained him."

I took a step, waiting for someone to challenge me. When no one did, I broke into a run again, fleeing from the marketplace. With a sinking feeling, I realized if the invaders had come here, then nearby Nanking had likely already fallen. Would Peking be next?

All of this was useless to ponder over now. In Shanghai, we did not look up, we did not look out. It was a city in pieces, fused back together, and we preferred to live in our pretty part of the mosaic. Shanghai never had a chance.

IT WAS my own failing that I hadn't seen what was developing. The foreigners were right before us, shipping in opium and kidnapping laborers against their will. Ren would say I was too focused on what was happening in the foreign concession and not what was happening in our streets.

It wasn't what was happening in the streets that I had missed. I had failed to see how much Ren had changed.

My last memory of him plagued me as I rushed through the streets. Ren's cold stare as he tied the strip of red cloth around his forehead and cut off his queue. He must have made the decision long ago. All those moments over the last days when my brother had suddenly gone quiet, suddenly gone cold with me. He'd already been gone.

Once I was clear of the market, I was close to my neighborhood. I used the back streets, favoring blind pockets and alleyways whenever possible to navigate a path home. As I passed over the last bridge, I spied what looked like a gentleman's top hat underneath the span of it.

It was a *Yangguizi* and not just any Westerner. It was Dean Burton. What was that devil doing in Old Shanghai?

He was pressed against the base of the bridge, but poked his head out to look for someone. He appeared relaxed, with a hand in the pocket of his long frock coat. It was a uniquely Western habit I'd come to recognize—resting one's hands in a pocket. At first, I'd thought it to be a deterrent against pickpockets, but apparently, it wasn't. Burton had laughed when I asked about it at the Dragon's Den.

Apparently, he found me very amusing.

At the moment, I found him to be the least amusing thing in the world.

I swung my legs over the bridge and landed on the side of the canal. Burton turned abruptly and his hand tightened on something inside his pocket. The moment he saw it was me, he relaxed and let his hand slip to his side.

He had a weapon inside his coat. A gun.

"Miss Wei—"

I shoved him with both hands until he was hidden in the shadows. "Mister Burton, you should not be here."

"Miss Wei, *you* shouldn't be here." Burton looked similarly vexed at the sight of me. But I at least looked like I belonged in this part of the city.

Along with the long coat, Burton had also put on a black top hat which added to his already glaringly noticeable height. It had been less than two hours since we'd seen each other last. He must have left the concession shortly after I had.

"It's the Heaven and Earth rebels," I told him.

"I know. I'm here to help—"

"How could you possibly help?"

We hushed as several dock workers passed above. I listened to their voices, but none were familiar to me.

"How many are there?" Burton asked once the group had passed on.

"I don't know. Too many."

Considering there was no red cloth to be found in Old Shanghai, there could be hundreds of sympathizers within the city alone.

"I suspected something was happening with those earthquakes," he replied. "I'm supposed to meet someone here."

He peeked out again, looking left and right. With his pale skin and ridiculous hat, he was so conspicuous it hurt my eyes. I took the hat and tossed it deep into the shadows, ignoring his bark of protest. It was probably very expensive.

"These rebels do not like foreigners," I told him sharply. "Old Shanghai doesn't like foreigners."

"This is very important business. My guide was to meet me here."

"How did you even get into the city?"

"I know people." He met my gaze steadily, blinked once, and said no more.

Of course. Dean Burton was a wealthy businessman. All doors in Shanghai were open to a man with the right bribe.

"Everything will be fine if we can take care of this quickly. This may even keep matters from getting worse."

Burton spoke in a soothing tone, with a hint of patronization that made me narrow my eyes at him. Perhaps he was so calm because it wasn't his part of the city burning down.

I started to ask Burton what sort of business he was involved in, but a gunpowder rickshaw chugged onto the bridge above, settling down in a puff of black smoke.

The rickshaw was fitted with a bicycle in front and a carriage for passengers in back. The driver at the pedals was a thin, cricket-like man in thick spectacles. He wouldn't have had the strength to pedal the transport all day, but the chain drive and gears were fitted to a gunpowder engine. Once ignited, the rickshaw practically propelled itself with the slightest effort on the pedals.

Burton started out from beneath the bridge and I tried to pull him back. He looked over his shoulder at me. "It's all right. Trust me."

I followed reluctantly behind him as he climbed up from the canal. I felt responsible for Burton. He was in my neighborhood and so clearly out of his element. If a Westerner was harmed in Old Shanghai, it would only make things worse. There would be war between the foreign brigades as well as the rebel army.

"Sir." The driver bowed at the waist in greeting.

Burton switched from English to the Canton dialect. "Old Wong, we will need to take this lady to safety before we pick up the package."

The driver gave me a sideways glance. "Yes, of course, sir. But we should go quickly. Where is the package located?"

"Wong is a longtime associate of mine," Burton explained, switching back to English. "There is enough room to seat two of us in here."

Why the choice to address me in his Western tongue? Perhaps it was habit—it was how we had always conversed in the concession. Over Burton's shoulder, I could see Wong watching us intently.

Burton invited me forward with a wave of his hand. Ladies first, another Western convention. It occurred to me that Burton assumed he was protecting me, just as I assumed I was protecting him.

As Wong stood from the pedals to help me onto the rickshaw, I caught the flash of red beneath his jacket.

I halted. "Mister Burton," I remarked in English. "Your rickshaw driver is part of the rebellion."

Wong's gaze darted toward me. From the glimmer in his eyes, I knew he understood me perfectly well. I backed away, grabbing onto Burton's arm to drag him with me. "Run."

"Come out here!" Wong shouted to someone unseen. "They're escaping."

We made it to the end of the nearby alley only to have a youth of perhaps sixteen years drop into our path. He wore a red sash tied around his waist and brandished a long knife, one of the marks of the Small Swords sect. I still had my steel daggers hidden in my palm. I took aim, ready to launch an attack—only to be wrenched back.

Burton had his giant hand on my shoulder. "Stay back," he commanded, shoving me behind him.

Cursed Western chivalry.

There was no safety behind him. Another youth had appeared, also armed with a long knife. This one was taller and broader than the youth at the end of the alley. The rickshaw driver Wong stood back to watch the fight. Though Wong's arms and legs were like sticks, that didn't mean he wasn't dangerous. I kept the old man in the corner of my eye as the second assailant closed the distance between us.

There was hesitation in the boy's step. I took a dagger in each hand, the curved shape fitting into my palms. The silk cord dangled between them. Few opponents knew how to defend against a rope dart. There were too many angles of attack to guard against.

The youth pointed his knife at me, his grip overly tight. I could see his hand trembling.

Behind me, I could hear the sounds of scuffling as Burton fought against his attacker. Each of my heartbeats sounded like thunder, and a rush of blood and heat seared through me.

I let the dagger in my right hand drop down, its weight pulling the silk rope across my hand to create tension. At the other end of the rope was the other dagger, the two ends serving as weight and counterweight. Many of Shanghai's gangs carried weapons merely to intimidate, but rarely used them. I carried mine for use.

I advanced, stepping past the long blade to sling the rope around my opponent's wrist. With a quick jerk, I reeled him in and struck at his throat with the edge of my palm.

I pulled the dagger back into my grasp as the attacker doubled over. I turned to see Burton punching his opponent's already bloodied face. The youth dropped to the ground and stayed down.

Burton straightened and turned to me, his eyes growing wide in alarm. Wong had moved from his rickshaw. The old man drew a pistol and aimed it at Burton.

Because of course Burton was the dangerous one between us.

"Stop," Wong demanded.

I dropped my dagger again, this time letting the rope slide down near the ground. Catching the silk with my foot, I looped it and sent the dagger shooting out at Wong. A snake striking at prey.

The steel weight struck against the bones of the old man's hand. Wong cried out and dropped the firearm.

A sharp tug on the rope brought the dagger back to me.

All three of our assailants were down around us. I made sure before turning to face Burton.

"Where did you learn that?" he asked, astonished.

It was, as the *Yangguizi* liked to say, a long story. I grabbed onto his arm and dragged him away from the alley.

"Missionary school," I replied.

Chapter 4

O ld Shanghai cleared quickly, leaving only the rebels out on the streets. Anyone we encountered was marked by a red sash tied around their waist or arm. The rebels had formed into patrols to scour the city.

"Bring out the *taotai*!" the parade shouted. "Bring out the coward. Bring out *Taotai* Wu."

We ducked into the alleyway to avoid them. It was unlikely they would let me pass peacefully now that I had a large, pale-skinned *Yangguizi* by my side.

I held my breath as the mob came closer. Burton pressed himself against the brick wall beside me as the parade marched by. His yellow hair fell disobediently over his forehead.

Only when the footsteps faded did we dare to speak.

"Are you all right, Miss Wei?" Burton asked.

"What made you so stupid to come out here?" I demanded.

He stared at me, jaw dropped open. I'd never said a harsh word to him over whiskey and cigars.

"These men are killers," I said. "They'll kill you."

Burton let out a long breath. "I know who they are. The Heaven and Earth rebels have been terrorizing the countryside."

"And others too. The street gangs of Old Shanghai—they've joined the uprising."

"Which ones?"

What did he know or care of the local sects of Old Shanghai? It pained me to think of Ren's place in all this. It should have been my brother and I together. We'd hide away, wait for the right time to make our escape.

"Which street gangs?" Burton asked again. "Who are these men?"

I looked up to see the foreigner watching me, the blue of his eyes startling in their sharpness.

"The Small Swords and...and I think there must be more. The factions from Canton, Fujian."

There were too many to account for.

The various sects had come from different regions to find work in Shanghai. They'd banded together due to a common origin and language. There were unspoken boundaries between the factions that were observed and respected. Somewhere between the magistrate's arrests and the *taotai*'s attempt to militarize his police force, the gangs had united into something greater.

And they'd dragged my brother in.

"We've been hearing of the Small Swords for months, but no one was certain who they were," I explained.

Though there were many weapons used by the rebels, the ones from Old Shanghai seemed to prefer the long knives our attackers had used.

"The Small Swords," Burton echoed thoughtfully. "What do they want?"

"I don't know."

I pressed a hand over my eyes. *Ren.* Ren had grown angry at the Emperor. At the forced labor camps and factories.

"The Heaven and Earth rebels want to proclaim their own kingdom," Burton offered. "And destroy whatever is old and traditional in the process. Uprisings are not always so coherent."

I opened my eyes to see him probing at a cut in his coat sleeve. The heavy material had been sliced open, but the blade had failed to draw blood.

"You were lucky."

He regarded me with a faint smile. "Stupid and lucky. What side do you belong to, Miss Wei?"

I shook my head wearily. "There are no 'sides' in Shanghai, Mister Burton."

Or there were too many sides.

The foreigner had some knowledge of Old Shanghai and its many sects, but his understanding was incomplete.

My parents had been part of a secret sect centered around meditation and Buddhist prayer, the worship of the Eternal Mother. The order had existed for centuries, since the Han Chinese had fallen to the barbarian Manchu army. Its members trained in order to band together and defend one another against the abuses of the Manchu government.

There had been a time when my people had grievances with the Manchu government. The last major rebellion had been a mere generation ago. Our only aim now was to survive and support one another. And build our strength for when the next fight arose.

"We can't stay here forever. We must find a place to hide," I suggested. "When it's safe I can try to smuggle you back to the concession. I do have some friends."

I could tell by the set of his jaw he was going to be hard-headed. "There's still something I need to do," he said.

"You have no guide," I reminded him. "Your old one betrayed you."

He gave me a pointed look, saying nothing.

"No one will want to help you. You're a foreign devil."

His look became more pointed. He raised his eyebrows at me, pleading.

Stubborn. Stubborn and stupid.

Foreigners weren't allowed within Old Shanghai. And he was impossible to disguise.

"Mister Burton, what you want is not possible."

"Just one request, then. Can you tell me where I may find the Long One Temple?"

"Long One?"

"Yes, the Long One Temple."

My pulse skipped. "Do you mean *Long Quan?*"

He cocked his head, making a face. "It sounds the same to me."

I made a face back. "Come."

Burton was going to find nothing but trouble on his own. He was fortunate that Long Quan temple was close. It was also very familiar to me. I could get there through back alleys.

"Can you climb?" I asked him.

He shrugged. I thought he meant yes.

Checking to see the street was clear, I slipped back out and hurried across. The Westerner followed behind, his every footstep like the stomp of an elephant. Perhaps I exaggerated, but he was not quiet.

We slipped into another alleyway, scaled a wall. Scaled another wall. Burton was able to climb quite easily with his long legs, though by the end of the journey his dark suit was covered in brick dust.

Another tremor shook the ground just as we reached the temple. I stilled and ducked out of instinct.

"There were earthquakes at Changsha as well," Burton murmured. He moved in close, casting a shadow over me as his arm circled my shoulder. Not touching, but protective. He looked up at the surrounding walls. "The report said the rebels tried to tunnel beneath the city."

In Shanghai, they'd tunneled into the marketplace. Whoever this Dean Burton was, he did more than sell tins of biscuits and tea.

"You know a lot," I said, glancing up at him. The earth had stopped shaking.

His lashes were pale and his features rough and big-boned, but he wasn't an ugly man.

"I know people. I hear things," he said.

"How did you know about this place?"

He followed my gaze to the temple entrance. It was a simple wooden gate hidden among the surrounding houses. There was little to mark it as a place of worship.

"As I said, I know people. One of them asked me for a favor."

We went to the gate where I pulled on the bell string. After a long pause, the gate creaked open to reveal an elderly monk in brown robes with a shaven head. He greeted us with the customary bow, one hand set in prayer. His expression was serene as if the city wasn't on fire around us.

"Brother, we've come to light incense at the altar of the Golden Mother," Burton recited.

It was the first time I realized, despite the occasional misplaced phrase or word and the odd accent, Burton's command of our language wasn't poor.

The monk blinked silently as he took in the sight of the tall *Yangguizi* before him. He glanced then at me before waving us both inside.

We crossed the humble inner courtyard into the hall of worship. The hall was an empty chamber with bare walls and a humble altar set at one end. Over the altar hung a scroll with a painting depicting the Eternal Mother, or the Golden Mother, as Burton had called her. This wasn't a place for shiny Buddha statues and relics.

The white-bearded abbot awaited us at the center of the room, also dressed in a plain brown robe. Only a string of prayer beads around his neck differentiated him from the disciples. "My child," he greeted me. And then to Burton, "Our honorable guest."

He gestured toward the altar with a sweep of his arm.

"I—uh. I'm here for the package—" Burton began, before I hushed him.

I went to the altar and retrieved two joss sticks of incense to hold to the candle flame. I relinquished one to Burton and held mine between my palms. Smoke curled around us from the smoldering tips.

Burton glanced over his shoulder at the abbot and then copied my movements. He held the incense between his palms, hands raised, head down.

"You're known here," he whispered.

I didn't respond. Instead I closed my eyes and thought of Shanghai, of my brother. I took a deep breath to try to clear away those dark thoughts. The smoke was laced with camphor and sandalwood, slightly sweet. I breathed deep, cultivating what peace I could gather before moving forward to place the incense into an urn. Hundreds of sticks had been planted into the same urn. They had burnt down to just the ends, the prayers carried by the smoke into the sky.

Burton glanced at me uncertainly as he held out the incense. I set his stick into the urn as well. There was no reason a *Yang-guizi* couldn't pray to the Eternal Mother.

"Forgive my rudeness," Burton said as the abbot approached once more. "A friend asked me to retrieve a package from your temple."

His voice trailed off as the senior disciple returned with another person beside him. I only knew him because Ren had pointed him out once when he made an appearance at the marketplace during last year's Spring Moon Festival. He still wore the robes of office and his cap was adorned with a peacock feather to denote his high rank.

"Did your friend not explain what this package would be?" the abbot asked.

Burton, normally talkative in the way of Westerners, fell

silent as he stared at the official before him. "No, venerable sir. He did not."

The man who stood before us in his expensive robe and neatly trimmed beard was the appointed superintendent of Shanghai, whose offices had been raided that morning. It was *Taotai* Wu, the man the Small Swords rebels wanted dead.

Chapter 5

"**Y**ou came to smuggle *Taotai* Wu?" I asked, stunned.

Burton rubbed a hand over his temples. "Smuggle might not be the correct word. And while we are speaking of translation, '*taotai*' means governor?"

"Intendant," I corrected. "The head intendant."

He nodded, looking very tired. "That's what I thought. He's the administrative head of all Shanghai."

"Not a very good one," I pointed out under my breath.

Burton shot me a look.

Over the last hour, *Taotai* Wu had relayed the events of that morning. When the attack began, *Taotai* Wu's bodyguards had all donned red sashes in a coordinated effort. His newly recruited militia had turned on him. However, an informer had managed to warn the *taotai* in advance.

Wu managed to slip away to seek sanctuary within the temple. The district magistrate and his assistant had not been so fortunate. The tragic pair was stabbed to death, their corpses left lying over their desks.

The Small Swords were more than willing to shed blood for their cause, but they appeared to be targeting the city's administration. The lot from Canton were still angry about their arrest several weeks ago.

At the end of his account, Wu looked Burton up and down and asked him who else would be coming to his aid. The *taotai* had not liked the answer.

The monks quickly ushered Wu away and pulled me aside to speak privately. Three hours had passed since the uprising began. The temple had sent out runners to gather additional information, and most of the inhabitants of Old Shanghai had taken shelter to wait out the unrest. I was left to explain the situation to Burton.

"The Small Swords are still marching through the streets, searching for the *taotai*," I told him. "The city is in disarray. The militia has fractured and it seems the guards have abandoned their posts."

Burton rubbed a hand over his chin as he considered the report. "Do you think anyone will organize a defense against the rebellion?"

The bureaucrats barely had control over the city before all this happened.

"Many of the street gangs are sympathetic to the rebellion. Old Shanghai doesn't have the manpower or will to fight back," I replied. "The monks believe the best course of action is to move the *taotai* quickly during the confusion. Things will only get worse once the rebels consolidate power."

"The safest place for the *taotai* would be behind the walls of the foreign settlement," Burton reasoned. "It's under British and French control and protected by several armed brigades."

My chest tightened at his casual claim of foreign authority upon Chinese soil, but Burton was in some part correct. According to the reports, the Small Swords were concentrating their forces in Old Shanghai and ignoring the concessions in the Northern City. The rebels did not want to engage the foreigners.

"*Taotai* Wu may not be amenable to that plan," Burton said.

"He was expecting more…formidable protection."

It was not so much that a foreigner had been sent to retrieve him as much as Burton was only a single man with no escort or manner of weapons. *Taotai* Wu had expected at least a small battalion.

Rather than taking insult, Burton shrugged. "I'll admit I'm not much to look at, but I was supposed to have a guide and reliable transportation."

"Your trusted guide has reported your part in this to the Small Swords by now," I pointed out.

"Hmmm." He grunted and folded his arms over his chest, a deep furrow cutting over his brow. "We have a dilemma."

He was quite fascinating to watch: the open play of emotions, the habit of making statements that added little. There were so many extra signals to read and most of them simply noise. I'd watched him and his peers for nearly a year while serving whiskey at the Dragon's Den—which I had yet to point out to the Westerners was a ridiculous name. Dragons lived in the clouds, not in dens.

Yet Burton's reputation was what he claimed. He knew people and heard things.

"You must have secret channels out of Old Shanghai," I surmised.

He raised an eyebrow. "I might."

Burton had to have come through some hidden passage. Or perhaps he was able to bribe the guards to turn a blind eye. Either way, we needed to use the same way out.

"You've smuggled goods out of Old Shanghai into the concession before," I pressed.

"I wouldn't say that—"

Which meant he was saying it. "Mister Burton," I snapped. "We're co-conspirators here and time is short. Please refrain from being so...so English."

"I'm American," he corrected.

I fell silent and closed my eyes, trying to think of a way out of this mess. When I opened them again, Burton was watching me.

"Why are you helping me, Miss Wei?"

"Because you'll get yourself killed on your own."

"Is that all?"

I exhaled slowly. I wasn't loyal to the *taotai* any more than the monks at Long Quan Temple were. Our city was on fire and our loved ones in danger. My brother Ren was caught in all this. The worse the uprising became, the more entangled he'd become. I still held out hope there was a way back for him.

"I want to avoid any more bloodshed," I told him honestly.

The corner of his mouth lifted. "Even mine?"

"*Especially* yours."

The monks had returned with the *taotai* beside them. "What is your plan, most honorable sir?" the bureaucrat asked Burton stiffly in English.

Perhaps the Westerner was too distracted by the *taotai*'s accent to recognize the disdain.

Burton faced the man squarely. "I do have a plan, but the honorable *Taotai* Wu will need to shave his head."

There was an audible gasp from the attendant monk while the abbot bowed his head, palm to chest, and implored the Eternal Mother to protect us from misfortune. The *taotai* narrowed his eyes at Burton.

It was a solution only a foreigner would have suggested.

"A man's queue is his sign of allegiance to the Emperor," I explained.

"I understand, but these are extenuating circumstances. If we disguise him, we might be able to smuggle him across the bridge into the settlement."

Burton clearly did *not* understand. A loyal subject to the Emperor would rather die than cut off his queue.

"*Taotai* Wu would be dishonoring himself and renouncing the Emperor. He would be exiled forever."

Like my brother. Though if Ren was ever caught, he wouldn't be exiled. He would be executed as a traitor.

"The rebels won't be searching for a monk," Burton insisted. "The abbot can write up papers to provide a false identity."

With each word, I could see the *taotai* becoming more upset.

I had to pull Burton into the adjacent chamber. "When the rebels take prisoners, they forcefully cut off their queues. To the *taotai*, shaving his head is a sign of his surrender. It would be no better than handing himself to the rebels."

Burton looked back into the hall of worship. *Taotai* Wu was staring at us with great displeasure.

"You should apologize," I prompted.

"It was a good plan," he muttered beneath his breath before returning to the chamber. He did apologize, bowing low in a gesture of extra politeness.

Then Burton came back to me, looking very tired. "The second plan is more difficult. How many of you are there?"

"How many of…us?"

The corner of his mouth lifted in a smirk. "Come now, Miss Wei. We're co-conspirators here. There's no need to be coy. It's clear you're respected here—how many people can you round up?"

It took some time before I understood what Burton was talking about. This phrase "round up." It made little sense to me. Even when he explained it. Round—like a circle? Up?

And then the part when he was attempting to be coy. My people? Shanghainese? Chinese?

"Your clan," he insisted. "This secret society of yours."

I looked to the abbot and he back at me. We were not like the street gangs. Our sect was united around the spiritual message of the Eternal Mother. We had vowed to preserve and protect one another with silence.

"How many people do you need?" I asked him evenly.

"The more the better. Men, women. Young, old."

I couldn't ask so many to put themselves in danger. We

weren't aligned with the Small Swords, but we weren't aligned with the Emperor and his Manchu government either.

"*Taotai* Wu's life is in danger," the abbot reminded me. "We must prevent further violence."

"The more there are, the less danger there is to any one of us," Burton assured. "Like a herd. A roundup."

I frowned at that word again, which I still didn't understand. But I think I was beginning to understand his strategy.

The abbot sent word through his runners to find who among the sect were willing to help. For Burton's disguise, I sought out the laundress from my tenement for a set of clothes from Big Lo, the largest man in the neighborhood.

Burton removed his frock and suit to put on the pigeon gray tunic and trousers. The sleeves were still too short.

"You don't look Chinese," I told him flatly.

If anything, the disguise made his pale skin and yellow hair stand out more. The laundress thrust a wide conical hat into my hands and I handed it over to Burton.

"Better?" he asked, his face shielded by the brim.

I shook my head.

"It'll do," Burton proclaimed. "Let's go."

The two of us returned to the streets to look for a transport. I hoped the monks were correct—that the rebels were leaving most of the inhabitants alone. And though they didn't like foreigners, harming someone like Burton would suddenly involve the American legation. It was possible he was afforded some protection because of it. In any case, the two of us were now bound together in this mission. I didn't want to risk any of the others needlessly.

We found the gunpowder rickshaw on the bridge where we'd left it. The driver and his rebels must have continued on foot. Burton tried to fit himself onto the driver's seat and found his knees were folded up too far to work the pedals. We switched places, with me at the pedals and Burton in the carriage. The engine sputtered to life, but the rickshaw only managed the length of a street before sputtering out.

"*Puk gaai,*" Burton swore in the Canton dialect. "The gunpowder supply is depleted."

"We can try the local gunpowder depot," I suggested.

Burton gave the rickshaw a swift kick as he climbed off. We soon discovered the rebels had taken the store of powder at the local repository and set fire to whatever was left behind. This led to a series of more fervent swearing from Burton in several languages.

We found ourselves back at the rickshaw, hunched down on the ground beside it as we tried to devise a new plan. We were hidden for the moment. In the distance, I could hear a parade of rebels shouting. They were becoming more agitated with each passing hour.

Burton folded his legs and rested his forehead against his knees, shoulders slumped. Even collapsed like that, he was still enormous.

"What did you think the package would be?" I asked.

He kept his head down. "Usually it's letters, information. I suspected the rebel army would try to breach the walls so I figured my contacts had information that might help our defense."

Were all Westerners so free with information? Perhaps it was just that it had been a trying day and we'd found ourselves thrown together.

I was running out of time and options and there was something I needed to know from Burton. Something that had nothing to do with the temple or the gangs or the uprising. I might not have the chance to ask again.

"I know you are a spy," I told him.

"I'm not a spy." His denial was immediate. "I'm just a businessman," he continued after a pause. He turned his head sideways to meet my eyes. "I know people and hear things."

I nodded, unconvinced.

"Is that why you're so friendly to me at the club?" he asked. "Because you think I'm a spy?"

"Yes."

He made a whistling sound which I interpreted as either surprise or an arrogantly rude response. "You are much more pleasant at the Dragon's Den," he said, but with a wide grin.

Americans were very hard to understand.

I propped my knees up as well, mirroring his pose. With a deep breath, I weighed my options. Shanghai was on fire and I'd already lost so much this day.

"Do you smuggle opium?" I asked him.

"No. Never."

"Don't look so astonished. All of your gentleman friends at the club trade in opium."

He remained silent.

"Have you ever smuggled people? Coolie workers, I believe you call them." I turned to look directly at him, waiting for an answer.

Burton straightened, his frown deepening. "No," he repeated emphatically. "Never."

There was a specific reason I'd chosen to work in the foreign concession. There was also a reason I'd cultivated a relationship with this foreigner.

I couldn't look at Burton anymore so I stared at my shoes. The black fabric looked worn through from just the day's travels. A lump formed in my throat when I started to speak.

I couldn't say these things without thinking of Ren. Of him showing up at the school, claiming to be my brother and the missionaries refusing to believe him. *Papers*, they'd insisted. *Where are your records?*

My parents had been declared enemies of the Manchu government and sent away. And there were no records. My brother and I had been separated and I was sent to the orphanage as a child who had been abandoned. Again, no records.

I climbed out of the missionary window one night with Ren waiting below to catch me. I was ten, he fourteen. We then went to Shanghai where the worshipers of the Eternal Mother had taken us in, just as they'd accepted our parents. We vowed to find out what had happened to our mother and father together. But Ren had gone his own way and I was left to fulfill our vow alone.

I blinked back tears.

Not here. Not in front of this foreigner.

"My mother and father were sold off as indentured servants and put onto a British ship," I told Burton while I continued to stare at my feet. It was easier to say this in English. It was as if I was describing someone else's life. "They were sent far away. I hear there are colonies and plantations all over the world. On islands in the middle of the ocean. Places that grow sugar or opium."

I had tried to learn as much as I could, but my knowledge was so scattered.

When I did look up, he was watching me with concern, saying nothing. Gone was his charming demeanor, his grin, his look of good humor. Perhaps I was seeing his true face for the first time. Perhaps he was seeing mine.

"You know people and hear things," I said to him. "Will you help me find them?"

He nodded, breathing deep. Then he held out his hand. I had seen the gentlemen at the club do this upon coming to an agreement or making a deal. I reached out my hand and his strong fingers wrapped around mine, squeezing firmly.

"I also know things," I said finally. We had our own local stashes, smuggled away. "I'll get you the gunpowder."

Chapter 6

O ver the next hour, we resupplied the gunpowder rickshaw and I drove it back to the temple. I was also able to locate a few friends from the tenement. Liu came with his set of tools and Auntie Ma. Several others who may not have cared about *Taotai* Wu but wanted the unrest to end. Big Lo noticed Burton was wearing his work shirt but bit his tongue and said nothing.

"All they need to do is provide cover," Burton explained. "We are posing as a group seeking refuge in the foreign settlement. The Small Swords haven't done any harm to citizens, only bureaucrats. If we encounter trouble, if the rebels demand we clear the streets, everyone does exactly that. You run and hide. Don't challenge them."

The *taotai* exchanged his state robes for peasant clothing and shaved his beard. I took his robe and peacock feather hat to prepare for the second part of the plan. Liu was already at work, tinkering with his big wrench beneath the rickshaw.

"Are you certain you can do this, *Zágōng?*"

"Ha, making something not work properly is easy. Can you hand me that extra bit of pipe over there?"

Auntie Ma brought me a dummy dressed in *Taotai* Wu's

clothing. She'd stuffed him with straw and found a melon in place of the head. We arranged the dummy so it was huddled down inside the carriage. It took several tries and a large wooden stake speared through the melon to keep it from rolling off.

Burton came to stand beside me as we completed the final preparations.

"This cart looks exactly like a transport one would use to smuggle someone," I remarked.

Burton frowned. "Do you really think so, Miss Wei?"

"I do."

"We'll see," he murmured.

I tied my strip of red silk onto the front of the rickshaw. There was no knowing whether the Small Swords would honor the sign of allegiance and let us be.

When it was time to go, I threw a blanket over the Melon-head *Taotai* wearing his peacock feather hat. Then I took my position in the driver's seat. Burton would head to the bridge on foot with *Taotai* Wu and the others. I would approach separately in the gunpowder rickshaw.

"I'll take care of them," he promised, coming up to me.

I'd actually asked Auntie Ma and the others to take care of Burton.

"I'll be watching," he told me.

"Move quickly," I reminded him.

We rattled off advice to one another for a full minute before stopping. He smiled at me. I was too tired to smile back.

"I guess we just have to trust one another."

I nodded. Facing forward, I set my foot on the pedal to begin, but Burton stopped me once more.

"You can come with me."

There was no need to consider it. I shook my head, no.

"Things will get worse quickly," he said. "The supply lines, the loading docks will be cut off. They'll start scouring the city for enemies. The rebels will need to keep the populace under control."

Everything he said was true. "I belong here," I replied. "But thank you for your offer."

"About your parents—"

"I'll find you somehow. After all this."

"Once the smoke clears," he said.

The saying was very appropriate.

Burton hesitated once more. I could see his mind working to gather more arguments about how I should come with him, but in the end, he respected my decision. He tapped the handlebars of the rickshaw twice in farewell.

"Godspeed," he said, turning to join the others.

I waited, giving the group a chance to make some progress before I started the engine. I cycled forward as the gunpowder engine rumbled, propelling me toward the North Gate and out to the foreign concession. The streets had cleared in the late afternoon and Old Shanghai was eerily quiet. I passed by empty markets and shops. The patrol at the city gate had dissolved. Just outside, the silence gave way to a crowd of people gathered at the bridge that led to the foreign concession. Burton's instinct had been correct that the people of Old Shanghai would flee from the rebel army to seek protection.

I easily spotted Burton in his conical hat near the foot of the bridge. There were Small Swords patrols scattered in the area— I recognized them by the red headbands. I hoped Burton didn't appear so obvious to them.

It was time. I pedaled the rickshaw forward, heading toward the crowd. I had the attention of the Small Swords gang now. The red bands turned and started toward me.

I increased the speed on the pedals and the crowd parted, fleeing from my path as the gunpowder engine rumbled and coughed up black smoke. Liu had added a lever that would keep the engine engaged once I took my foot off the pedals. I cranked the lever and leapt from the rickshaw, just as the smoke bomb in the luggage compartment exploded.

The vehicle veered left and began to drive in circles, smoke billowing from the back. The Small Swords patrol chased after it and I heard someone yelling that they saw someone hiding in back.

Looking behind me, I saw Burton and his group had reached the bridge and were steadily pushing through. The rebels seemed to be staying away from the bridge itself, which was fortunate.

The crowd grew thicker around me. For the first time, I looked upon the people who were seeking refuge. Families had brought little more than the clothes on their backs and I could see the belongings that had been discarded by the side of the bridge when it became apparent there was no room. Some of the first comers had brought trunks of possessions which had now been thrown aside and subsequently picked through. A tablet from an ancestral altar was cast unceremoniously into the dirt.

Over the following days, the inhabitants of Old Shanghai would cower in their houses, many cut off from food, from water. No one knew what came next. Would the rebel army roll through and press every able-bodied man and woman into service? Would they force the populace to cut off their queues or lose their heads, as the reports from other conquered cities had claimed?

I forced my attention back to the patrol. They had reached the rickshaw and had pried the trunk open, releasing a great puff of smoke. Someone had taken hold of Melon-head *Taotai*. They threw the dummy to the ground in disgust, stomping him to pieces.

Unseen, the real *Taotai* Wu remained crouched beside Burton as he made his way toward the checkpoint gate. I would stay until Burton and Wu were safely within the concession and then I'd take the others back to the tenement.

The entire day was like a dream. I wanted so much to go home and find Ren there, sweating from a hard day at the docks.

A flash of red cloth brought me back to the present. On the far side of the bridge, there was a red headband moving fast through the crowd with the singularity of a tiger on the hunt.

Ren. I knew it without seeing him. It was how he moved and the way he held himself, sullen. Angry. I knew his movements as well as my own.

I stood and surged forward, pushing through the crowd, reaching for my rope dart and readying the daggers. The energy of the gathering had changed and I could sense the arrow of fear as it moved from man to man. The Small Swords rebels were on the bridge now, shoving people aside. At the sight of them, people began to fall back on their own. No one wanted trouble with the bloodthirsty rebels. They only wanted to survive this day.

The flash of my blades chased away those nearest to me. A line of sight opened up just as my brother charged toward Burton and the *taotai*. His knives were drawn.

I let my dagger fly, the cord of the rope dart snaking over my palm. The blade glanced off Ren's shoulder, not drawing blood, but setting him back. The impact alone would be hard enough to draw a bruise, but it wasn't enough to stop Ren. I followed with the second dagger immediately, letting it fly as I wound up the slack at the other end.

The rope dart acted as blade, as projectile, as a whip—whatever I willed it to be. Ren dodged the second dagger, but I brought the tail lashing around before he could recover. The silk rope wrapped around my brother's wrist with the weight of the blade guiding the path. The moment I felt it catch, I tugged hard on the line, dragging Ren off-balance.

Burton turned just as my brother recovered his footing. Ren struck like a cobra, his knife thrusting forward. Burton had just enough time to push the *taotai* away and toward the gate. The

British guards took hold of the bureaucrat and dragged him toward the concession. I watched helpless as Ren's knife plunged toward Burton's chest.

I screamed out Ren's name.

My breath caught as Burton reeled back, clutching at his arm. Blood flowed red through his fingers, but the blade had missed his heart. He'd managed to dodge away in time.

The crowd of refugees fled away from the gate, shoving past me. I blocked out the shouting, the mass of shapes and movement, and focused in on my adversary. My own brother. He turned at that moment, his eyes locking onto mine.

I cast out the rope again, this time hooking it around Ren's neck. Hand over hand, I reeled him closer, the silk cord constricting around his throat with each pass. His muscles strained as he fought against me.

The rope dart was an uncommon weapon. Few knew how to defend against it. In a fight, one blink, one breath of an advantage was all one needed to turn most battles. But Ren had been trained as I had been. Rather than fighting back against the coil at his throat, he moved forward, toward me. Stretching out an arm, Ren wound the rope around his wrist to remove the tension and eliminate my hold over him.

With a flash of his knife, he cleaved the silk cord in two. I stumbled back with my weapon destroyed. It was enough of a break for Ren to end this fight. He could have aimed a knife at my throat, at my heart—but I wasn't his target. He flew instead toward Burton.

Burton whipped off his conical hat to deflect the attack. Ren's steel knives pierced through the woven bamboo, cutting it to shreds. I moved in to counter with my dagger in hand. The rope was useless now, but the weighted blades were still sharp. I cut across Ren's forearm and sliced a thin line over his knuckles.

I was between the two men now. I faced my brother with Burton at my back. It took discipline for Ren to hold on to his weapons after those cuts. It took discipline for me not to waver despite the sickness in the pit of my stomach.

I'd drawn my brother's blood after we'd spent our lives searching for one another. Protecting one another. It was like spilling my own.

"Ren," I pleaded. "Elder Brother."

He met my eyes and I saw the parts of him I'd failed to see all along. The unbridled anger. The stark hopelessness. I already knew the answers to the questions I'd been asking all day.

My brother hated the Emperor. He hated the corruption and abuse of the Manchu government, which we'd fought for generation after generation. For Ren, this had started long before us, long before even our parents. Blood was the only way to pay this debt.

"Ming-fen." There was no emotion as he spoke my name. There was nothing but cold knowledge.

My brother didn't want to fight me, any more than I wanted to fight him. I sensed Burton's presence at my back, felt him reaching into his tunic.

The gun. I'd forgotten he had a gun.

The guardsmen at the gate had their rifles trained onto me as well as my brother. They wouldn't intervene in a Chinese dispute, but the moment one of their people was harmed by one of ours…

Ren wasn't afraid to die. I'd always known that about him and I was afraid for him.

There was no choice left. I fell back, my shoulder blades pressing against Burton to urge him back behind the line of guardsmen. Back into to the foreign concession where he would be safe. If I moved away, my brother would kill Burton because he was nothing but a foreign devil after all. Then the rifles would fire in retaliation, filling Ren with black powder and iron.

With each step, I severed the last ties to my brother. We were no longer of one mind. We never again would be. My vision blurred with tears as I crossed into the settlement. The gate swung closed then, cutting off my view of Ren and the crowd of refugees behind him on the bridge.

For a long time, I stared at the closed gate, struggling for each breath. My chest felt as if a boulder had been set on top of it. When I turned around, it was as if every last drop of blood had been drained from me. *Taotai* Wu had been led away into the custody of the consulate. Burton stood with a hand pressed to the wound in his arm, out of place in Chinese clothing.

I moved past him without a word, stranded and cut off in my own homeland.

Chapter 7

That night, I sat on the roof of the Grand Hotel, watching airships retreat from the river. Fires continued to burn on the rooftops of Old Shanghai. Here and there, the citizens were banding together to try to extinguish them.

"There you are, Miss Wei."

I turned to see Burton with a glass of whiskey in hand. He was back in his dark suit with all the little buttons and pockets. Carefully he stepped out onto the roof, the glass balanced precariously in one hand. "I didn't know you could climb out here."

"It's the only place I can see the city from inside." I turned back to Old Shanghai. A red banner had been hung over the North Gate and red flags flew from the guard towers. The Small Swords had taken control with the backing of the Heaven and Earth army.

With the *taotai* gone, it hadn't been difficult. There was no one to challenge their authority.

Burton settled down beside me. "More residents of Shanghai are gathering on the bridge with every hour. The foreign legation is trying to determine who to let in."

"Because you are on our land, after all," I pointed out.

He raised his hands in a gesture of surrender. Which didn't mean he'd actually surrendered. "I'm just telling you what I know. Drink?"

I shook my head at the offer. He lifted the glass in a silent toast before raising it to his lips. While he drank, I searched Old Shanghai with my eyes, wondering where Ren was. Would I ever stop looking for him?

"That man—the one who attacked me. You knew him?"

Burton's voice seemed to come from far away. I continued to stare into the fire and smoke of Old Shanghai.

"My brother," I replied tonelessly.

Silence descended, heavy and oppressive.

"Tell me what you know about the White Lotus Society," Burton said finally, setting down his glass.

I scowled. "That is a name the Manchus use to cast suspicion on anyone they don't like. We prefer to call ourselves Ming loyalists."

He listened, absorbing the information. I was beginning to see how all Burton's noise served as distraction. Underneath his pleasant demeanor, he was storing away every detail.

"The White Lotus Society has been implicated in several rebellions," Burton began. "It stands to reason your parents might have been accused of being White Lotus before they were condemned. That could provide a way for me to search for them—"

I sat up so quickly my hand swung against Burton's glass. He rescued it without spilling a drop.

"I made you a promise, didn't I?" he said, meeting my eyes.

The grateful look I gave him must have made Burton uncomfortable. He glanced away and finished the rest of his whiskey in one swallow.

He cleared his throat nervously before speaking again. "Miss Wei, I should thank you for saving my life on the bridge today."

"I didn't do it for you." I'd done it for Ren, so I didn't have to see my brother killed in retaliation front of me.

"Well, I'm alive all the same because of you. So, thank you, Miss Wei. I'm…ah…in your debt."

"Think nothing of it."

"Yes. Indeed." He coughed once. Picked up the glass to take another drink only to find it already empty. "Since you are here all alone because of me, I thought. Well. If you needed anything…"

Why was he acting so strange? Could it be—

"Are you asking me to be your mistress?"

"No!"

I narrowed my eyes at him.

"No," he repeated in a more subdued tone, smoothing a hand over the front of his jacket. "I meant to say there is a room at the shop you can take. In return, perhaps you would consider working for me."

He *was* asking me to be his mistress. I shot him a poisonous look once again.

"No," he insisted for the third time. "You can help me get information, find things. A lot of people won't even talk to someone like me. I think we work well together, wouldn't you say?"

"I don't think I would," I replied flatly.

I must have communicated my wishes incorrectly because Burton found my answer amusing. He grinned and seemed to actually take my contrary response as agreement.

It wasn't a bad option, working for this man. The foreign concession would be my home for the foreseeable future and Dean Burton had proved to be a good person.

The pain of losing my brother and my home in one day was still a raw and open wound, but there was still hope.

Shanghai was still there. I could see it—the wall and the dwellings and the friends I'd left behind. I could still *feel* them.

Just as my brother was somewhere in Old Shanghai, still alive. I hadn't lost my home or my brother yet. Not completely.

In the meantime, working with a businessman who knew people and learned things sounded more useful than being a sing-song girl in a gentleman's club. And he'd agreed to help me find my parents.

"I will consider your offer, Mister Burton," I replied evenly.

He looked surprised. "You'll *consider* it?"

Apparently. he thought his proposal was too good to refuse.

I rose to go. "I will think about it."

It wasn't a bad offer. Actually, there was little else I could do, but this was still Shanghai. One did not make a deal without at least bargaining a little. I reached the trapdoor that led from the rooftop back down into the hotel.

"Well, when might you have an answer?" he called after me.

"Tomorrow." I looked back to see Dean Burton staring at me in puzzlement. "Perhaps," I added as an afterthought.

He had too much of the advantage between us. The least I could do was keep him guessing.

Author's Note

The most interesting thing about "Big Trouble in Old Shanghai" is that, other than the wuxia-style kung-fu action and steampunk elements, everything else was inspired by the historical record.

The story features two minor characters that have very little screen time in Gunpowder Alchemy. Here was my chance to finally explore those characters.

As the name implies, the story was conceived as an "East Meets West", wuxia-style action adventure. The character of Dean Burton, a.k.a. "Mr. Burton", is not modeled after Jack Burton of Big Trouble in Little China. His name, however, is not purely coincidental.

Ming-fen and her brother Ren are children of so-called "White Lotus" rebels—though this was a name that the Qing government assigned to any group of dissidents in order to brand them as rebels. In kung-fu mythology, there are several White Lotus styles of fighting.

The Small Swords Rebellion was an actual occurrence when several gangs within Shanghai banded together under the banner of the Taiping rebels and took over the Chinese portion of the city. The rebels held the city for nearly a year and a half before being overthrown by a foreign armies.

From historical accounts of the Small Swords Rebellion:

Several earthquakes rocked Shanghai prior to the start of the rebellion

Leading up to the fateful day, there was a run on red cloth in all the shops. The rebels used red cloth to signal their allegiance to the revolt.

Many rival gangs from different geographical regions were active in Shanghai at the time. They were associated with different work crews in the city.

The city government was attempting to crack down on gangs. To do so, they were trying to recruit other gangs.

Taotai Wu, the head of Chinese Shanghai, did manage to escape. Using his foreign connections, he escaped to the American legation outside of Old Shanghai.

The Small Swords Rebellion for the most part left the foreign settlement alone as those areas were under control of the British, French, and American forces.

As a result of the rebellion, many citizens of Chinese Shanghai flooded into the foreign settlement. Refugees on land that had once belonged to them.

For more information about the Gunpowder Chronicles, sign-up for Jeannie Lin's mailing list to receive updates on new releases, appearances, and special giveaways.

PART II

The Island of the Opium-Eaters

Chapter 1

I live upon a madman's ship, cast away on the endless ocean.

There was a time when I had a home and a name that held some honor. I was Sagara Satomi, daughter of Lord Sagara Shintarō, a man who was loyal to the shogunate—but not loyal enough. And not in the ways they demanded. By the time I set out to sea, my home and my family name had long been destroyed. I was already a soul without roots which made it easier to leave my homeland behind.

The master of the ship was one Yang Hanzhu, a man who had a reputation in Nagasaki of being a mystery. *Shina-jin*, wealthy, and a trader of some sort. Now that he was known to me, Yang Hanzhu wasn't what I'd expected. He appeared to be just over thirty years of age, making him perhaps eight years my senior. Not a fresh-faced youth, but surprisingly young for one who lived in a fine mansion and bribed port officials into asking few questions.

After a month of passage on this vessel, I'd found Yang Hanzhu intensely private and more than a little eccentric. He remained out of sight most of the time, locked inside his workroom.

It was said he was an alchemist and there were stores of volatile and powerful reactants kept below. Trespassing into the forbidden areas would lead to immediate abandonment on the nearest shore.

The harshness of these rules did not cause me any alarm. My father had been an artificer and an engineer. I had grown up roaming his workshop, hiding among half-constructed automatons. I was familiar with men of science and their peculiarities.

Those days of wonder when my father had still been alive seemed so distant now. The memories were rare and contained, like lightning trapped in a jar.

Over the last week, rain had kept us trapped below deck. I'd spent too many days lying in my berth, staring out the porthole at gray storm clouds. This particular day was clear by comparison. We could see a hint of sunlight through the wisp of clouds. The promise of warmth lured all of us out into the open air.

This morning, I reclined against a bulkhead on the main deck to clean the double-barreled *Tanegashima*. I had brought several of my firearms with me to tend to them. The salt air was enemy to the metalwork and they required constant maintenance.

The vessel itself was a Shina junk ship fitted with battened sails made of red silk and reinforced with lightweight steel spines. The sail assembly was designed to harness even the barest of ocean breezes. When the wind was fickle, the ship could be powered by its gunpowder engine alone. When it was running, the roar of it could be heard throughout every deck.

Today the wind was favorable and the engine silent. It was the sort of day that had everyone in good spirits.

Makoto, my fellow countryman, stood nearby with his sword sheathed at his side. He wore the kimono of the samurai class, though with the sleeves and length shortened to allow for easier movement. He was plain of face, but strong in presence, with a swordsman's lean build.

His gaze was fixed out over the water with an expression that was full of longing. I knew he looked toward Nippon, the country we had both forsaken. We hadn't been away long enough to lose sense of where the islands were located.

The crew had initially assumed we were companions but were quickly disabused of that notion. Makoto and I had barely known one another when we'd boarded this ship, though we had watched side-by-side as the shores of Nippon disappeared into the horizon. The pain in my chest had been sharp and unexpected.

Sakoku was the law of Nippon and had been for two hundred years. Foreigners were not allowed to enter, but our people were also forbidden to leave. I'd known when I set foot on this ship that I would not be allowed to ever return to our shores. Makoto had known it as well.

The swordsman had left Nippon for his own reasons. In typical samurai fashion, he spoke little of it, but I'd learned that he was searching for someone. A merchant's daughter who had once resided in Nagasaki. As for me—I didn't know what I was searching for. Stepping onto this boat had been an act of defiance. I would not stay and wait for death as my father had. A samurai would insist that this was cowardice, but my family was samurai no longer.

Today was a rare day indeed as Yang Hanzhu had also come above deck. He stood at the bow, flipping slowly through a tattered book. The ocean breeze stirred through the pages and I wasn't convinced he was reading them. After an interval, he closed the book with a snap and slipped it into the pocket of his coat.

That was one of Yang's peculiarities. He didn't dress in the way of Shina or Nippon, preferring instead the Western style. His long coat was fashioned from tanned leather and cut squarely over his narrow shoulders and extended down to his knees. He left the coat unfastened, revealing a white linen shirt and a row of buttons. Compared to kimono, the clothing was overly complicated.

His face was sharp, composed of strong angles and a slight crookedness in his mouth that hinted of mischief. Yang's most striking feature was his hair which had been hacked off at shoulder length. The significance of such a drastic change was understood even in Nippon. A man who had cut off his queue could never return to Shina.

Yang extracted a spyglass from one of the coat pockets now and extended the instrument toward the horizon. Whatever he was searching for, it didn't take long. Yang collapsed the tube and tucked it away, producing a cigarette from his breast pocket in its place and lighting it with a tinder device that closed with a snap. He took a long drag from the cigarette and exhaled slowly.

A cloud of smoke billowed around him as he continued to stare across the water. Another one of the oddly Western habits he'd adopted along with his appearance. I wondered if Yang's smoking habit was a replacement for the opium pipe. In Nippon, we considered opium to be a disease of the *Shina-jin*. For all I knew, all of Shina consumed the drug. Nippon had witnessed how the poison could take down an entire empire. Opium was strictly forbidden from entering our borders.

With a sideways glance, Yang caught my eye and started toward the main deck. Bitter smoke wafted toward me, scratching the back of my throat. Yang noticed my reaction and flicked the cigarette aside before closing the distance between us. I stood as he approached.

"Sagara-san." His greeting contained all the appropriate words, but far from the proper amount of respect.

"Yang-san."

Makoto edged closer. The swordsman insisted on acting as my protector though we owed no allegiance to one another. I was fallen nobility, but he was fallen samurai. I suppose that meant I still held rank over him.

Yang's gaze flickered momentarily to the swordsman before returning to me. "Tomorrow we will drop anchor near a shore. I humbly ask that you accompany me when we disembark."

"I would humbly ask for what reason?"

His eyes glinted with amusement. "More to the point, I would ask that your firearms accompany me."

"Can your crewmen not protect you?"

Yang shrugged. "The more protection, the better. And I've seen how you shoot."

He'd only seen me fire once when we were escaping Nagasaki. Together we'd fought off armored assassins sent by the shogunate. From that battle, I knew Yang Hanzhu did not show fear in the face of danger. Yang was apparently expecting a good deal of it wherever he was going tomorrow.

"What do you need protection from?"

The corner of his mouth lifted, not quite a smile. "I wish I knew."

I stared hard at him without wavering.

"We are headed to an island," he relented. "Off the coast of Guangdong province to the south. We'll approach in the night and drop anchor on the eastern shore opposite the mainland."

Opposite the mainland to avoid any patrols.

"Are you smuggling opium?"

Yang met my gaze directly but didn't answer.

"I know you have opium on this ship." I'd seen a case of it loaded at the last port.

"The last thing I would smuggle is opium."

Implying he would smuggle other goods. That wasn't my concern. In Nagasaki, I'd been considered an outlaw for selling firearms to foreigners, and wasn't one to pass judgment. Most importantly, Yang had offered me safety and passage on this ship. He'd refused any form of payment and it always made me uncomfortable knowing there was an imbalance between us.

"I'll go with you, Yang-san, as I owe you a debt."

"Tomorrow, then." Yang grinned and turned to leave, lighting a fresh cigarette and taking another drag. Before moving too far, he turned to address me a final time. "You could have refused, Sagara-san. Honor no longer binds anyone on this ship. There is only free will."

Chapter 2

"Where do you think he's going?" Makoto asked once we were below deck.

I replied with silence. Yang had asked for a favor and I'd assented. It was impolite to pry into his affairs beyond that. Perhaps I was still samurai at heart.

We retired to the sleeping berths. As the only woman on board, I was given a small compartment separated by a curtain. Inside, there was a single wooden bunk with a woven bamboo mat. The bunk served for both sitting and sleeping. On days when the weather kept us below deck, this tiny corner of the ship was all I had to fill the hours.

I was used to spending my days roaming the hills of Nagasaki. Debt or no, I welcomed the promise of setting foot onto land and stretching my legs beyond the confines of the ship. For now, I was here because there was nowhere else to go. The chance for a new life, even one contained in a vessel at sea, had to be better than a slow death retracing the same worn pathways of the past.

Alone, I climbed onto the bunk and opened my father's journal. The familiar and constant smell of salt air and musty wood surrounded me. There was just enough light filtering in through the porthole to read the scrawled characters. These were the notes he'd kept during his studies, but to me they were disjointed and unintelligible. He'd done extensive experiments on *elekiteru*, the invisible force harnessed in lightning that could be created by the spinning of wheels, by chemicals.

Specific metals have shown an affinity for elekiteru, my father wrote. He'd been fascinated with the discoveries and advancements of the gaijin in the West. I had inherited his knowledge of metalwork and gunsmithing, but not his propensity for scientific investigation. The shogunate would have preferred Father limit himself to making weapons of war for their armies. His inquisitive nature had gotten him killed.

Between the sway of the vessel and the dim light, reading the journal was making me dizzy. I lay back and closed my eyes, thinking about the island. Yang Hanzhu was not a cautious man or a reasonable one. And now he was asking for protection from an unknown threat on a strange island.

In Nippon, I lived under the constant threat the shogunate would send their assassins after me, just as they had with my father. Perhaps I didn't know how to pass the days without that weight over me. I was too eager to walk into danger, just to remember the taste of it.

I fell asleep thinking of the empty rooms that had been my home for the last few years. This ship wasn't any different. More people, but just as empty. Except Yang Hanzhu.

His madness was so familiar it was comforting.

The ship sailed through the night. By morning, I peered through the porthole to see the silhouette of land through the early fog. Just before sunrise, the crew gave notice we were to prepare to disembark.

I had already prepared my weapons and a travel pack. As I readied myself, I heard a voice on the other side of the curtain.

"Sagara-san."

I pulled the curtain aside to reveal Makoto fully dressed in a dark-colored kimono with two swords sheathed at his belt. The only thing sharper than the katana was the gleam in his eyes. Makoto looked every bit the warrior, ready for battle.

"I'm coming with you."

"I would be grateful for your blade, Makoto-san."

He looked surprised. We'd clashed in the past discussing the virtues of the sword versus the gun. Unlike Makoto, I didn't care about pride or aesthetics. Weapons were tools suited for specific functions. As certain as I was of Sagara weaponry, each firearm was only good for one or two shots, at best. In comparison, swords did not need to be reloaded.

I holstered two pistols into my belt and tucked a third, smaller weapon into my sash at the small of my back. It was a weapon of last resort, only of use at arm's length. I draped a light *haori* jacket around my shoulders for warmth. It fell below my hips, ending mid-thigh, and was loose enough to allow easy access to the weapons. After living alone in the hills of Nagasaki, I'd adopted more masculine clothing, though there was nothing strange about it on this ship. Here, everyone outfitted themselves in the odds and ends they'd encountered on their travels.

I checked my rifle one more time and slung a powder bag over my shoulder.

"The *tojin* isn't telling us everything," Makoto warned, using the name for wealthy businessmen who had inhabited the mansions of Nagasaki.

"No one ever does."

My father had been full of secrets: sending forbidden messages to the Ministry of Science in Peking, creating inventions and taking his knowledge of them to the grave.

Makoto followed me to the stairs and we ascended into a thick veil of fog. The crewmen were loading into a rowboat rigged onto the stern side. Yang Hanzhu watched over the operations, smoking another cigarette. The island loomed about two *ri* away across not-so-tranquil waters.

"Is that a dock?" I gestured toward the wooden structure along the shore.

71

"I prefer we keep our distance."

I didn't challenge him. It was his ship, and, as I'd acknowledged before, he was somewhat erratic.

Five men seated themselves in the rowboat and then it was our turn. Yang stepped in first before turning around to offer his hand. The gesture took me so off guard that I merely stared at him. Eventually I ignored his offer to board on my own. Unnecessary contact was…unnecessary.

Rather than take offense, Yang smiled, his eyes sparking with an inner light. He continued to regard me as I took a seat beside him and I couldn't imagine what it was he was seeing. I had little knowledge of how I looked to others, or how I looked to myself, for that matter. The only thing I could discern from Yang was that however it was I appeared to him, I wasn't invisible.

Makoto was the last one in before the crew cranked the rig to lower us into the water. The rowers fought against the tide, but we managed to make progress and landed on the beach before too long. A dense line of trees protected the rest of the island from view. Yang stationed two crewmen as guards while the rest of us continued inland.

No one came to greet us and the dock was in disrepair, the wood cracked and worn.

"Guangdong was ravaged by opium even before the war," Yang explained as we entered a wooded area.

"And after the war?"

"Now our entire empire has been ravaged," he replied dryly. "Grand Chancellor Lin once dared to take a stand against the opium trade. He banned the sale of it and confiscated over two thousand chests from the *Yangguizi* in the port of Canton. Then he destroyed the entire supply, a portion of it by fire and the rest by dumping it into the ocean. A grand and tragic gesture."

"Tragic," I echoed.

"Shortly afterward, the *Yangguizi* piloted steamships into our harbors, destroyed our citadels, and forcibly enslaved our people to the drug."

Yang finished the last part in a rush, like a bad taste he wanted out of his mouth.

Shina's downfall was a warning to Nippon. Our island empire had tried to shut itself off from the world, but the Western steamships had come to Nippon all the same. They had arrived at the same time I had left, grand and tragic.

We continued through the trees. There appeared to have once been a path from the docks, but it had become overgrown.

"Our people have been using opium medicinally for thousands of years. Why were we falling to this now? I tried to discover what made this opium from the *Yangguizi* so much more addictive. In my studies, I came across an anomaly—an alteration in the formula." A deep line cut across his forehead. "I came here to seek out how that happened. And why."

Yang hadn't spoken of this until now. He'd meant to keep the knowledge secret to all but the few of us he'd brought onto the island: Makoto, myself and three of his crewmen.

"Opium affects the mind and induces a dream state and feelings of detachment," Yang continued. "This new strain causes complete detachment."

My heart thudded. "What does that mean?"

"It turns men into animals, ready to attack anyone in sight."

My hand edged toward the pistol in my belt. I scanned the edge of the trees for movement. Beside me, Makoto was doing the same.

"I've come to believe there was a reason Chancellor Lin made such a reckless move," Yang continued, unperturbed. "The *Yangguizi* demanded retribution after their shipments were confiscated, but the Chancellor refused." Yang's jaw hardened. "He knew what was happening was worse than addiction so he destroyed the opium."

And sparked a war. Yang's theory sounded mad, but the entire conflict was madness.

"Do you believe there is evidence of the tainted opium on this island?" I asked him.

"This was a haven for opium smugglers. The island was seized during the ban ten years ago, but any recent record of it has disappeared."

The surrounding trees began to thin as we moved along the faded dirt path. The scouts at the front of our party came to a stop and signaled to Yang they'd found something. There was a wooden shelter in the center of a clearing ahead. Weeds had grown tall around the structure and the panes of glass in the windows had been broken. There was no movement or sign of any life inside.

"Let's go see, friends." Yang's light tone held an ominous ring.

Our party moved as one unit with Yang taking the lead. Makoto moved in closer to Yang, his hand hovering near the hilt of his katana. Makoto was meticulous about not committing to action too soon, but I preferred to err on the side of caution. I drew my pistol from its holster.

One of the doors was slightly ajar and Yang reached for it before I took hold of the sleeve of his jacket. He glanced back over his shoulder and our eyes met. Wasn't this why we'd come? He'd asked for protection.

Makoto moved past us while Yang's gaze remained fixed onto me. The corner of his mouth lifted crookedly.

Wood scraped against the ground as Makoto dragged the door open. I let go of Yang's arm to follow Makoto inside, weapon ready.

For the last three years, I'd been alone in Nagasaki without friend or family. I knew how to keep myself safe, but I was unaccustomed to being in the company of so many others. Yang fell into step behind me.

The interior was dim and the air was thick with dust. An array of vats was arranged in the center of the room in a honeycomb-like pattern. The building appeared to be some sort of distillery. A murky, unidentifiable smell filled the air. I stepped close to see the vats were stained with a black tar.

Yang produced a folding knife from his coat pocket and bent to scrape at the residue. "I'll need to perform some tests."

He'd come prepared. Out of his pocket came a glass vial which he used to collect a few scrapings. Yang took a few more samples as he wove around the vats. Then he took to inspecting the network of pipes that snaked around the room, feeding into the containers. Beneath the vats appeared to be an iron grate.

"A furnace," Yang explained as I bent to peer below. "They were cooking something here."

"Opium?" I asked.

"Refining opium isn't a complicated process. It's quite simple."

Yang made another circuit, trailing a hand over the iron-works as if they could speak to him. The crewmen wandered through the room inspecting the equipment curiously. I glanced at Makoto who had paused at the entrance to inspect the doors. He touched a hand to the wood, his brow furrowed.

I was about to ask Makoto what he'd seen when Yang waved us on. "Come. There's more island to explore."

I holstered my pistol as I took position behind him. The utter emptiness of this place set my teeth on edge. There was a ghostly quality to how everything had been abandoned.

"Those are scratches," Makoto reported, coming up beside me. In front of us, Yang gave the doors a passing glance. I examined the doors as we passed.

Makoto was right. The surface was jagged and gouged, but the scratches were so abundant I had mistaken the roughness for the natural grain of the wood.

"What could have done that?" I asked Yang.

Silence. Yang kept his back to us, moving back to the remnant of the path. Whether he was lost in thought or deliberately ignoring me, the result was the same. Yang Hanzhu was inscrutable when he wanted to be. There was no penetrating his wall of silence.

"The door was also forced off its hinges," Makoto insisted. He maneuvered to the front of the party to confront Yang. "Was this island raided during the war with the *gaijin*?"

"The island is not a military target. It was well hidden," Yang replied. Then, quieter. "It was hidden on purpose."

The air hung heavy around us as we continued through the woods. I couldn't place the sense of unease that permeated the island, a constant prickling on my skin.

It wasn't long before we encountered another building, this one built of stacked brick and mortar. It was smaller than the first, with shuttered windows on every side. Our party readied our weapons once again; Makoto with his sword and me with my rifle in hand for the approach. We reached the door and pushed it open before stepping back.

There would be no shooting here. The building was also empty.

There were rows of worktables inside set with unfamiliar-looking devices. On one wall was a large cabinet fitted with many drawers. There were also shelves filled with glass bottles and containers.

"A laboratory," Yang declared, browsing the cluttered shelves.

I moved to open the shutters while Makoto paced through the room to inspect each hidden corner. Sunlight streamed in, murky through the cloud of dust and cobwebs.

Yang paused to pick up a flask that had been left on one of the tables. He inspected the contents before swirling the flask. There was residue on the sides of the glass and a sticky layer of liquid at the bottom.

Glass crunched beneath my boots as I followed Yang through the laboratory. The place was in disarray. Apparatuses tossed aside, broken glass everywhere. At the end of one table lay a heap of ash and paper.

Yang sifted through the pile, raining ash onto the ground. "They burnt everything."

One scrap of paper fluttered to land at my feet. A red seal had been stamped onto it. I presented the scrap to Yang who gave it the barest of glances.

"The Ministry of Science."

He discarded the paper, letting it slip through his fingers. The puzzle pieces in my head dropped into place.

"You were a member of the Ministry."

"Yes."

He kept on moving through the laboratory, stopping at the medicine cabinet at the far end.

"During the Opium War."

"Yes." He opened the small drawers one by one, giving each only a cursory inspection. "My specialty was gunpowder. Gunpowder alchemy."

"The Emperor of your country sentenced many scientists to death after the war."

"But not me. Not me," he said, taunting and sadly triumphant.

Nippon hadn't suffered the same kind of defeat, but the shogunate had become similarly wary of Western influences. Anyone who had an interest in Western studies and inventions suddenly became suspect.

"My father—" A knot formed in my throat as I prepared to speak.

"I know about your father, Sagara Satomi," Yang replied quietly.

I had forgotten myself, mentioning something so personal among strangers. The eerie stillness of the laboratory reminded me too much of my father's abandoned schoolhouse, once a place of study and learning. The imperial assassin had walked in during a lesson and Father calmly instructed the students to leave. When they returned, he lay still at the head of the class, his throat cut.

I cursed the memory for returning now. Here. Yang turned to me and our gazes locked for too long a time. I needed something to focus on to fight back the tears and there was nothing but him. I traced the sharp curve of his cheekbones with my eyes, the strong line of his chin, trying to reduce them to shapes with less meaning. I could see the skip of his pulse in his neck, the rise and fall of his chest as he regarded me.

He was the first to turn away.

"Let's see what else is on this island," he announced.

The laboratory was left abandoned once more.

Chapter 3

"I don't like this place," Makoto said as we continued into the woods. "It's full of dark spirits."

"I wouldn't have taken you for one who believes in ghost stories," Yang replied.

Our party fanned out as we walked with Yang at the center and Makoto and I on either side of him. The crewmen formed the front and rear guard.

The path once again disappeared under a growth of weeds and bramble. The wild grass grew as tall as the tops of my boots, nearly up to my knees. I kept my gaze trained on the surrounding brush while the two men conversed.

"Not ghosts," Makoto insisted. "Spirits."

I didn't know what brought Makoto to this conclusion, but I couldn't help but agree with him. The hairs on the back of my neck rose higher with each step.

Suddenly Yang came to a stop and I did the same, looking about warily. There was no sign of any movement through the dense growth of trees. When I looked back to Yang, his head was cocked to one side.

"What is—"

He raised a hand, demanding silence. "It's quiet here," Yang said.

He was right. I'd sensed something was unusual about this place, but I couldn't explain why. Now I knew: the island was too still. There was no scurry of wildlife among the leaves and twigs. We couldn't even hear the chirp of birds.

Makoto looked over at me. "Ghost Hill," he said grimly.

Ghost Hill was a place steeped in lore and superstition. Yang shot us a puzzled look. At that moment, we saw two figures hunched on the ground up ahead.

We slowed our step and as we approached we could see it was two men. Their clothes were smudged and gray and torn to rags. The lines of their bones jutted sharply through the worn cloth. They were bent over something. When Makoto called out to them, their heads swiveled lethargically toward us.

The first sight stole my breath. Their faces were too inhuman to be called a face. Thin and wasted with gray skin, sunken eyes and a hollow black hole of a mouth. As if their tongues had been soaked in tar. The one closest to us had a shred of flesh hanging from his teeth as his jaw worked. On the ground between them were the remains of an animal that had been torn apart. A dreadful silence surrounded us.

We were paralyzed with shock when the ground started rumbling. A strangled cry rose from one of the crewmen at the perimeter. He fell to his knees as the creatures grabbed hold of him.

Suddenly they were everywhere.

A horde of dark bodies tore through the brush, rushing at us. Arms, legs, the white gnash of teeth. Creatures that looked to be little more than skin stretched over bone. I didn't know what I was staring at. Men. Beasts. I only knew to raise my rifle and aim at the center as one of them rushed at me.

The first shot exploded. I'd hit one of the things in the chest. He fell back, but more advanced. The horde trampled over the fallen creature with a sickening crunch of bone and flesh. The wave was nearly upon us. From the corner of my eye I caught the flash of Makoto's two blades. Yang moved closer to me. In his hand, he held two pale stones.

"Run," he commanded before throwing the stones at the foot of the horde.

With a flash of light, smoke billowed into the air. My eyes stung as the cloud surrounded us. I tried to wave through the smoke when Yang appeared beside me and grabbed my arm.

I followed him, running blind. Behind us I could hear the growl and snarl of the horde. As the smoke cleared, there was no sign of Makoto or the others. I glanced back over my shoulder to see the feral creatures pushing through the smoke in a tangle of bodies.

We ran faster, tearing through the woods with branches whipping against me. There was a thicket ahead and we ducked into it, hiding among the trees. Yang leaned forward, hands grasping his knees as he tried to catch his breath. My heart pounded like a hammer inside my chest.

"We have to find shelter," he said.

We could try to return to the refinery, but we'd risk encountering those things. "We can go back toward the water," I suggested. "Get back to the boats."

Hopefully the others would do the same.

The sound of a snarl set us back on alert. Yang slung one of my rifles around his shoulder and we started running again. I wasn't sure if he knew how to fire it, but I was grateful for the lightened load. Gradually the sounds of pursuit faded behind us. We slowed our pace and I took the opportunity to lift a steel-handled pistol from my belt.

I checked to ensure it was properly loaded. "Do you know how to use this?"

"I have some experience."

I presented the weapon to Yang, grip first. The way Yang took hold of it told me enough. I wouldn't have to worry about being shot in the back by a nervous hand. He completed a quick inspection, checking the chamber himself. I handed him more bullets which he pocketed.

"We don't have enough ammunition to fend off the afflicted," he said grimly.

"What are they afflicted with?"

"Opium. The drug has destroyed their minds."

A branch snapped to our right. A gaunt figure moved swiftly through the trees with more scrambling behind him. Once again, we set off. I knew why we were being hunted. These people, if there was any bit of humanity left in them, had been left on this island. They had caught and devoured every animal in sight to keep from wasting away from hunger.

We needed to find a safe place to hide, regroup. If we were caught out in the open, the horde would overwhelm us.

As we started across a clearing, I spied more of the afflicted roaming nearby in the trees. I pulled Yang back behind a fallen log and crouched down, praying the wild grass was tall enough to hide us.

My stomach sank as I heard more of them in the brush. "They're gathering. Like a herd."

Yang opened his palm to reveal another of his smoke bombs. "This might get us through. The path starts again over there." He gestured toward the bare patch of dirt at the far side of the clearing. "We'll follow it, see where it leads."

Breathing deep, I readied my rifle. I'd have to shoot and run at once if the creatures attacked. I met Yang's eyes and he nodded. It was time.

We sprang from the hiding spot together, but only made it a few steps before we were sighted. With a vicious shriek, the creatures charged toward us. Yang waited until we were halfway across the clearing before deploying the smoke bomb. Though the cloud blinded me, I kept on running. I could sense the dark shadows moving closer on either side of us.

One of them clawed toward me when we emerged from the smoke. I jammed the butt of my rifle into it, catching it squarely in the chest. Then I pushed past, not caring whether I'd felled it or not. If we slowed down, the creatures would overwhelm us.

As soon as we reached the path, I saw it. Yang spotted the building at the same time. We both sprang toward it, sprinting as fast as possible. The double doors at the front were unlocked and left ajar. I slipped inside with Yang immediately behind me. Together we pushed the heavy wooden panel shut.

"Is there anything to bar the door with?" Yang asked.

I searched around. We were in what looked like a stable. In the dim interior, I could make out pens arranged against opposite walls with a narrow corridor between. At the far end of the stable, a ladder led up to a loft area. We abandoned the door to run for the ladder. I began the climb first with Yang following closely behind.

At the top, I dragged myself onto the wooden platform and swung around, unhooking the rifle to take aim. I waited for the creatures to break into the stable, counting the seconds. Yang pulled himself up from the ladder and also turned to stare down at the floor, chest heaving. The front door remained closed.

Exhausted, I fell back against the wooden slats. My words came out in gasps. "Can…those things…climb?"

Yang collapsed beside me, forearm propped over his eyes. "I don't know."

If the afflicted could climb the ladder, only one would be able to reach us at a time. We'd be able to fend them off, but it would only be a matter of time if they surrounded us.

"If they start circling, we need to run," I told Yang. "Otherwise we'll be trapped."

He didn't reply. For a long time, all I could hear was our labored breathing. I listened for the clamor of footsteps closing in. For the animal snarls of the afflicted. They never came.

Yang and I turned our heads to face one another.

"We're safe," he said, his chest rising and falling.

"For now," I replied.

I didn't believe it. I don't think he believed it either. This was all far from over.

———

THE LOFT WAS CONSTRUCTED from wooden slats and lay beneath a window through which we could see the grounds at the front of the stable. There were the remnants of several mats up there. The material had rotted away, but perhaps the loft had once been used for sleeping. We also found a broken gas lamp, though the wick was burnt to a stub and there was no oil to light it.

Yang took advantage of the fading daylight to search the area with his spyglass. "There's a rise over there. Maybe a cliff top."

He handed me the instrument to confirm. I closed one eye and peered into the glass, locating the formation he was speaking of. It was the highest point of the island. From that high point, we might be able to find Makoto and the surviving crewmen. At the very least we could signal the ship.

The sound of grunting below drew my attention. Two of the creatures wandered toward the stable. The clothing they'd once worn was torn away leaving them nearly naked. The exposed skin was torn and bleeding. They didn't show signs of knowing we were here.

"Do they ever tire?" I asked, retreating from the window. I didn't want to risk those things detecting us.

"They don't appear to," Yang replied, sitting down with his long legs stretched out before him. "They'll also ignore pain and don't exhibit any fear. All they feel is hunger."

It was hard for me to believe these creatures were once human. "The opium has taken everything from them."

"It's a new kind of sickness."

We took the opportunity to drink from our flasks and share a handful of dried dates. We'd brought little else in the way of provisions.

Yang leaned back against the wall, looking abnormally calm given how we'd been running for our lives not too long ago. He seemed capable of locking fear away like the closing of a gate.

"Have you ever smoked opium?" I asked curiously.

"I have."

"Why?"

He shrugged. "I'm *Shina-jin*, aren't I?"

I couldn't tell if he was serious. In Nippon, we thought of opium as a uniquely Chinese affliction. We guarded fiercely against its import, fearing the same rot would set in among our people. Shina was weak for succumbing to it. But now the *gaijin* had forced their way onto our shores nonetheless.

"It's like being in a waking dream. Your thoughts, your movements are slowed as if moving through water," he explained.

"One takes it not to wake, then."

"Opium dulls pain in the mind and body."

"It seems a coward's way out," I decried. "Pain is unavoidable."

"You'd prefer a quicker exit with a sharp blade. The samurai's way."

I started to argue, but clamped my mouth shut instead. I had no traditions anymore, just as I had no country.

"The horde outside was in a rage. Not like a dream at all," I said.

Yang nodded slowly, gravely. "Maybe for them it's the opposite. A nightmare."

The sky was growing dark. Another quick glance showed the stragglers hadn't left. I retreated to the opposite wall, propping my back against it to mirror Yang Hanzhu's pose. "Will your crew come looking for you?" I asked after a long silence.

"Perhaps."

He was less concerned about it than I would have expected.

"Will your Makoto-san come for you?" he countered after a beat.

"He's not my—"

"I imagine that one would die for you."

"Makoto-san is a fallen warrior. He is looking for a cause to die for." The words sounded more bitter than I intended.

"And what is your cause, Sagara-san?"

The question caught me off guard. "I have no cause."

"Not true."

Whatever my purpose was, I couldn't name it.

"Why did you leave Nagasaki?" he probed.

"I would have died if I stayed."

"So?"

"Maybe I just liked your ship," I snapped.

The corner of his mouth lifted in a smirk. I let my head fall back against the wall and closed my eyes. I was accustomed to days upon days of long silences. I opted for silence now and Yang Hanzhu seemed to be of similar disposition. Silence didn't make him uncomfortable. Occasionally we glanced outside to see the wretched creatures roaming aimlessly yet they refused to wander away. Could it be that they remembered there was flesh and blood not far away? I shuddered at the thought.

"We should have marked the building so the others would know we're here," Yang suggested after the next long stretch.

"We could do so now."

"Or we can run," Yang replied. "We'll have to make our escape sooner or later."

I opened my eyes to see him watching me intently. The thought that he had been doing so the entire time made the back of my neck uncomfortably warm. A respectable gentleman would know enough to avert his eyes.

"Which will it be?" I asked him.

"What do you say?"

I glanced outside. The evening was upon us.

"There are too many of them out there and we won't be able to see. It would be best to stay here until daylight."

We'd have to make an attempt to flee while we still had the strength. We'd gone nearly the entire day with little food and we couldn't count on Makoto-san and the crew finding us. They also had to find a way to survive.

"We'll stay until morning, then," he conceded. "Yang Hanzhu is merely an alchemist. Sagara Satomi has been surviving on her own since she was a child."

My mind wandered back to Nagasaki. To Ghost Hill. To the nights spent sleeping outside under the stars because I couldn't bear to stay inside.

"I wasn't alone," I corrected.

"The Sagara clan was condemned by the shogunate. Who would dare to disobey?"

"We should take turns keeping watch," I said, avoiding the question.

"You first. It will be a while before I can sleep," Yang offered. He took a journal from his pocket and began to scribble something. I closed my eyes and listened to the rasp of the stylus against the paper. The sound of it was enough to bring me back to a time farther back. To a time before blood stained the walls of our home. I fell asleep to the sound of Yang's writing, of knowledge being committed to memory.

I AWOKE with a start into a drowning darkness, gasping for breath. Every muscle in me tensed, as if just coming from battle. To my horror my face was drenched with tears.

"Sagara-san." Yang's voice was close in the darkness. I could sense his presence but he didn't reach out to me. "You were dreaming."

A sliver of moonlight peeked through the window. Gradually my eyes adjusted until I could make out his shape before me.

"I—I'm sorry." I don't know why I felt the need to apologize.

"You're trembling."

"No." I wiped at my eyes. The murky threads of my dream unraveled around me. I tried to catch hold of them before they slid away. What had I been dreaming about? The panic receded leaving only a sense of shame. It was unsightly to show such weakness.

"Here."

Yang started to remove his coat, but I held up a hand to ward him off. "How long was I sleeping?"

Slowly, he released the edges of the jacket. "A few hours."

"I'm fine."

Yang nodded. "All right."

He sat back but didn't retreat. We sat there for the space of the next breaths, just out of arm's reach, saying nothing.

I broke the silence. "You should rest now."

"I can do that."

I wanted him to stop watching me so closely. Even if it was with concern.

"This isn't fear," I told him.

He tilted his head, not convinced.

"I wasn't afraid in the dream." I swiped the back of my hand roughly over my eyes again. "It was the kind of dream where…where you're looking for something and you can't see it. You can't even remember what it was."

My throat constricted. The cold, empty feeling remained in the pit of my stomach. It wasn't real. Just a feeling conjured by my mind, yet I couldn't banish this sense of loss.

"It was just a dream, Sagara-san."

His voice resonated between us, two people stranded on this too-quiet island. There was a depth and gravity to it that soothed me.

"I wouldn't have asked you to come as my bodyguard if I thought you were easily frightened." Yang had settled in across from me with one arm draped over his knee. Completely at ease. He pushed a length of cropped hair away from his face.

"Why do you go about like that? With the clothes and the hair," I ventured. The shape of the stiff jacket squared his shoulders and created a silhouette akin to wearing armor.

"Burn the ships, as the proverb goes." Yang delighted in the irreverence of it. "Cut your hair and you've cut all ties to the Emperor."

"You've condemned yourself as a traitor."

"I didn't want there to ever be any doubt."

The room had darkened to the point where there was nothing but voice between us. Just the sound of our words and a sense of presence.

"I was a traitor to my Emperor the moment I set foot on your ship," I confessed.

"Is that when it truly started?" Yang asked quietly.

My rebellion against the shogunate had started long before. This man knew nothing about me, but he understood that part of me. It had started the moment the daimyo had marked my father for death. The moment I'd left my guardian to roam Ghost Hill—a ghost myself.

"I sold firearms in Nagasaki," I confessed to him. "To countrymen. To foreigners."

"Why?"

"Because I wanted to feed myself." I could have left it at that, but I wasn't finished. "And I wanted to disobey."

Yang Hanzhu wore his rebellion outwardly. He wanted to tell the world that he was an outlaw by choice. My rebellion had always been hidden inside. I had been trying to tell myself that I no longer belonged in Nagasaki.

For the last ten years, my dreams were plagued by the shogunate's assassins. They'd come in mechanized armor with swords sharp enough to cut a man in half with a single blow.

Those wretched creatures in the woods weren't the most frightening things I'd ever faced. I'd spent most of my life daring the shogunate to come for me the way it had come for my father. The armored enforcers had come eventually. They'd been more formidable than the worst of my nightmares. Gleaming metal killing machines.

But I survived. I defeated the assassins with weapons made with my own hands, using the skills my father had passed on to me.

"You and I are free, Sagara-san," Yang concluded.

"You and I?"

"You and I," he insisted. "We are our own masters. I like that about you, Sagara-san," Yang continued. "When adversaries attack, you shoot them dead. When I speak, there appears to be more than just a glimmer of understanding in your eyes. Should either of us set foot in our homelands, we'd be hanged as traitors. There's no reason we can't roam the earth together until the last of our days."

"I think you're teasing me, Yang Hanzhu."

"Well, if we are to leave this island, it will be together or not at all." He glanced up at me from his reclined position, looking very serious. "Let's get off this island, Sagara-san."

Then he closed his eyes and said no more. For all I knew, he'd fallen immediately asleep.

As Yang took his turn resting, I took my turn at the watch. I went to peer out the window into the darkness below. It was then, staring into the night, that I remembered the part of the dream that had devastated me so.

I dreamt that I was still on Ghost Hill. That I had never left.

The most frightening thing was that all my efforts to fight back, to escape, had meant nothing. I was still trapped. I was still alone.

Chapter 4

We lowered ourselves down the ladder during the orange sky of dawn. The sun had just begun to peek over the horizon and the view was clear from the loft window. When I reached the ground floor, what had appeared to be holding pens for animals looked different in the light of day.

The cells were much smaller and the doors fitted with iron bars. Yang came up beside me as I stared at an empty enclosure. Though we said nothing, I imagined he was thinking the same thing I was.

It didn't look like an enclosure for livestock.

"Come on," he said grimly.

Yang stood at the stable doors. I positioned behind him, rifle drawn and ready.

We'd mapped out a rough course through the trees in case we were separated, but staying together was a matter of life and death.

Yang gave a signal it was time and I acknowledged it with a nod. I took in a deep breath as he pushed the doors open. After surveying the area outside, Yang advanced and I followed. We moved as quickly and quietly as we could. The plan was to find higher ground and create a signal to alert the rest of the landing party—if they were still alive.

We continued along the empty pathway without another living thing in sight. The afflicted had moved on or perhaps they were sleeping. They were human, after all. We did our best not to rouse them if that was the case.

"Stay vigilant," Yang said. "They'll appear docile until they see someone."

"How do you know so much about them?"

"Some of my crewmen were afflicted. I tried to find a cure."

"Were you successful?"

He didn't answer.

We encountered another building on the way toward the cliff. I shook my head furiously when Yang started toward the door. He shot me a hard look. Whatever negotiation had taken place, apparently, I lost. He approached the structure with pistol raised and I had no choice but to follow.

This building was larger than the stable...or whatever the last place had been. Inside was a long chamber with mats and blankets strewn along the floor.

"Dormitories," Yang surmised.

"We should go." The hairs on the back of my neck rose as I stepped along the pallets. Unlike the other places we'd seen, the dormitory hadn't been completely stripped. Yet it was clear from the layer of dust covering the room that nothing had been used in a long time.

Yang stooped to pick up a brown bottle left among the mats. He turned it over in his hands, then waved the opening beneath his nose. My impatience rose. I knew what that faraway gaze meant. He was ensnared by his scientist's sense of curiosity. Nothing could break the trance.

"This wasn't merely used as sleeping quarters," he amended, looking from one end of the chamber to the other. "This was a sick ward."

"For whom?"

"Opium addicts would be my guess." He picked up an empty yellow paper packet and gave it a cursory inspection before letting the paper flutter to the floor. Many more of the yellow wrappers were strewn about in the chamber.

A disturbing history was beginning to form. The people would have been packed in here, more prisoner than patient. Had they all become like the horde we'd encountered? Any who hadn't succumbed to illness would have been attacked by the others. The thought sickened me.

"Why would they be brought here?" I asked.

"Isolation. To keep them away from opium until they could be free of its influence."

Except an addict was never free. That was the cautionary tale that we had been told across the sea in Nippon. Once poisoned by the drug, a soul was caught in its grip. Opium had enslaved a once great empire, hadn't it?

"We should go," I repeated forcefully. "Now."

Yang took one last look over the chamber, searching for lingering clues. Finally, he decided there was nothing else to find. We left the ward as quickly as we had come.

THERE WAS another ward not far from the first. The doors on this building had been thrown open. One glimpse of the inside showed it had been torn apart violently.

"Leave it." There was nothing for us to find, and the horror of what had happened tore at my soul. "There are too many ghosts here. We should not disturb them."

Yang gave me a quizzical look. "Can there be ghosts if these people are alive?"

"Are the afflicted still living?" I countered.

There was little humanity left in them. A clean death would be mercy. For my part, I wanted nothing more than to leave this island. It was too desolate of a place. A dying place without promise. The sickness and hopelessness of addiction had infected the very air we breathed.

"The empire keeps ships away from these waters with ghost stories," Yang remarked after we left the second dormitory behind. "There are rumors of shipwreck and ill-fortune around this island."

"Like Ghost Hill," I murmured.

"You keep on mentioning this place."

I took in a deep breath. "My father built his academy in the hills overlooking Nagasaki Bay. The name was born when the locals noticed no birds would nest there. It was abnormally quiet, like this island, but the reason wasn't because of ghosts. Before his death, my father constructed a tower. It relayed signals using a strong electrical current. The air would become heavy with it, so much that birds and other creatures sensed it and stayed away. After my father was killed, no one thought to dismantle the tower. The gears and wheels continued to turn, producing the current."

Was the signal tower still functioning? In time, all my father's creations would cease to function. Or the shogunate would destroy them.

"Sagara Shintarō was a remarkable scientist," Yang declared. "Your father's death was a waste."

His anger surprised me. Anger for someone he'd never known.

"Sovereigns are threatened by knowledge," he went on. "How could they not be? Their power comes from nothing but an accident of birth."

As we continued our journey, I listened to his litany regarding power and the responsibility of those who sought knowledge. Much of it echoed my father's sentiments, but my father had remained loyal to the shogunate and the Emperor to the end. He'd just believed the loyal needed to intervene, even if it meant subverting orders.

The earth rose ahead of us to a rocky hill that blocked the

shore. Our plan was to climb the formation and start a signal fire. Our party had a better chance of detecting the signal above the forest floor. We could even attempt to signal Yang's ship.

We started toward the foothill, moving with quiet determination. It was only a matter of time before we escaped this cursed island.

I abandoned all hope of a quick rescue when we reached the base of the cliff. The horde had gathered there, at least twenty of them. Many of the creatures lay sprawled in the dirt, looking weak and emaciated. The others roamed the area in circles, like a pack of wild dogs on the prowl.

"Why are they gathered here?" There was no discernible source of food. Why didn't the afflicted wander away to search for sustenance?

"Perhaps they encountered the barrier of the cliff and stopped. The tainted opium has robbed them of rational thought."

Whatever the reason, there was little point in theorizing. We needed to get to the top of the hill and create a signal fire. Our own sources of water were pitifully low and hunger gnawed at my insides.

"They appear weak. We might be able to outrun the majority of them and fight off the rest," I suggested.

"It's too much of a risk. I've seen the afflicted lie still as if in a trance only to launch into a frenzy at the sight of possible prey. A starving animal is the most dangerous kind."

"Perhaps we can draw them away—"

Yang's eyes lit up. "Fire," he declared triumphantly. "They're drawn to fire."

"No animal is drawn to fire."

"Except the human animal. The smoke and movement will lure them. They won't touch it, but it will draw their attention."

The plan was simple. We gathered piles of dried grass and wood and built a set of markers leading back to the sleeping quarters. Igniting the fire was easy. Yang Hanzhu was a gunpowder alchemist and I had a good supply of it.

We started in reverse order with the sleeping dormitory first. The bamboo mats provided enough material to feed the fire. The building itself was dry wood. As flames rose to engulf the building, I couldn't help but feel we were cleansing the island of the plague that hung over it.

From there we ignited the other bundles to lure the horde. Then we crouched low in the brush and waited.

It wasn't long before plumes of smoke rose from the dried grass, drawing the horde away from the hills. One by one they rose and dragged their withered bodies toward the fire.

"What if Makoto and the others see the fire?" I asked as the last of the afflicted shuffled past.

"All the better. That would mean they're close. They'll find us faster when we signal from up there."

I checked the foothills again for any sign of danger before we started up. There were no trails cut into the rock, so we had to search for natural footholds and handholds as we made the climb. I grabbed fistfuls of wild grass to drag myself up. After an hour, we had slipped back one length for every three we gained, but we were making progress. Yang pulled ahead of me and lifted himself onto a ledge before turning around to offer me a hand. As I reached for it, my eye caught something just over his shoulder.

Yang took hold of my waist to help me onto the rock. Once I regained my footing, I turned upward to take a better look. At the top of the hill, hidden behind an outcropping of rock, was another building.

The structure was positioned to overlook the sea as well as most of the island. The sight of it was enough to renew our resolve. We searched for a way up but found nothing.

"There must be something on the other side of this hill," Yang reasoned.

Carefully, we made our way around to the side facing the

ocean. Once there, Yang's guess proved correct. We found a thin trail cut into the rock. It led to a contraption tangled in vines. Together we pulled the vegetation away to reveal a two-man hand crank attached to a large iron wheel.

"It's a lift." I followed the attached cables up the face of the cliff. "The carriage is there."

What we could see of it was overgrown. Yang stood on one side of the crank while I stood on the other. We gripped our respective handles and tried to turn. The attached wheel groaned in protest.

"It must have been years since this was in use. Try again. Slow and steady," I assured him.

The wheel groaned again, but gradually began to move. The carriage encountered resistance from the vines, but as we pulled harder on the levers, the growth snapped away. The compartment resembled a cage and looked large enough to fit the two of us. The lift had likely been used to raise supplies up to the watchtower.

"The transport was in raised position," Yang remarked. He had removed his coat and rolled up his shirtsleeves. The muscles in his forearms tensed and stretched as we worked the crank in tandem. "It was used to take something up there the last time it was operated."

"And it never came back down," I finished for him.

It was possible someone had raised the carriage to keep it from damage or to prevent anyone else from going up, but that hardly made sense if the island had been abandoned. Nervous anticipation knotted in my stomach as the carriage completed its descent. What would we find up there?

Once we settled the cage onto the ground, there was another dilemma. How to get back up.

"It took both of us to bring it down," Yang remarked.

I climbed into the cage to inspect the controls on the side panel. "I believe we can raise the platform from inside. Come, I'll show you."

Gathering his things, he climbed in beside me. "Engineering isn't my area of expertise."

There was a spring-loaded mechanism attached to the cables and the main wheel. "The act of lowering the carriage raised the counterweight. See the tension coiled here? We should be able to release this lever here and the carriage will reverse."

Yang looked skeptical. "I suppose we can just pull the lever and see."

He had more trust in chemicals and their properties than in machinery. Bracing a hand against the sides of the cage, I released the lever.

Nothing happened.

Yang looked at me expectantly.

"Something must be broken," I said.

I inspected the panel and control mechanism again, tracing the lines and gears before climbing back outside.

"Out with you too," I ordered brusquely when I caught Yang still watching me from inside the transport. "Help me raise this compartment so I can look at the cable attachments."

We turned the crank to raise the cage up to waist level. Then I made sure to lock the wheel before slipping underneath. It didn't take long to find the problem. The gears were clogged from the broken vines. That and a combination of rust prevented the mechanism from turning.

I only had a few of my tools, but they would do. Grabbing a punch tool, I crouched beneath the carriage and set to work removing the vegetation from the gears.

"How long do you think this will take?" Yang asked. He remained outside to keep his eye on the wheel and ensure the lock stayed in place.

"Fifteen minutes, perhaps twenty." I jabbed at a chunk of vine stuck in the gears. After a few minutes, my fingers were sticky from sap, but I was making progress.

"This is fascinating, Sagara-san. I didn't realize you were mechanically inclined." I could hear the admiration in his tone.

I kept working. "My father was an engineer. He was always designing some complicated machine. I'm not like him." I had finished clearing away one attachment and moved on to the other cable. "I don't have his talent for invention. Seeing something that should work and fixing it is simple."

"I would disagree."

"My father would make these moving automatons. In Nippon, we called them *karakuri*."

"The puppets. I've seen them in tea parlors."

"These were much more intricate."

I was hidden beneath the transport now. Yang's voice came to me from outside. The barrier between us, being able to hear but not see each other, made it easier to speak to him.

"There was one *karakuri* he created that towered over the tallest of men. Father fitted the automaton with armor and called it—called him—Yoshiro. He was so lifelike. After Father was gone, Yoshiro would follow me around and stand guard over me. Whenever something broke inside him, I could open up his panels and figure out what was wrong. I kept him functioning for many years after—"

My throat constricted with an unexpected flood of emotion.

"What happened to him?" Yang asked, breaking the stretch of silence.

"He…he finally broke down. As all machines do."

I was speaking about my father's mechanical puppet as if he were a friend, a brother even, rather than an elaborate toy. Maybe I was a little mad myself.

When I emerged from the shadow of the transport, Yang had lit a cigarette. He stood beside the carriage, taking a drag.

"Can you find the pliers?" I asked.

He bent, cigarette balanced between two fingers, and sifted through my pack. He retrieved the tool and handed it to me. I disappeared underneath to pull the thicker vines out of the gears.

"How much more time?" Yang asked.

"Five minutes."

Most of the growth was cleared away. We would be ready to try again soon.

"How much longer now?" Yang asked no more than two minutes later.

"Why are you so focused on the time?" I came out from under the transport.

"The fires have died out. It looks like our companions are returning."

He gave a nod toward the high grass. The horde of afflicted were roaming back toward us, closer with each breath.

"Why didn't you *tell* me?" I demanded.

Yang shrugged and took another drag from his cigarette, blowing out smoke in a leisurely stream. "I figured you would work better if you remained calm."

"That's nonsense. I...you should have—" Arguing only wasted more time. "Get back inside." I grabbed my belongings and might have been less than civil as I shoved Yang and then myself into the carriage.

Five of the afflicted lurched toward the lift. The moment they saw us, they broke into a run and I quickly pulled the lever to activate the transport. The mechanism whirred as the gears started to turn, which was promising. We rose up a foot before stopping again, which was not.

"*Kono kasu,*" I swore. "Not you," I amended when I saw Yang staring at me.

He smirked. "We're about to be eaten and you're apologizing to me?"

I narrowed my eyes at him before jumping back out. "If anything comes near, shoot it," I shouted as I slipped back beneath the transport to dig away at the remaining growth.

Pulling out the thinnest punch tool, I slid it into the edge of the main gears. I gave myself to the count of ten, tracking silently as I worked. Outside, I could hear the growls of the afflicted growing louder. There were more of them. My heart hammered inside my chest and my hands started shaking, but I forced them still.

I kept on working, counting. At ten, I hurried back up into the transport. By then, the horde of afflicted had grown. The leaders of the pack had nearly reached us.

Yang had his pistol aimed as I took position by the control panel. I could see hands reaching up, torn fingers clawing at the bottom of the lift. There was one lurch and then another before the transport began to rise. I breathed deep, exhaling sharply as the carriage finally traveled beyond the reach of the horde. The writhing mass of bodies below grew smaller and smaller as we rose to the top of the cliff.

Chapter 5

We exited the carriage of the lift with weapons drawn. From there, we had a clear view of the watchtower and it became evident the structure's camouflage was intentional. The sides of the tower had a rough stone finish which blended in to the surrounding hill. I couldn't detect any movement within.

At the wooden doors, Yang called out twice to announce our arrival. When there was no answer, he pulled on the iron ring and the door creaked open.

It was dark inside, but the interior lacked the stagnant, musty smell of all the other buildings on the island.

"Someone has been here recently," Yang remarked.

There was no dust on the wooden table and stool in the main room. There were other items of use near the stove: a pot, ceramic bowls, a small stack of wood for the fire. I paused at the wall beneath the window. A field of marks had been cut into the wood.

"One for each day?" I ran my fingers over the scoring, taking a rough count. "Over two years."

Yang came up beside me and gave the crude calendar a

cursory glance before moving on. "This back room seems to be used for storage."

We made a brief inspection of the area. There were a few sacks of rice along with preserved squid and salted fish. Several casks of oil were set near the wall. The rest of the room was desolately bare save for a trunk in the corner. Yang opened it to reveal a stash of yellowed paper.

"Records." Yang rifled through them and I could see his eyes light up with the promise of information. "They've been tossed in here without a care. If there's anything of interest, it will take time to sift through."

Shaking his head in disgust, he picked up a handful of paper before tossing it unceremoniously back into the trunk.

Our exploration led us up the stairs into the tower. There was a single galley at the top with several windows arranged on every side. I took one while Yang went to another. From my outlook, I could see into the woods below. The sleeping quarters we'd torched were easily identifiable. Smoke rose from the remains of our fire.

"Come look at this." Yang beckoned me over to his aperture and I went to stand beside him. Shoulder-to-shoulder we looked down onto a yet undiscovered building tucked into the canyon. A high fence of wooden stakes had been built around the perimeter.

"What do you think that could be?" I asked.

He stared at it a long time, as if weighing his answer carefully. "Something very important to someone."

I started at the sound of the door creaking open. I pulled my pistol from my belt as we hurried down the stairs, spilling into the main room to come face-to-face with a thin, bearded man holding a basket.

"So," he began, his voice rasping against his throat. He looked us both over in turn. "You made it here."

THE MAN INTRODUCED himself as Hu Bin and invited us into the lighthouse. Inside, the three of us sat on the floor with an oil lamp set between us. He poured us a brew of what he called root tea, which I attempted to sip very slowly. It was bitter with a somewhat oily residue, but given that Hu had been stranded for so long, his attempt at hospitality was admirable.

Our meal consisted of a scoop of boiled rice, a piece of yam root, and a handful of some sort of brown nut.

"Silkworm," Hu explained after I bit into a nut that turned out to not be a nut. "Very easy to grow."

I chewed around the mealy worm texture and swallowed bitter tea to wash it down. What we had before us was likely a feast for the hermit. In truth, I'd eaten nothing but dates over the last day. Boiled silkworm and yam wasn't so bad.

"Are there any other survivors here?" Yang asked.

"Only me."

Hu had his head down as he dug into his meal. Yang waited until Hu finished eating before continuing his questions.

"What happened to the others?"

Hu looked up, wiping the back of his hand over his mouth. Deliberately, he took a drink of his tea and regarded Yang with a dagger-sharp gaze. "Are you an opium runner?"

Yang returned the stare.

"I saw your ship," Hu continued. "It's the first to come since the last one left. I didn't know if they were returning to rescue me or execute me."

"Who are 'they'?" I asked.

"The Imperial Ministry," Yang replied before Hu could answer. "But, my friend, you can be assured that I am not with them."

Hu looked over Yang's clothing and his shorn hair, which hung loose about his neck. It was in stark contrast to the older man's queue, which he'd kept neatly braided even while in exile.

"You're an outlaw," Hu accused.

"Against the very authorities that left you here."

Hu cast his eyes downward, head bowed. We waited for him to speak, but he said nothing.

"I can offer you passage on my ship," Yang offered. "I do not deal in opium or any other form of smuggling. All I ask of you is your story."

The hermit rubbed a hand over his temples, slowly shaking his head back and forth. "I thought I would die here. I would die alone on this island."

"Tell us what happened, friend."

Hu sighed long and loud. "One morning, the boats were all gone. We thought they would come back. At least to bring more supplies. When months went by with no word, we knew we had been abandoned."

"There was someone else here with you then," I prompted.

"Four of us. We were brought here to tend to the addicts. Care for them through the cravings and withdrawals. Once cured, they would be returned."

"So this was an opium refuge." I could see the furrow in Yang's brow deepening. "So far from the mainland?"

"Opium reclaims nearly every man once he leaves a refuge. There is no escape when the poison is everywhere. Here, we were isolated from such temptation."

Yang's jaw grew tight. The story set his teeth on edge. "Why was the refuge abandoned?" he asked evenly.

"I don't know." Hu downed his tea, rubbed his hand once more over his forehead. He looked genuinely troubled. "We never knew. After the boats left, we continued with our duties, but as time went on, supplies dwindled. The addicts became agitated, then violent with withdrawal pain."

"In my humble experience, that is not typical of opium smokers," Yang remarked, his tone remaining flat and controlled.

"You haven't seen what I've seen." The words poured from Hu now, as if he'd been waiting for a long time to purge himself of the memories. "The poison destroys everything. The worst of the addicts became mindless with need. They demanded food, more opium. We were overpowered. They killed two of us with their bare hands. Myself and one other… His name… How can I not remember his name?"

Hu bowed his head again, striking his head with his fists as he choked out a sob. I looked over to Yang, at a loss for what to do. His expression was unreadable.

"Jiang!" Hu suddenly blurted out. "It was Jiang. We gathered what supplies we could and retreated up here. Left the addicts to the rest of the island where they've become nothing more than animals. I thought I would die here. I thought I would die here."

The old man retreated into himself, rocking slightly with his shoulders hunched. What could we do but watch in silence, hoping the worst would pass?

Eventually it did. Hu regained his composure, breathing deep and wiping his eyes.

"What happened to Jiang?" Yang asked quietly.

I shot him a look, but Yang remained focused on Hu, watching his every expression. Hu didn't answer. Instead he shook his head slowly and began to collect the empty bowls.

"There's a beacon up in the tower," Yang continued. "I need to signal my ship. They'll come for us when they see it, perhaps within a day. You can leave with us."

Hu nodded, docile. All his energy had been spent in confession. "One more day," he murmured. And then again, "I thought I would die here."

AN HOUR LATER, Yang and I carried firewood and a drum of oil up the stairs to light the beacon. It was at the topmost point of the tower. Yang had to climb up on a ladder to reach it. I stood beside him, handing up tinder and wood and oil as requested. When it was lit, I could see the warm orange glow from below.

"Now we just need to keep it lit," Yang said, coming back down. "My crew should be able to see it from the other end of the island."

"Much better than sending up smoke," I remarked.

Yang nodded. We settled back, sitting against the wall of the tower and looking up at the fire for a few minutes.

"There's enough oil for Hu to have lit the beacon long ago," Yang observed.

"Perhaps he was afraid. The Ministry had left him here to die. Any ship that came might have been sent to make certain of it."

Mistrust of those in power was something Yang and I both understood, but he was not convinced. "His story about the refuge doesn't ring true. Addicts don't become violent upon withdrawal."

"He seemed to believe it."

Yang shook his head. "There's something he's not telling us. I've heard myths that opium corrupts one's morals. That opium turns one into a demon. If only opium smoke did induce such violence. We might have been able to fight back against the foreign devils."

"Something strange did happen to the addicts here. You suspected there was an altered formula."

With a long sigh, Yang let his head fall back against the wall. Even though he was still, I could sense his agitation in every muscle.

"Do you have nightmares?" he asked finally, by way of distraction.

It was obvious Yang was thinking of the previous night. I closed my eyes, wanting yet not wanting to seek out the memories. "I often dream of the assassins who killed my father. I never see them, but I can hear them moving about in their heavy armor. Just the metallic clang of their footsteps coming closer."

"But that's not what frightens you. I've seen you face the infamous *hitokiri*."

"Dreams are a different matter. In nightmares, you're help-less—unable to move. A single moment can seem to last for hours—"

I remembered then what had affected me so last night. I was on Ghost Hill back in Nagasaki. I could hear the *hitokiri* in the fog, but I couldn't see them. Something rolled at my feet. It was a helmet. When I picked it up, there was no blood. Only a tangle of copper wire where the neck would be.

"What is it?" Yang asked gently.

I shook my head. This memory was mine alone. "Something I lost that can't be replaced," was all I would reveal.

I had poured too much meaning into Yoshiro even though he was a construction made of gears and wire. Once the automaton was gone, it wasn't that I had nothing left. I was forced to realize I'd had nothing there all along.

The beacon fire flickered and I used the excuse to go check on it. I stoked it with the poker and watched the sparks dance before climbing back down the ladder.

"We'll take turns on watch, same as yesterday," Yang suggested. "Maintain the beacon."

Keeping with the routine of the previous night, I placed the pack with my weapons within reach and laid down on my side with my arm as a headrest. The position allowed me to watch Yang. Once again, he took the journal from his pocket and began to write.

"Do you do that every evening?"

He looked up, surprised by my attention. "It's how I remember the finer details of the day."

"Would you forget if you didn't do it?"

"It's a way to think things over a second time, make connections I might have missed."

"My father kept a journal." It was the only possession of his I'd managed to keep. "Most of it is meaningless to me, but I still read it all the time. It's just notes and observations. Many small thoughts."

"The same here."

I shifted, trying to find a comfortable position. Then I let my eyes close.

"Today I made a note that Sagara Satomi is mechanically inclined," Yang said. "Also, that there is a compound in the canyon below that may hold a secret. One never knows when a small idea becomes a big one."

I didn't realize how tired I was. Already I was starting to drift. "Did you ask Old Hu about the building?"

"Better to see it with my own eyes. We'll reunite with the crew and then go take a look."

Yang continued to write in his journal. I fell asleep beside him while he gathered his memories, wondering if it was sometimes better to forget and clear away the clutter of the past. How else could one ever make room for something new?

Chapter 6

"Sagara-san."

A hand gripped my shoulder to rouse me from sleep and I awoke with a start. It took a moment to recall what was happening. Our first and second shift had gone by without incident. It had to be several hours past midnight.

"Do you smell that?"

Something was burning. I looked first to the beacon, but Yang interrupted. "It's down below."

Jumping to my feet, I grabbed my pack and rifle. We hurried down the stairwell, feeling our way in the dark, and were met with the crackle of a fire burning in the hearth. A stack of papers curled and blackened beneath the flames.

With a curse, Yang grabbed the poker and tried to rescue the papers, stirring up a rain of ash that circled the room like gnats. They were too far gone.

"That lying dog—"

Lighting a gas lantern, Yang ran for the door with me close behind.

"He's destroying the evidence," Yang growled.

We ran to the opposite side of the tower, tearing through a

garden. Hu was nowhere to be seen, but I could hear movement at the edge of the cliff. It was another lift.

Hu carried a lantern with him. We tracked him by its glow as the transport carriage traveled downward toward the ground. The bottom was too far away to see, but we heard the creak of the cage and then Hu appeared to move back and forth, in and out of the transport.

"He's taken the oil drums," Yang said through gritted teeth. "He's going to set fire to everything."

We rushed to the hand crank. The muscles in my back and arms burned as we pushed hard, turning the wheel as fast as we could to reel the transport back up. Yang practically jumped inside, moving to the edge to stare out the bars. I released the lever on the control panel to set us in motion.

All we could do then was wait, watching the ground as it grew closer and closer. I had just become accustomed to the falling sensation when the transport lurched to a halt, tossing the two of us together. Fighting to remain steady, I reached for the controls. The carriage swayed precariously with every movement.

The controls did nothing. "Hu sabotaged the lift."

We were stranded and it was too high to jump.

Yang was unperturbed. "No matter. Down is the easy part."

He hooked the lantern onto the cage and opened the door.

"What are you doing?"

I watched in disbelief as Yang climbed out and reached for the counterweight rope. I sank to my knees with my arm outstretched, trying to pull him back.

"Watch." His tone demanded my attention. "Watch very carefully."

He wrapped his leg around the rope so that he was intertwined with it. Then he did the same with his arm, twisting it around the line so that it rested against his coat sleeve. "Wrap the rope around your arm and leg exactly like this. Once you're secure, gradually loosen your hold to slide down. Don't touch the rope with your hands."

He slid down a length, as if to show me it was nothing at all. "No matter what happens, don't let go."

Then, with no more than a nod, he was off. I watched as Yang slid down the rope, using his body to control the speed of descent while I cursed him as a madman. My heart pounded as he neared the ground. He'd made it safely and I was left with no choice at all. I could stay up here, swaying in the wind for eternity, or I could climb out and risk being battered against the rocks below.

Breathing deep to steady myself, I eased myself out to the edge and gripped the cage door as I searched for a foothold. The wind had begun to pick up, tossing my hair into my eyes. I had to climb onto the outside of the cage to reach the rope. Trembling like a leaf, I looped my leg around and then my arm, just as I'd seen Yang do. Gingerly, I released my weight into it, still holding on to the cage. My chest was so tight I could barely breathe.

"It's not too far down," Yang called up. That was a lie. He sounded *very* far away.

Holding my breath, I let go of the cage. The sudden drop pushed the air from my lungs, but my scream was cut short when the rope caught me. The length of rope formed a harness, gripping against the sides of my boots and jacket.

"Release the rope slowly," Yang instructed.

I tried to do exactly as he had described. The evening wind grew stronger, whipping me back and forth as I clung to the rope. The coiled fibers slid past as I dropped, rubbing hard against the crook of my arm. Whenever the descent became too fast, I hugged my body against the rope to slow my fall. Whereas Yang had sailed down, I was making my way in fits and starts, inch by inch.

"Almost there," Yang encouraged. I could barely hear him past the rush of the wind.

"Just go on," I shouted back.

Hu was far ahead of us. Yang would be too late to stop him if he waited for me.

"You're very close. Relax your hold. You'll slide down faster."

My mind wanted to comply, but my arms and legs clung stubbornly onto the rope.

"I'll catch you," Yang promised. "Just slide down."

Taking in a big breath, I held it and counted in my head. On three, I loosened my grip and began to slide down the rope, picking up speed as I descended. It seemed I fell for an interminable amount of time before crashing into a hard body. Yang's arms closed around me as we struggled to our feet. A rush of elation flooded through my veins as I finally allowed myself to breathe.

"Nothing broken?" Yang asked.

He didn't leave any space for an answer before he was rushing off. I followed, pistols ready.

The compound was surrounded by a tall enclosure built of wooden stakes. The large gate was open and Hu's lantern glowed through the windows. He was inside the central building which, unlike the other structures on the island, was reinforced with iron bars on the windows.

The cold wind whipped through the narrow valley, howling in the darkness. A fire roared to life at one end of the building, the rush of air fanning the flames. Another fire sprung to life inside, the flames growing until we could see nothing else through the windows but the blinding flash of orange.

Yang only made it to the front entrance before he fell back. He raised a hand over his face to ward off the smoke and heat.

"Hu, come out of there," he implored.

I ran up behind him. Over Yang's shoulder, I could see Hu with a jug of oil in hand. He turned and splashed it onto the dancing flames, making them jump higher. Then he threw the jug into the fire in a clatter of broken pottery. When Hu turned to face us, his shoulders were sunk, resigned. There was a darkness in his eyes that no fire could penetrate.

"Jiang wanted to leave, but I couldn't let him," he cried out, his voice ragged.

"Please come out!" I shouted in desperation, but Hu didn't flinch. All around him I could see the reflection of fire off an array of glass tubes and beakers. It was another laboratory, one much larger and more elaborate than the one we'd found earlier.

Hu raised his voice to a shout. With each word the flames licked closer. "It was better to die here, I told him. So everything would be forgotten. No one would ever know."

Glass shattered from the heat, one container after another. I could see the tears on Hu's face as he turned around to walk deeper into the laboratory. For one awful heartbeat, I saw the ghost of my father, resigned to die. I considered running to Hu Bin, to this stranger I'd known less than a day. Anything to not stand by helpless once again.

A growl from behind us broke through the horror. I swung around to see the opium horde. They'd been drawn by the fire and now they were crowding toward us, reaching.

I shot the first one through the head. He fell away, but the others kept coming. They were void of any reason, of any fear.

"Run," Yang shouted over the roar of the blaze.

I shot again and broke away from the fire. Unfortunately, there was nowhere to run. We were backed up against the wooden barrier. Ten or more bodies surrounded us while more crowded in behind them. Yang took out the closest one with his pistol, gaining us only a few seconds to do nothing. I fired off both shots of my rifle, each one hitting home and each one equally useless.

The horde swarmed thick around us, two bodies pushing forward to fill in for each one that had fallen.

I reversed the rifle to use the butt as a weapon and prepared to fight. Yang reached into his pocket to load another round. It would be his last. The horde was too close to reload after that.

We were side by side when Yang turned his head to look at me. Inexplicably, he started moving away.

"I'll draw them, you run," he shouted.

"It won't work—"

"If we separate, it'll divide them. You find an opening and run." Yang raised his pistol and fired his last shot. Then he retreated toward the lab as the horde closed in on him.

His words came back to me.

If we are to leave this island, it will be together or not at all.

With a cry, I raised my rifle and ran to Yang, swinging hard at the horde. I connected with the back of the first one's skull and jammed the butt into the next one, shoving it back. Once again, Yang and I were face-to-face. The flames from the laboratory burned bright behind him. No more time for clever strategy. There was nothing to do but fight.

The flash of a blade gleamed through the darkness. A body fell away at the back of the mob. The blade flew again, tracing a silver path in the firelight. Makoto appeared amidst the horde, both blades unsheathed. Gunshots could be heard at the perimeter. Yang's crewmen had also joined the fight.

I smashed my rifle against the mass of flesh and bone before me. My blows did damage, but the afflicted continued to push forward. They felt no pain to deter them. I struck again, hitting one in the skull hard enough to take him down. Beside me, Yang fought as well, positioning himself at my back.

Makoto cut a path toward us while we pushed through to him. The rest of the crewman flanked us as we finally broke through the swarm. I shoved one of the creatures into the fire as it reached for me. Then I ran. We all ran.

"The boat," Makoto panted. "It's on the beach."

We raced through the woods in the dark. Branches whipped across my face and the leaves crunched beneath my feet, but I was running blind. I followed the others, moving like a herd.

Then I finally heard it—the sound of water crashing against the shore. A surge of energy flowed through me.

We broke through the tree line. Moonlight shone against the pale sand and I could see the rowboat by the water.

The horde was still behind us, snarling and relentless. I trudged through the sand and nearly threw myself against the boat. We grabbed onto the sides of it, all hands at work to drag the vessel into the surf.

"Now," Yang commanded. The boat was afloat, finally free of the shore. I practically threw myself inside. One by one, the others jumped in, with Yang hauling himself aboard last.

I barely righted myself as the crewmen took the oars. They pulled us out to open water where our ship was anchored. I looked back to see the afflicted clamoring on the shore. A few ventured into the water, but only far enough to be pushed back by the waves. Behind them the sky glowed orange from the burning laboratory.

"How long will they survive there?" I wondered, watching the black figures prowling on the shore.

"Not long," Yang replied.

We turned away from the island, leaving the opium refuge and its forsaken inhabitants behind.

Chapter 7

S ilence descended when we returned to the ship. We didn't speak aloud of what had happened at the refuge. We didn't know how to speak of it. The ship's captain set a new course and we sailed away, leaving the desolate island behind.

Gradually, we filled in the parts of the story that were missing, but only amongst the few of us who had been to the island. We spoke in hushed tones. While the two groups were separated, Makoto and the crewman had been able to return to the landing boat. They made camp there and intended to recruit a larger search party to find us. Before they could send word to the ship, the horde swarmed the beach.

They surrounded one of the crewmen. When he couldn't make it to the boat, the others were forced to watch as the horde tore him to pieces and devoured him.

"They were like *kyonshī.*" Makoto spoke of the living ghouls of Nipponese lore, still shaken by what he'd seen.

They'd rowed the boat back to ship where they had spotted the beacon tower. The fires then led the newly formed rescue party to us.

As soon as we were back on board his ship, Yang disappeared into the laboratory. The crew was accustomed to his habits and gave him his distance. After Yang didn't come above deck for three days, I broke the rule to call on him in the laboratory even though it was forbidden.

Surprisingly, the door wasn't locked.

I entered to see Yang Hanzhu swirling a flask filled with clear liquid. He'd removed his coat and was wearing a white linen shirt with a row of neatly fastened buttons. His sleeves were rolled up past his elbows. Yang continued to work, refusing to acknowledge my presence.

I'd come to ask about his welfare, to see if he was eating. To see if he was still distraught from all that had happened on the refuge. He'd lost two men, and in the most violent way possible.

"Did you find anything?" I asked instead.

"The tests on the composition of the samples have been inconclusive. Which is not unexpected. We all want knowledge to strike like lightning, but most inquiry is—" He paused, looking suddenly tired. "Unrequited."

I was reminded of my father and his singular focus during an inquiry. The world ceased to exist. Interruptions were unwelcome enough, but to interrupt and ask about his progress was unforgivable.

Yang raised the flask up to the light once more, then broke away momentarily to meet my eyes. Slowly, he set the glass down. "You needed me for something?"

"I wanted to see if you were well."

"Well enough. I survived an island of opium-addicted cannibals." He nodded toward me. "I believe somewhere in there you saved my life."

I shook my head.

"No, you must have," he insisted. "It's why I brought you and I like being right. So humbly admit I was right."

If anything, we had helped each other, hand-in-hand, so they say. Now we were connected by that debt.

One particular occurrence did intrigue me. "On the cliffside, how did you know about how to slide down the rope?"

"I grew up on ships, climbing up the mast, hanging from rigging. Additionally, those who are not familiar with heights often overestimate their measure. I'm sure it appeared to be ten *bu* high, but it was really probably around nine *bu*."

My stomach lurched recalling how I had clung to that rope in the darkness with the wind rushing around me.

"Yang Hanzhu is not just some wealthy know-nothing giving orders," he continued with a self-satisfied grin. "If everyone were to be washed overboard, I could sail this ship by myself."

"Such humility."

Yang grinned. "What would you say? You and I alone, sailing the world."

The look he exchanged with me was more than warm. Heat rushed up my neck, but I wasn't certain how to respond. Something had happened between us on that island. Something much deeper than the first flush of attraction or even the casual flirtation Yang was affecting now.

The mood suddenly changed. Yang braced his hands against the table, head down. The silence grew heavy.

"What I needed was in that lab, Sagara-san," he said fiercely. "All the answers. Destroyed."

He looked ready to strike something, but he stayed with his head bowed. Unmoving.

"As one of the Emperor's gunpowder alchemists," he went on, "we thought the answer to the war was in our firepower. In our cannons and gunpowder and the ratios which would yield the greatest power." He exhaled long and deep. "But we were wrong. What defeated us was at once something simpler and more complex. Opium *was* the weapon. It's still the weapon."

Amazingly, I understood him. It was how my father had approached the world—with formulas and ratios. My father would disappear into his workshop and Yang into his laboratory. It was both cold and comforting to think the answers could be found here, in tireless and meticulous experiments. It was a comfort to believe there were answers to be found.

But I just found more questions.

"It sounds like there's much work left to do," I replied gently.

Yang nodded gravely, then turned and moved closer, stealing my breath as he closed the distance between us. He touched his fingertips to my cheek and his eyes were dark and unreadable.

I flushed hot, my skin tingling with awareness as he watched my face. My pulse pounded, but still he continued to wait. Asking.

I must have moved first or maybe he did. His lips pressed against mine and my knees, my entire being weakened with that first touch. I'd been alone for so long, never even considering anything like this. I kissed him back and felt his presence opening to me, leaning closer. An ache grew in my chest as our breath mingled.

Then the kiss was over. Without warning, Yang moved away and turned back to the work table. I was left at a loss, heart pounding, confused by the sudden break—what had happened? Yang made a motion toward the flask, but his hand fell away. He stood with his head bent. Lost in thought.

Maybe he was as lost as I was. We were doing things out of the natural order, though I had no idea what the natural order should be.

"Someone I knew fell prey to opium," he confessed, looking at his hands. "Someone I cared for very much. I thought if I could find a cure. If I could find the one correct answer... But human minds and bodies are complicated, aren't they? They defy rigid formula."

Finally, his gaze returned to me. I knew no one else who looked like Yang Hanzhu. The angles of his face seemed less sharp, more welcome. The tilt of his jaw less mocking. His appearance, not Eastern, not Western, was no longer so strange to me. I could still feel his mouth against mine.

"Satomi," he said softly.

It had been so many years since anyone had called me by my given name. I wasn't yet ready to speak his name so freely, but I placed my hand onto the table to bridge the gap between us. He reached out and our fingers intertwined briefly before Yang slipped free to return to his work. I left him to his inquiry.

As I exited the lab, I was more convinced than ever I was on a madman's ship.

I had been around such madness all my life. Maybe that was why there was something about these strange circumstances and the eccentricities of Yang Hanzhu that felt curiously like home.

He was impulsive by nature, yet methodical by approach. His was a mind that remained occupied with a hundred things at once. My soul was no less cluttered, but we were both on a journey, both searching. We had time to find one another and an endless ocean before us.

Author's Note

THE ISLAND OF THE OPIUM EATERS

This was the first story to come to life from the collection. Yang Hanzhu is my favorite secondary character of the *Gunpowder Chronicles* series and immediately after the end of *Clockwork Samurai*, I wanted to know what happens to Hanzhu and Satomi after they sail off together.

Opium-Eaters weaves together several facts and conspiracy theories around the crisis of opium addiction in Qing Dynasty China. Though we frequently hear of Commissioner Lin Zexu's seizure and destruction of foreign opium shipments, what's less well-known is that Lin spearheaded a major opium cessation program, essentially your 19th century anti-drug campaign.

The program included, along with the seizure and banning of opium sales, cessation pills and opium refuges (drug detox centers). Fringe theories suggest that Lin didn't destroy the seized opium, but rather created morphine which was distributed as an anti-opium treatment.

That, combined with several street drugs today touted as "zombie" drugs, inspired the idea of the opium-induced zombies of "The Island."

Who wouldn't love the chance to explore a madman's island, a la *The Island of Dr. Moreau?* So "The Island of the Opium-

Eaters" serves as my entry into the "mysterious island" genre of pulp fiction.

For more information about the Gunpowder Chronicles, sign-up for Jeannie Lin's mailing list to receive updates on new releases, appearances, and special giveaways.

PART III

Love in the Time of Engines

Chapter 1
QING DYNASTY CHINA, 1831 A.D.

The gunpowder crawler churned along, gears grinding over the wide, dirt road that led to the imperial capital. Anlei was seated in the hold, wedged between large drums of black powder along with her books and brushes.

She'd hitched a ride with the gunpowder trader as he'd passed through Anhui province three days earlier. Since then, the crawler had carried her over two thousand *li* toward the imperial city of Peking. After the first day, she'd learned to ignore the noise, but the rattle of the engine grew louder.

"*Uncle.*" She stood, her footing unsteady as the transport vibrated beneath her. "Uncle Po!" she called again, waving frantically at him.

"We'll be at the next relay station in a few hours," Uncle Po shouted back from the driver's seat.

For the last three days, she'd tried to stay out of the old trader's sight as much as possible. She wasn't yet comfortable with her new appearance, and the less he saw of her, the less chance he had to see through her disguise. Unfortunately, there was a whining, wheezing noise coming from the engine below. Even with her limited experience of machinery, Anlei was certain this was not a good sound.

"There's something wrong—"

The trader remained facing forward, unable to hear anything above the engine's rumbling. Anlei blew out a sharp breath and started picking her way through the containers to move toward the front. Suddenly, a sharp boom shook the entire transport. Anlei grabbed onto a barrel to keep from falling, and her spectacles slipped from her nose.

The engine sputtered before going quiet.

"On my mother's grave!" Uncle Po swore. He wasn't actually family of any kind, but he seemed to favor a familiar tone of interaction which involved cursing and sharing personal details even though she was a stranger. Or maybe this was how all men conducted themselves in the presence of...other men.

Po hauled himself from the driver's seat and lumbered to the side of the wagon. A tell-tale tongue of black smoke rose from the exhaust pipes. "Fetch me my tools, son."

Son.

That was reassuring. A month ago, Anlei had shaved back her hairline and braided her long hair into a traditional queue. She'd wrapped her breasts tight with a band of cloth. The high-collared mandarin jacket she wore was buttoned all the way up to her chin to cover up the lack of knot at her throat.

Anlei had become Shi Han, a young scholar traveling to Peking.

She found the tools inside a heavy burlap sack which she handed down to him. Anlei remembered to pitch her voice lower before speaking. "Did the engine overheat?"

Every time she spoke, she feared she'd be discovered. Hopefully, this feeling would pass — she had a long time until the imperial examination.

"What does the gauge read?" Uncle Po asked as he tinkered with the valves outside.

She wiped at the meter on the engine panel with the edge of her sleeve. "The needle's stuck."

Po swore some more as he fitted the lifting device beneath

the carriage. Huffing loudly, he started working the crank. Anlei wondered whether she should offer to help. Was it rude to step in or rude not to? Before she could decide, Uncle Po had raised the transport an extra hand's length. He lowered himself onto one knee and attempted to peer underneath. "You're small. See if you can take a look."

Anlei hoped Uncle Po was more focused on the engine than on her. She flattened her back against the dirt to slide beneath the transport. The air below was hot, strong with the scent of burnt oil and sulfur.

"Check the water pump," Uncle Po prompted.

She inched in further. The machinery at her family's paper mill had been driven by a gunpowder engine, an archaic one that broke down twice a week. Mechanics and *zágong*, fix-it men, were expensive, not to mention too far from the village to call on quickly. She'd learned how to keep the mill running with sheer will and axle grease.

"There's a leak," she reported. A quick sniff showed it to be water and not oil

Probing around, she found a tear in the rubber hose connecting the pump. The repair took them the next hour with Uncle Po giving instructions and handing her tools from outside while she loosened the fittings and attached a new length of hose. By the time she emerged, she was pouring sweat and covered in dirt.

Uncle Po poured water into the radiator chamber while they waited for the engine to cool. The only shade to be found was on the side of the crawler. Anlei crouched beside the vehicle, scrubbing her hands on the grass to clean off the grease.

"You have some mechanical ability," the old trader said with a hint of approval.

"My family runs a paper mill."

"Most scholars wouldn't get their hands dirty," he said with a chuckle.

Uncle Po had now taken a liking to her which was not good

at all. To her dismay, he called her up to the driver seat to keep him company when it was time to go.

He wound the starter crank to prime the engine and, after a few stutters, it coughed loudly and roared to life. The air filled with the smell of sulfur.

"What is that you're always reading?" Po asked as he climbed up beside her.

"Mathematics. I'm studying for the imperial examination."

"That's very difficult. You must be a very smart young man."

Impostor.

She adjusted her spectacles and bowed her head humbly. Even the eyeglasses were part of the ruse. It felt better having a barrier to shield her from the outside, even if the barrier consisted of two thin lenses and a wire frame.

The exam was notoriously difficult. In a given term, very few men were granted degrees. If one was a woman, the exam wasn't just challenging. It was an impossibility.

In the realm of problems, this one was far from unsolvable. It helped that her mother had never had her feet bound—Anlei had simply disguised herself as a man.

She'd even created a small device with a pump that could be hidden in her palm. If she ever had to "relieve" herself, she could use it to dispense a stream of yellowed water from an artificial bladder strapped beneath her clothes.

Anlei had thought of everything. Well, not everything. But she'd thought of a lot of scenarios.

Uncle Po had no further interest in talking about the imperial exams. Instead he launched into another one of the adventures he'd had hauling gunpowder to the far corners of the empire. This story involved an opera troupe he'd traveled with.

They reached the posting station just before nightfall. Uncle Po unloaded the entire shipment of gunpowder, standing by while station agents weighed and measured it. Gunpowder was heavily taxed and regulated by imperial authorities, which made it a target for smugglers. Several armed guards surrounded the scales while more hovered around the perimeter.

This was where they would stay for the night. Anlei parted with a coin for a room at the inn. It was an extravagance given that her string of cash had to last her the entire term, but she needed some privacy to clean off and look presentable. By tomorrow, she'd be in Peking where the true test would start.

Once inside the sleeping compartment, Anlei removed her jacket to brush off the dirt. There was a spot of oil on her sleeve which she hoped wasn't too visible given the darkly colored material. Carefully, she unwound the binding cloth around her breasts, wincing as the circulation returned.

For the first time in days, Anlei was able to breathe in deeply. Over the next year, she could never forget herself. Never let down her guard. She could not, literally, even allow herself to breathe freely.

She washed quickly and dressed again. Better to not take any chances of being discovered, even far away from the capital.

There was a thin bamboo mat on the floor where she was meant to sleep. Anlei sat upon it and took out her writing case. There were no windows in the room, so she had to light a precious candle as she prepared her brush and ink.

It was a letter to be sent back to Anhui province, to the school Anlei had once attended. Mistress Wang had run an academy there for both male and female students. Anlei had studied there for five years, from the age of fourteen, but while her male peers expected to take the civil exams one day, her education was looked upon as a curiosity. Something she engaged in as a diversion.

As if the very act of pursuing an education didn't take great effort and sacrifice. Anlei's parents didn't even think she was going to school. Mistress Wang had told her mother and father that she needed a handmaid. Her teacher had paid a wage to Anlei's parents every month just to have her come to school.

Maybe Mistress Wang had done that because Anlei alone

understood her mistress' work hadn't come from boredom or mere curiosity. Her studies had come from a driving need to learn. And excel.

A year ago, imperial messengers had come to Anhui province with a special summons for "scholars of undiscovered talents in science and mathematics." The imperial palace was attempting to recruit people from the "far hills and mountains" outside of the traditional academies.

Mistress Wang had started preparing men's clothing and setting aside money. Anlei had even assisted her teacher in the preparations, assuming the entire time that Mistress Wang was planning to disguise herself and take the exams. Her mistress was accomplished in mathematics and astronomy, and recognized as a rare talent within the province.

Looking back, Anlei could see that her mistress must have already known that she was dying. Mistress Wang had already started sending her manuscripts away to trusted colleagues. A month after the summons, she'd dismissed all of her students. Anlei had been devastated to be sent back to the paper mill.

Several months later, Anlei received a letter written by Mistress Wang herself. The letter told her that her mistress was already gone—and that she had one final wish.

A tear slipped down Anlei's cheek and fell onto the mulberry paper as she began to write. She addressed the letter, not to Mistress Wang, but to her widowed husband.

Thank you for your kindness and generosity. Tomorrow I will be in Peking.

She paused with the tip of her brush hovering over the ink stone. Those simple words seemed so inadequate given what Mistress Wang and her husband had done for Anlei. But was she bold enough to write the next line, the one hidden in her heart? She dipped the brush into the ink.

I will not fail.

This was her one opportunity. Her only way to honor her teacher's legacy.

Once the ink had dried, Anlei folded the letter and started another one. This one was even harder to write. It was to her father and mother, who didn't know she was on the road to the imperial capital. They didn't know she'd changed her hair to wear a man's queue. They didn't even know she'd studied mathematics.

The next morning, she took both letters to the relay station clerk. She posted the one addressed to Mistress Wang's husband, but hesitated on the message to her parents.

When Mistress Wang had fallen ill, Anlei had returned to days of drudgery stripping mulberry bark and feeding it to the pulping machines. Before her studies, she'd never thought life would be any different, but now the grind of the mill set her teeth on edge. Her days felt as blank as the pages of mulberry paper they churned out.

She was her parents' only child, a lone daughter. Her only duty was to care for them when they grew old. Take over the mill when it was time.

To rescue her, Mistress Wang's husband had come to ask for her in marriage. He'd paid her parents bride price taken from his late wife's savings. That had also been part of Mistress Wang's plan.

Her father and mother were practical people. They accepted the money, wished Anlei many children, and that she be well taken care of. Anlei poured them the ceremonial farewell tea, and wished them good health and long life. All the while, she'd known it was a ruse. She was not leaving to be married.

Anlei pictured her mother and father working the mill, two cogs turning one wheel, day in and day out. In harmony, but without joy. For them, it was enough. For her, it couldn't be. She had learned there was such a thing as infinity.

In her parents' eyes, she had once belonged to them. Now she belonged to someone else, as daughters were destined to do. Anlei could send them this letter telling them the truth, or she could leave them in peace, believing the lie.

Anlei crumpled the paper into a ball and slipped it into her pocket.

She belonged only to herself now.

ANLEI ALWAYS IMAGINED Peking would be a grand and golden city of towering pagodas and graceful stone bridges. Opera houses and temples.

Perhaps there was grandeur somewhere in this massive sprawl, but from down in the streets, Peking was a place of mud and camels and too many carts being shoved through crowds. The roads suffered beneath the stamp of a thousand feet and every shop looked alike. She was far, far away from the lonely paper mill by the river.

Uncle Po had taken leave of her in the marketplace, with a vague instruction to "just follow that main avenue down there". Anlei slung her knapsack of books over one shoulder and hefted a roll of paper in her arms to set out for the Imperial Academy.

She quickly learned that in Peking, streets did not run straight. Instead, the hutong alleyways wound around the walled residential courtyards. Shops stood along the walls of the alleys and where there wasn't a shop, there was a street vendor set up on a steam cart, a wheelbarrow, behind a stack of crates, or with nothing more than a bamboo mat and a basket of goods. Every street looked like a main thoroughfare. East was the same as west.

An hour passed while she wandered the hutong maze and there was nothing that looked like an Imperial Academy.

Flustered, Anlei stopped at a public pump to splash water over her hands and wash her face. The roll of paper she'd brought as a gift to the Academy was growing heavier by the moment.

Anlei waved down a passerby to ask directions, but he merely shouted something unintelligible at her before he hurried off. Then she got caught in the tide of foot traffic, and was swept along, unable to get her bearings. When Anlei finally pulled away, she swore she was back where she'd started.

She knew it would be difficult getting admitted to the Academy, but at the moment it seemed like the streets themselves would defeat her.

Setting down the scroll of paper at her feet, she wiped the sweat from her forehead with her sleeve before hefting the offering back up. It was then she spied a young man across the street dressed in scholars' clothing. It was the same outfit she was wearing; a mandarin jacket in dark blue buttoned over a black robe. A close-fitting silk cap covered his head.

His features were well-defined, and his skin bronze in tone from the sun. He looked more accustomed to riding across windswept plains than studying old books at the Academy.

The stranger moved with a purposeful stride, his long legs cutting like blades through the crowd. He was far from approachable, in fact he might be the most intimidating person she'd met so far, but she'd resolved to live boldly, hadn't she? The man turned to catch her staring and now Anlei had no choice but to approach.

Taking a deep breath, Anlei wove through the crowd toward the dark tower standing before her. His head and shoulders rose above the surrounding crowd.

"Sir," she greeted awkwardly. He watched her with a curious expression and she hoped it wasn't because she looked too out of place. Nervously, Anlei pushed her spectacles up onto the bridge of her nose. This was possibly her first interaction with a scholar, with someone associated with the Academy.

She came to a halt before him, realizing, too late, that she didn't even know how close she should stand to someone like this in terms of etiquette or custom. She'd never dealt with anyone man-to-man as an equal. Were they equals?

Anlei found herself a pace or two closer than intended with a view of too much chest. She tilted her head up to the stranger staring down at her, his piercing expression more than a little daunting. He had a distinguished appearance with cheekbones cut high and sharp accompanied by a nose that curved like an eagle's beak.

"Uncle," she said, striving for a more familiar address that still preserved respect.

"Uncle," he echoed, frowning. "Do I appear so old to you?"

Her face heated. "Elder Brother," she amended. "Do you know of the Imperial Academy?"

His eyes were set deep and had a hint of copper to them. She had never seen eyes like that. They were sharp and focused and she swallowed as they narrowed on her. Luckily, he didn't linger on her face, but shifted his focus to the scroll clutched in her arms.

"You're a student at the Academy?" he asked.

"Yes. I mean no."

His eyebrows raised at that.

"Well…I hope to be."

The stranger's frown deepened. "You don't know if you've been admitted?"

Her stomach knotted. "I have a petition. There was a special summons sent out to Anhui province. I suppose other provinces as well—"

Why was she pleading her case to him? They had just met in the street and this churning, skittish feeling in her stomach wasn't helping her concentration at all. Her carefully crafted strategy was already falling apart. She was saying too much which made him skeptical of every word that came out of her mouth.

The tall stranger made her unaccountably nervous. There were things she was supposed to say and ways she was supposed to say them and she knew nothing of it. Meanwhile his presence seemed to take up all the space in the lane. The passersby flowed around them like a stream over rocks. He would never get swept away and dragged through the streets.

"I am to have an audience with the headmaster," she added weakly.

The heavy paper slipped in her arms and she shifted the weight onto her other side, attempting to balance it against the books slung over her shoulder.

"My home village specializes in paper-making," she explained. This is a gift for the Academy."

He nodded faintly, as he watched her struggle.

"I was told gifts were——-not unwelcome," she added uncertainly.

Finally, the corners of his mouth lifted. There was such a gravity about him. The high cheekbones and the commanding line of his jaw evoked such weight and seriousness that just the slight relaxing of his expression allowed her to breathe easier. The tightness in her chest loosened.

Anlei took the fact that he didn't offer to help with the paper or her books as evidence he was convinced by her disguise. She was at least grateful for that. This was the hardest conversation of her life.

"Gifts are not unwelcome," he agreed with a look that was not unkind. "I'm Jin Zhi-fu."

"Shi Han from Anhui province." Though she'd practiced it out loud on her own, it still sounded strange.

"The Academy isn't far."

He began walking, once again moving with a purpose, but he did edge toward the side of the lane. It was an invitation to join him and she darted forward to fill the space.

"Anhui province," he echoed, his brow furrowed thought-fully. "Anhui is well-known as a center of mathematics."

Her heart raced. She was in conversation with a student of the Academy. He was cultured and well-read and perfectly groomed while she was covered in road dust and engine oil.

"Many respected mathematicians have come from Anhui," she concurred. "Mei Wending, certainly. My master was a great admirer of his..."

Jin Zhi-fu's gaze drifted away from her in disinterest. She meandered onto some nonsense about geometry and had to bite her tongue to keep from babbling.

She continued walking beside him in silence. It was strange to even be doing that, matching strides with a man. For the first time, she noticed the lacquered block box tucked beneath his left arm. It was inlaid with mother of pearl to form a dragon design.

"Is that meant for the Academy?" she asked.

"Gifts are not unwelcome," he replied, echoing her earlier sentiment.

Her heart did a little leap. She'd at least made some impression on him. "It's very beautiful."

To her surprise, he lifted the latch with a flick of his thumb and opened the lid. Inside was a metal instrument with a steel barrel the length of her forearm. It was polished to a gleam.

"Is that a firearm?" she asked.

He nodded, promptly closing the lid. "From the trading port in Macao. It's Portuguese in origin."

She had no idea where that was. Nor had she ever seen a fire weapon so compact and intricate. The paper she held seemed lackluster and plain in comparison.

Where was Zhi-fu from to have acquired such an item? She considered him out of the corner of her eye, hoping she wasn't too conspicuous about it. Like her, he was certainly not from Peking, but she wasn't experienced enough to recognize any regional nuances in his accent. He spoke and conducted himself with the rigid manners of an aristocrat and, though the two of them wore similar attire, there were tell-tale embellishments in his jacket that marked him immediately as being above her in class and wealth. Silk for him rather than linen, the brocade pattern in the cloth. Yet his look was sun-drenched with a striking physicality.

A set of triple arches lay ahead, towering and painted in a brilliant shade of red. Her breath hitched in her throat. There was no mistaking that they had arrived. On the other side of the gate was the center of learning of the entire empire.

Perhaps that was an exaggeration, but it was certainly where all scholars aspired to study.

"The Imperial Academy," Zhi-fu announced as if introducing an old acquaintance.

Anlei paused at the entrance, feeling much like a carp about to jump through the Dragon Gate. Zhi-fu was already through. She took a deep breath before stepping beneath the decorated archway.

The main hall in the interior courtyard of the Academy was a palace onto itself, lined with red pillars and a sweeping rooftop. It towered high over gleaming stone walkways. A row of majestic locust trees lined the pathway leading to it and the branches were in full bloom. She could see the famed Temple of Knowledge.

The enormity of what she had done stunned her. Anlei took a moment to stand in the center of the courtyard, among the old, wise trees, to absorb the moment.

She was inside the Imperial Academy. And no heavily armed guards had appeared to demand she leave.

Jin Zhi-fu had moved ahead of her. Probably eager to extract himself and continue about his affairs unhindered. She started to call out her thanks when two porters pushed through the front gate, rushing past them carrying a large trunk suspended between a set of poles.

Zhi-fu stepped back, brushing against her as they once again ended up side-by-side. A parade came through in twos with each pair of servants hefting large trunks draped dramatically in red silk.

"Kuo Lishen," Zhi-fu muttered.

A well-dressed young man emerged at the tail end of the procession. His nose had a slightly crooked look to it and his tidy beard tapered down to a point like the tip of a dagger. The newcomer turned and immediately saw them, or rather he saw Jin Zhi-fu. Anlei remained invisible.

She assumed this new arrival was Kuo Lishen. He strode across the stone tiles of the courtyard as if he owned them.

"Jin Zhi-fu," he greeted, breaking into a grin. "Time to win this battle, my friend." Kuo struck Jin Zhi-fu's shoulder with a brotherly air.

"Before we're too old to fight any longer," Zhi-fu replied.

"Never."

"You're trying your hand at bribery this year?" Zhi-fu nodded toward the caravan which had disappeared into the complex of buildings on the west side of the Academy.

Kuo laughed. "Whatever it takes."

Anlei was caught between wanting to slip away quietly or linger on to learn more.

"Thank you again, Elder Brother Jin," she ventured. "I should be—"

Kuo Lishen continued over her, as if she'd never spoken. "To tell the truth, what I've brought is much more valuable than gold and silver."

He lowered his voice then and Zhi-fu stepped in closer, his shoulder angled just so to form a barrier that most definitely left her outside. Anlei considered forgetting her manners and simply fading away. Being forgotten so quickly didn't sit as well with her as she imagined. She had started to hope Jin Zhi-fu might be a friend.

Zhi-fu frowned. "What is inside those trunks?"

"Something that will change everything."

Anlei took one step backward and another. At that moment, Kuo's gaze found hers. His expression suddenly sharpened, dark brows furrowing as he took in her measure. Suddenly, another sort of person took his place. A shrewd and calculating person hidden beneath the swagger.

Her heartbeat quickened. Could he see through her

disguise? Her palms started sweating and the edge of the scroll folded and crinkled beneath her fingertips.

He doesn't see anything, she scolded herself. No one does. She had to remain confident. Kuo Lishen's gaze eventually slid harmlessly over her. Her own fear would expose her before anyone else if she couldn't remain focused.

Let the upperclassmen fight over who was at the head of the class. She was still fighting to be admitted. She left the two of them and navigated toward the interior of the Academy, looking for the headmaster's office.

When she asked for directions, she was sent to the innermost courtyard where the administrative offices were located. Once inside, she presented her request to the clerk. She was surprised when he disappeared only to return a moment later, beckoning for her to follow him.

Anlei smoothed a nervous hand over her cap and jacket as she followed the corridors. Then there she was, standing just inside the entrance to the headmaster's office.

The windows were shuttered, leaving the room dim and cool. She was grateful. The darkness would make it harder for him to see her.

"Headmaster Sun," she greeted, bowing awkwardly.

"Young Master," he greeted. "Come in."

She took a small step inside, became overly cautious that the step might be too womanly, then followed with a bolder step. She squared her shoulders for good measure.

"Honorable Headmaster, I have a petition to enroll in the Imperial Academy. And there's this…this special notice here. For scholars of mathematics."

He beckoned her forward. She presented the gift as well as the other papers before taking a step back.

The palace summons had appeared so important back in her province, but now it seemed flimsy in the exalted halls of the Imperial Academy. She hoped it held true, that she hadn't based her dreams on shapes in the mist.

"You never studied at the University in Anhui," he said.

"No, Headmaster. I received instruction at a private school." Taught by a brilliant woman they would never have allowed inside the Academy.

She bit her lip nervously as Master Sun inspected the petition again, the frown lines cutting deep across his forehead. "I take it you are well-versed with the Computational Canon."

"Yes, Headmaster," she replied dutifully.

She wasn't.

She stood, forcing herself to remain still. Her very presence in this office was built on a palace of lies, one stacked on top of another. A bead of sweat formed on her brow, but she was too scared to wipe it away.

Without a word, Master Sun set the papers aside. Using a metal rule, he sliced through the scroll of paper. Then he picked up a brush and dipped it in ink, writing in quick strokes down the sheet. When he pushed it toward her, Anlei's pulse began to pound.

Numbers and symbols. It was a math problem — one she'd never seen before.

"If you are truly an undiscovered talent, then you have great expectations to fulfill," Master Sun declared.

He sat back in his chair to wait.

Chapter 2

As Zhi-fu watched hapless young Han disappear toward the headmaster's office, he wondered which conversation he preferred to be trapped in. Han with his awkward uncertainty or Kuo Lishen with his unabashed bravado.

"Come out with us tonight." Kuo Lishen hadn't changed in the two years since the last examination term. His invitation was more command than request.

"Already?" Zhi-fu asked.

"Always." Kuo lowered his voice, but not low enough that anyone couldn't overhear. "What did I tell you? It's about connections."

"And yet—" Zhi-fu's wave encompassed the breath of the Academy's courtyard. "Here we are again."

Kuo snorted. "Luck, influence, talent, in that order."

"You must be the unluckiest soul around."

Zhi-fu hadn't fared any better. It was his third time taking the imperial exams while Kuo Lishen was an old celebrity in the scholar's quarter by now. He'd failed to pass three times, making this year his fourth 'charge'. They liked to speak about it as if they were generals taking the field of battle rather than failed scholars vying for recognition.

"My luck has changed." Kuo looked to the corridor where the procession had disappeared. "Yours as well."

"What did you bring, Kuo?"

Kuo regarded him in all seriousness before breaking out into a grin. "Come out tonight and you'll find out."

With a laugh, he strode away. Zhi-fu was left to visit the offices and drop off his tribute, the Portuguese firearm. The headmaster was not available to meet him nor any of the lower Academy officials. He left his gift with a clerk along with a letter written by his father, an appointed official of the Ministry of War assigned to the frontier defense.

The Academy instructors knew who he was by now. They knew who his father was. They knew his family name. He'd read thousands of pages, solved hundreds of equations over the last two years. Luck first, then influence, then skill.

He was beginning to wonder if any of it mattered.

Zhi-fu returned to the main courtyard just as the young scholar Han emerged from his audience with the headmaster, if he'd even been allowed a hearing. The boy slumped against the corner of the administrative building; head bowed. Zhi-fu felt the pang of disappointment tugging inside his own chest. Shi Han was a tradesman's son from the provinces, without proper schooling or pedigree. The boy hadn't even passed the provincial level exams.

Seeing such fresh-faced optimism had reminded Zhi-fu of his own dreams the first time he'd set foot in the Academy. When he believed that hard work and talent would earn him success. Han was probably bright in comparison to his peers in the village school. Someone had foolishly gotten the boy's hopes up. Zhi-fu hadn't wanted to tell Han he'd probably made the journey for nothing.

He considered going to Han now. Surely, he deserved a few conciliatory cups of wine for his troubles. Han would experience the full cycle of a scholar's heart break in just one day and be able to return home without sacrificing a year of his life.

But when Han lifted his head, a wild light flickered in his eyes. His round face registered confusion and disbelief, but above it all, he was *glowing*. By the time Zhi-fu came to stand before him, Shi Han's grin spanned from one ear to the other.

"Good news?" Zhi-fu asked.

The boy straightened with a jolt. He bit back his smile and ran a nervous hand over his jacket. The afternoon sunlight caught in his spectacles as he nodded.

"Congratulations, Shi Han from Anhui province."

It was only the first step on a long, hard road, but Zhi-fu didn't need to tell the young scholar that. He'd learn soon enough on his own.

Han cleared his throat before speaking. "I…uh…do you know of any place where I might find lodging, Elder Brother? Perhaps a place that does not require too much money."

The boy really was unprepared. A few coins a day was barely enough to crowd oneself into a tenement for laborers. Any less than that and he'd be out in the streets with the beggars.

"Come with me," Zhi-fu said. "I may be able to help you."

Fortune seemed to favor the young scholar so far. Han fell into step beside him, a hundred times lighter than he was before. And not just because he was no longer dragging that roll of paper through the streets.

"I hear there are hundreds of candidates for the imperial exams," Han piped up.

"For the mathematics examinations. If you consider the civil and military exams as well, the number is well over a thousand candidates."

"An entire city!"

"Sometimes it feels like it."

In the years the imperial examination was administered, the

lodgings, teahouses, and eateries enjoyed an influx of business as students crowded into the hutongs. Silver poured into Peking.

Shi Han was still floating in the clouds. "And we have a year before examination week. What do you think the examination hall will be like?"

"I know the examination hall too well," Zhi-fu replied glibly. There was no use hiding it. "This is not my first sitting."

"Oh, well, I…" Han proved to be less adept with words than he was with numbers as he struggled for a response. "I hear that it's quite common not to pass the first time. Second term candidates are much more prepared."

"Then I must be triply prepared."

Han clamped his mouth shut and kept it shut, letting his gaze wander from one side of the lane to the other. Zhi-fu took no insult. The past was the past and now he knew what to prepare for. There was no time to be blinded by pride.

Not to mention, there were scholars who attempted the exam every year it was offered. They could be seen on examination day, seventy and eighty-year-old elders, still attempting to pass. Zhi-fu thought there was a name for those determined academics—he was probably better off never finding out what it was.

He continued to push through the crowded street with Han trailing behind him. They turned off the main avenue and were met with a moment of quiet.

"Where are you from, Elder Brother?" Han asked.

"My family is from Jilin province in the northeast. My father is a commander in the garrison there."

"The frontier defense," Han sounded impressed.

He wouldn't have been if he knew the distant post was one that was overlooked by the imperial government. The banner armies had little to do but stand guard over the last years and had been all but forgotten. He supposed that meant the Jilin frontier defense was fulfilling its duty to the Emperor, but Zhi-fu was eager to find a different way to serve their country.

He braced for the usual question. Why wasn't he taking the military examination?

When the question didn't come, Zhi-fu glanced over his shoulder. Han had fallen behind and was caught on the doorstep of one of the pleasure houses. A courtesan with painted lips and a green silk dress beckoned him closer, her handkerchief waving like a pink butterfly.

Zhi-fu went to retrieve the boy, taking firm hold of the boy's shoulder. "Careful, there."

"Zhi-fu, you're back," the courtesan smiled prettily at him, fluttering her eyelashes. "We missed you."

Shi Han's eyes widened like two great pearls.

"Good to see you, Lily," he replied stiffly. He directed Shi Han away from the establishment. "The pleasure quarter has been the downfall of many a scholar. That's why there are so many lovesick poems written about courtesans."

Han's face flushed a deep red. "I didn't—I wasn't…"

He gave the boy's shoulder a good-natured shake. "Don't worry. No one is watching you here. Enjoy your time, but don't lose sight of what's important."

"Don't lose sight of what's important," Han echoed, nodding obediently.

Of course, Zhi-fu had an invitation to a drinking house that very night, before the term had even begun.

"Here we are."

They had reached a courtyard residence situated at the corner of the lane. The front gate was constructed of worn wood and it creaked on its hinges to reveal an atrium lined with rooms. It was one of many such apartments that filled the quarter, each one crowded with hopefuls from every corner of the empire. By now, the chambers would all be rented. In a few weeks a few rooms might open up as scholars dropped out, either defeated by the intensity of the studies or because they had run out of funds. For now, the place was full.

Zhi-fu left the young scholar in the courtyard while he went to search out the landlord. Han remained standing in the very same spot, clutching the strap of his satchel when Zhi-fu returned.

"You're in luck, young master," the landlord drawled, sauntering past them. Han glanced at Zhi-fu questioningly, waiting for his approval before moving to follow the portly landlord. The man led them to the far corner opposite the gate, stopping before a narrow door which he pushed open with a flourish. "Best room in the house."

Han peered inside skeptically. Zhi-fu could see a few sacks of grain stowed inside the narrow space along with some wooden crates and a pile of pots and other implements.

Han stared at the landlord with a look of confusion. "This is a storage closet."

The man shrugged without a trace of shame. "Four walls, a roof overhead."

Once again, Han looked to him for some sort of acknowledgment.

"It's this or communal housing," Zhi-fu replied.

Apparently, the boy didn't know what that was.

"The poor house," the landlord offered cheerfully. "Where the lice and rats also bunk down."

"This will do fine then," Han replied stiffly.

The landlord gave a self-satisfied nod and named a price that he knew wouldn't be negotiated. Then he was off to his next errand. "Clear it out for me, young master, and I won't charge you anything until next month."

The youth glowered, clearly having picked up by now that the "young master" address was not a sign of respect.

Zhi-fu folded up the sleeves of his jacket. Without a word, they got to work. For the next half hour, the two of them took turns slipping inside the narrow closet to haul items out. Good thing the boy was so slight. Zhi-fu barely fit inside, but Han's smaller size seemed much better suited to the room. If it could even be called a room.

"There," Zhi-fu pronounced as he dragged a broken wooden broom and a bucket out of the closet. "Done."

Han wiped his sleeve over his brow. "I'm in your debt, Elder Brother."

"Think nothing of it."

"Where are you staying?"

Zhi-fu pointed to the next door over. Incidentally, the largest apartment in the residence.

"Neighbors," Han declared, a bit too cheerfully.

Zhi-fu had a sense he was embarking on something more than an acquaintance. Debt had a way of forming those bonds.

Kuo Lishen said it was important to make connections, and here Zhi-fu was, hard at work on it. Shi Han was a penniless papermaker's son on his first trip to the big city. With a hundred questions on his tongue and another thousand in his eyes. A prize connection, indeed.

Yet there was an earnestness about the boy that made others want to help him. Zhi-fu had been drawn in himself even though Han promised nothing in return.

It was freeing to look at someone and seek nothing. Nothing more than what was offered on the surface. Such fresh-faced honesty was rare given the competitiveness of the examination halls.

"Well…till tomorrow then," Han said. He hefted his travel pack over his shoulder. The thing must have weighed more than he did.

"Take care, Shi Han."

The boy ducked into his closet while Zhi-fu returned into his chamber.

Inside the room, his belongings had already been arranged by the porters. His desk was set by the window where there was good light. He'd paid a coin to a fortune-teller to assure proper placement to promote focus and good energy. The trunks hadn't yet been unpacked so he set about doing so, digging out his collection of well-worn books to place on the shelves. It was all there, the required canon of mathematic compendiums and scientific writings.

His calculation and measurement devices filled another trunk. Then his writing implements. He arranged them on the desk along with a set of blank journals.

Zhi-fu then sat at the cherry wood desk and closed his eyes, breathing deep. The beginning of another examination period. He wanted to believe this was the year when he'd finally succeed.

Was he any wiser? Smarter? More determined? He couldn't answer anymore. What he kept wondering was whether it really had anything to do with him at all.

He'd been tempted to blurt it out to Han the entire way there. Most will fail. Don't get your hopes up.

Shi Han was another fresh-faced hopeful from the provinces, out to conquer the world. Peking flooded with the likes of him every three years with each examination period. It wasn't too long ago when Zhi-fu had been that fresh-faced scholar; eighteen years and at the top of his local academy. He'd come to Peking only to be taught a lesson in humility.

He'd been foolhardy that first year, taking success for granted. He'd never known anything but success until Peking. After his first failed attempt, he'd gone home in shame to his family and doubled his efforts. For the next period, he'd come back more determined, more resolved. He knew every book in the canon, had studied every solution the masters had designed. He had been certain, certain that he would pass that year, which had made his failure all the more devastating. His father hadn't spoken to him for a month after his second failure.

Now at the age of twenty-five, Zhi-fu was truly an Elder Brother when it came to the candidates for the exam. He'd seen upper classmen come and go. The majority of the candidates who had been in his original cohort hadn't passed either, but after one or two attempts, they had stopped subjecting their families to such shame. They had accepted positions as tutors back in their hometowns, raising up the next generation of hopefuls.

But there was no teaching position or clerkship for him. It would either be an imperial appointment or the garrison. A life of science and learning or cannons and gunpowder.

He reached for his copy of the *Wucao suanjing*. He had been gifted it on his fifteenth birthday. It had been written over a thousand years earlier, designed to be a computational manual for civil servants entering the five governmental departments. Opening up to the first page, he began to read through instructions for bureaucrats. One-thousand-year-old instructions for stodgy bureaucrats.

He didn't get very far before shutting the book. He'd studied this very same book cover-to-cover over ten times. It wasn't that he lacked focus. He lacked faith.

The sky was beginning to darken outside which meant that they would be lighting the lanterns at the drinking houses. Kuo Lishen had promised to let him in on the big secret. Something that would change everything.

It sounded like more manipulation from Kuo Lishen. Of course, it was manipulation. It wasn't that Kuo wanted his company. Though Zhi-fu could hold his drink, he wasn't known as the life of the party. Kuo just reveled in the idea of bending others to his will.

Still…

It had been quite a parade of trunks with a grand air of secrecy.

Zhi-fu straightened his desk one last time before stepping outside where he was met with a rhythmic clicking sound. Click, click, click like the chatter of teeth.

He looked over to see Han perched outside the door of the storage closet. The young scholar had reclaimed a wobbly stool they'd removed earlier and he sat with his back against the door frame, book balanced on one knee with a wooden abacus balanced on the other. Deft fingers flew across the beads. Then the youth would pause, inspect the pattern, and mark something in his book.

Already studying hard.

Shi Han looked up momentarily and their eyes met. The boy's spectacles overshadowed his face, giving him an owl-like appearance. Behind the lenses, his features were soft and rounded. Zhi-fu had never heard of anyone below the age of eighteen passing the imperial examination. It took that long to pass all the prerequisite local examinations. Yet Han looked suspiciously younger than that.

Zhi-fu gave a brief nod which Han returned. Zhi-fu considered inviting him out, but Han was so intent on his studies. The boy would need that level of focus and dedication. He would need that and more.

Zhi-fu turned to head out of the gates. Behind him, the clicking of the beads resumed. Han working diligently away at his calculations.

Silently, Zhi-fu wished Han all the best. May he would succeed where others had failed.

"WHY DO you think you failed last time?" Kuo Lishen poured another round of drinks as he asked the question.

They were sitting at one of Kuo's favorite drinking spots, a local tavern on the corner of the Guojizan hutong. It was a stone's throw from the Academy which always offered the possibility that an official might come by for a drink.

"You studied pretty hard, right? Night and day."

It was an open wound for Zhi-fu, so of course Kuo insisted on jabbing at it.

"I should have studied harder."

Kuo Lishen made a rude noise. "You wouldn't have passed no matter how hard you studied," he declared, tossing back his liquor to punctuate the statement.

"Then why didn't you pass?" Zhi-fu countered.

Kuo slammed his cup open side down on the table to show he'd finished his drink. "I didn't study hard enough."

There was a sparse crowd at the drinking house tonight. The term had just begun after all. Tonight's patrons were here to reunite with old friends and take measure of the new class.

They had started the night with a group of their fellow classmates, but now it was just the two of them left. Regardless, Kuo Lishen always acted like he had an audience. Zhi-fu had been here for an hour and he was starting to conclude that this evening was indeed a waste of time.

"I suspect you didn't pass because of who you are," Kuo Lishen continued, wagging a finger at him.

"You think I angered someone?"

Kuo Lishen looked annoyed. "I don't mean Jin Zhi-fu, specifically. I mean who your father is. Your family."

Zhi-fu frowned at that. He righted Kuo Lishen's cup and poured the next round out of politeness. In truth, he was pretty much done drinking until Kuo had brought up this bit about some personal vendetta getting in the way of his examination score.

"I hadn't heard of any feud—"

"You wouldn't ever hear of any. Do you realize that you and I are the same? Even though your family has a military appointment and my family is just of the lowly, extremely wealthy merchant class." Kuo leaned forward which meant Zhi-fu had to do the same. "The scholar-elite doesn't want us to be added to their exalted ranks."

Zhi-fu drank, the liquor searing a path down his throat. He didn't like hearing what Kuo Lishen had to say, likely because there was truth to it. He'd been asked by Academy officials repeatedly if he would consider taking the military exams.

"So how is that ever going to change?" Zhi-fu asked. If Kuo Lishen truly had something to show him, he had better do it quickly. Zhi-fu's patience was hanging by a thread.

Kuo Lishen smiled. Then the smile widened to a grin.

"Come with me, Jin Zhi-fu."

As he stood, a heavy weight hung onto his shoulders. The truth was, Zhi-fu was tired. Not physically. It was only a little past the Hour of the Rat, just past the middle of the night. Not late at all in the realm of the student quarter.

Zhi-fu was tired of the games, the subterfuge. He almost wished the examinations would begin tomorrow. Then this year could be done with and he would know he wasn't suited for anything more than the life of a soldier like his father before him. And his grandfather before that.

The proprietor was at the door to bid Kuo a fond farewell with an invitation to return any time. A nod of acknowledgment was all that was required. No need to dirty any hands with money. Kuo's family wealth was beyond that. Only families like that could afford for their favored sons to keep attempting to pass. Failure was expensive.

When Zhi-fu had arrived for his first examination period, Kuo was already known in the quarter. An elder brother everyone wanted to have. His name was spoken among the candidates, if not with respect, at least with affection. Elder Brother Kuo, who knew everyone.

Kuo had sought out his acquaintance within the first months, but Zhi-fu had kept his distance. He was a serious student, intent to bring his family honor through the examinations. Kuo had made occasional inquiries, provided a careful word here and there. Only after the results had been read aloud, and Zhi-fu's name conspicuously missing, had he reached out to offer his full friendship.

"You are me, dear brother, one year ago," Kuo had said, pouring him a cup of warmed wine. "And me, today, for that matter."

They drank solemnly. Talked about the exam. How the best failed.

The second year they'd been closer friends throughout the

period and unfortunately hadn't fared much better. Now Zhi-fu was feeling that Kuo had accepted failure as a habit. He feared he might be doing the same.

"This is the way back to the Academy," Zhi-fu said as Kuo led them down the lanes.

"Correct, Jin Zhi-fu. We're going back."

"The gates will be closed."

Kuo hushed him. "Gates are never closed for those who have the key."

Kuo's key was a tael of silver that he pressed into the watchman's hand. The two of them then slipped inside the quiet courtyard of the Academy, a single lantern between them as they ambled through the blackness.

They moved through the complex to the buildings in the back. Zhi-fu had rarely been to this part of the Academy. It was where the archives and relic rooms were located.

"Several months ago, I heard rumors of a great crash near the border of the Kingdom of Bhutan, near Assam," Kuo began.

A knot of anticipation formed in Zhi-fu's stomach. "What sort of crash?"

Kuo's family administered to matters of commerce in the southwestern region near the Yindu border which included some of the most prosperous tea and silk routes. More recently, it had also become a crossroads for the trade of opium.

"Some of the traders had scavenged parts from the wreckage. My father put out a bounty on scavenged wreckage and they appeared to be from the hull of some kind of vessel. A ship."

Zhi-fu frowned. The Bhutan-Assam region was landlocked. "From a river boat?"

"From an *airship*."

Kuo paused dramatically before pushing the store house doors open. Zhi-fu raised his lantern to illuminate the room.

The relics had been moved to the corners to accommodate

the large crates that Kuo had delivered that morning. The containers had already been opened and the contents laid out.

Most of it was wreckage, as Kuo had described. Unidentifiable. But there was a large hunk of iron laid out on a workbench in the center of the room.

Zhi-fu's heart pounded as he approached. Tentatively, he placed a hand onto what was unmistakably a piston. "It's an engine."

"My family went through great effort to acquire these pieces. We made a point of gifting this to the Academy rather than the Ministry of Science," Kuo said.

Zhi-fu circled the wreckage, wishing that he had a better light source. They knew little of the inner workings of the Western ships. Fire wheel boats and hot air balloons. Much of it was dismissed as fable.

But this was no balloon.

"We are not prepared for an attack by air," Zhi-fu murmured.

Kuo snorted. "Spoken like a military-governor's son. Your mind always goes first to war."

"And yours to profit," he retorted.

Kuo took no offense. If anything, he accepted the remark as a compliment.

Zhi-fu placed his hand inside the iron structure, feeling along the jagged edge where the metal had been torn apart. As if he could discern its secrets by touch alone.

Their gunpowder engines were used to power land transports and industrial machines. They were known to be volatile, requiring frequent maintenance. Attempts to power larger vessels using black powder had failed—it was too dangerous.

Kuo came to stand beside him. The lantern light flickered dimly over the ugly, black fragment of metal. Somewhere in that misshapen mass, dark and twisted, lay the future.

"The Ministry of Science is going to need new blood," Kuo Lishen declared. "Not the same old tired bureaucrats."

Zhi-fu stared at the gears, evidence of unforeseen Western advancement. Their empire frequently traded with the West, purchasing shipments of opium. They were thought of as fledgling nations while the Qing Empire had thrived for over a thousand years. Western learning was looked upon as a curiosity, but had they been blind?

"You're right, Kuo Lishen," he agreed. "This is going to change everything."

Chapter 3

Anlei started awake in darkness. It was morning. Was it morning? Such was the peril of sleeping in a room without windows—or rather a storage closet. There were no windows to let in the light.

She had stayed up studying, not wanting to waste a single night. Now she had the sinking feeling she had woken up late.

With a lead weight in her stomach, she threw open the door of her narrow chamber and was hit across the face with a glaring ray of sun.

Late. Late, late, late.

The courtyard outside was empty. The apartments had cleared of the students. She wiped the sleep from her eyes and attempted to straighten her clothes which she'd slept in from a combination of exhaustion and a lack of other clothes.

She brushed away the dust from her jacket and smoothed out her hair. Strands of it poked out from the tightly woven queue, but there was no time to redo the braid. She shoved her cap onto her head and grabbed her books. Then she ran.

The streets of Peking were as full and unfriendly as the day before. She wove around the pedestrians, narrowly missed knocking over a basket of steamed buns. Received a stream of abuse from the vendor which she ignored as she kept running.

She was panting and out of breath by the time she saw the entrance of the academy. She also saw with dismay that it was empty of any students. Everyone was inside, diligently studying. Though her lungs burned, she forced herself to keep running.

The courtyard was quiet and empty. She was going to be expelled on the very first day and sent away in dishonor.

She paused at the doors of the main lecture hall. Inside, the lesson was already in progress. Anlei wiped the sweat from her brow. She couldn't do anything about the sweat soaking her tunic beneath her linen jacket.

Tentatively, she set one foot inside. Then another. Everyone was bent over their writing desks, scribbling into composition books. She tried to slip into an empty spot on the bench in the back row. Unfortunately, there was space for only half a person and the student who occupied the seat glared at her as she knocked against his elbow.

She fumbled for her notebook while a flood of heat washed over her face. There were a series of mathematical problems written on the wall — she assumed that was what everyone was working on so intently.

"Late," the instructor proclaimed at the front of the room.

Anlei froze and shrank down in her seat, but it was no use. An army of heads turned as one to stare at her. Jin Zhi-fu was there among them, something akin to a grimace on his face.

She could feel the instructor's steely-eyed gaze on her as she finally found a charcoal pencil to write with. A water clock had been set at the front of the room; each click of the wheel counting down another minute. By the time she copied the first one onto the paper, the sound of scribbling around her had risen to a frenzied pitch. Letting out a slow breath, she stared at the problem and started her calculations.

The sounds around her faded. She started down one solution path only to scratch it out. The clock wheel turned, the small click marking another minute gone, never to be recovered. Anlei started again. Once she simplified the problem down, it turned out there was a standard equation that could be applied. She solved the equation neatly, feeling the pieces of the puzzle click into place in her mind.

The second problem required more extended calculation. She retrieved her abacus, setting it upon her desk and quickly resetting the beads. As she started the calculations, once again everyone shifted their eyes toward her.

Anlei glanced up and that was when she noticed each student had before him a mechanical device the shape and size of an abacus. Instead of the rods and beads, there was a set of dials.

She pushed her spectacles up against her face. If she could have folded herself into a tiny ball and disappeared, she would have. She slipped her abacus back into her satchel as quietly as she could and continued working.

There were only four problems total. The fourth one was, once again, one she had never encountered before. Minutes clicked by on the water clock as she stared at her paper. Then she started writing, the page quickly getting filled up with her scribbles and scratched out figures. In frustration, she turned the paper over to start again. Clean page. New approach.

Biting down on her bottom lip, Anlei started to work through. She was still lost in the equations when the other candidates around her stood to file toward the front of the room. She completed the final problem as best she could and rose, disappointment hanging around her neck like a stone. She picked up her notebook and joined the queue. One by one, the students set their books in a stack on the instructor's desk.

Behind him, the wheel of the water clock had come to a stop. It looked like a great sun with the spokes radiating out from his back like a mythological being. His beard was thick and black, but did little to hide the curl of his lip.

Anlei was the very last one to turn in her work. The moment

she set down the paper, the instructor stabbed two fingers on top of it.

"What is your name?" In the near empty hall, the master's voice sounded like thunder through the clouds.

Her own voice shook in response. "Sh-shi Han. From Anhui Province."

She added the last part because he was staring at her, eyes hard and black like a cobra's.

"Next time you are late, turn around and go home, Shi Han from Anhui."

Out in the courtyard, Jin Zhi-fu was assembled with a group of students. They looked to be older candidates. Ones who had experience taking the exams in previous sittings. They were hotly debating the problems and she only listened with half an ear as she tried to rush by, shoulders hunched. Zhi-fu broke away from the discussion to call out her name. Or rather, her assumed name.

"Shi Han."

She stopped and lifted her head.

"The next lecture is this way." He pointed over his shoulder.

In her haste, she had set herself in the direction of the main gate.

His mouth twitched in what might have been amusement. If Zhi-fu hadn't stopped her, she might have fled and never returned. Everything was so much more difficult than she'd imagined. And she'd imagined it would be hard.

"Usually students don't flee until the second week," he teased. A few of the students around him chuckled, but quieted when he glanced at them.

Even though he was grinning at her, his expression was still kind. She was grateful she'd met Zhi-fu the day before, if only to have one face in the Academy that wasn't a stranger's.

She turned to find the lecture hall. As she passed Zhi-fu and his group, she was too intimidated to join them, but she did manage a small nod even though her face burned with embarrassment.

Getting into the Academy hadn't been the hardest part. The hardest part was always going to be whatever moment was in front of her. And there was still a year left in the term.

THE STREETS WERE QUIET, but far from empty as Zhi-fu walked back to his room. The tea stand at the corner of the hutong was still open and he was surprised to see his neighbor there, the young and eager Shi Han, nursing a near-empty bowl of tea. His nose was in a book, the lantern-light glinting off his spectacles. As he read, his right hand hovered over an invisible abacus, tapping out a sum against the table top.

"Already vying for the top spot, hmm?"

Han's head shot up. The youth had a perpetually startled expression. "You're up late as well," he pointed out, his tone defensive.

"But I'm not doing anything nearly as productive."

The Western airship still weighed on his mind. A massive iron dragon sailing over the skies.

"I'm going over the problem set from today," Han explained.

Zhi-fu sat down opposite Han at the table. The owner of the stand came over to pour tea and then disappeared just as quickly. The boy was already back in his book. Nothing else existed.

"Don't tire out too soon," Zhi-fu warned. "There's still a long way to go."

"Can't waste any time," Han mumbled.

Peculiar boy. Zhi-fu had to admit, he was curious about this young man who had come from nowhere to be admitted into the Academy. Han was certainly persistent, but if persistence was enough to open the doors, the Academy would be over-flowing.

Three of their fellow students came to the stand next, jostling the table as they sat. They looked and sounded to have come straight from the drinking house.

"Brother Jin. Elder Brother." They greeted him briefly before falling back into their conversation, laughing. Han was momentarily jolted out of his calculation by their chatter. He cast a frown in their direction before resuming.

"Not the best place for studying," Zhi-fu remarked.

"I need the light."

Han indicated the lanterns hanging from the poles that surrounded the stands, then turned his attention back to the problem set. The beloved abacus was laid out on the table, and his fingers flew over the wooden beads, click-clacking away.

Zhi-fu reached out and took hold of the instrument. Something had to be done. He was going to go mad listening to those beads.

"What are you—?"

"Come on," Zhi-fu stood and tossed down a coin for the tea. "You need a calculating device."

Han grabbed his things and chased after Zhi-fu as he strode down the hutong. He stopped at a shop with an engraved sign over the door, the largest shop on the lane. Though the markets were officially closed, there were plenty of pawn shops that operated in the unregulated night markets.

The pawn broker was seated behind a counter, leg crossed over knee in a leisurely pose. His eyes tracked to them as they entered.

"I prefer the abacus." Han made a swipe at the instrument, but Zhi-fu pulled it out of reach.

"This is a merchant's tool. You need a calculator for the work you'll be doing."

"I don't have any money," Han said under his breath.

"The broker may be eager to sell at a good price. The

supply is high." Zhi-fu pointed to the overflow of calculating devices laid out across two shelves. Imperial scholars had a reputation for running out of money.

Han bit his lip, looking entirely uncomfortable. Zhi-fu suddenly felt like a lout for dragging Han here. He could have handled it more discretely instead of forcing Han to lose face.

"Don't worry," Zhi-fu dismissed, moving to sift through the devices. "I consider this an investment."

"What sort of an investment?"

"An investment in peaceful sleep. It sounds like an army of crickets in the next room whenever you start on this."

Han clamped his mouth shut as Zhi-fu evaluated the devices. After turning and testing the dials and number wheels, Zhi-fu selected one that was in good condition. Han insisted on keeping his abacus, however.

"It was my father's," he said, tucking it carefully away in his satchel.

They ended the night on a crate outside of Han's room, with Zhi-fu going through how to use the various dials and readings and machine. Han was a quick learner and there was something satisfying about helping out the lower classman.

Kuo Lishen would have scoffed at the idea. Shi Han was a poor student from the provinces, without a sliver of wealth or influence to repay him with.

When they were done, Han murmured his thanks. He'd taken off his spectacles to inspect the number wheels. It was the first time Zhi-fu had seen him without them.

Zhi-fu squinted down at him. Han looked different when his eyes weren't hidden behind glass. His expression was sharper, brighter. Not so...lost.

Han became aware of the sudden scrutiny and shoved the spectacles back on, hooking the wire frame over both his ears.

"It's-late. Sleep-well-see-you-tomorrow!"

His words blended together in his haste and Shi Han disappeared into the storage closet before Zhi-fu could reply.

Zhi-fu retired to his room and lit the lamp at his desk. He considered reviewing the day's lectures as Shi-Han had done, but it was late. He wondered if the young scholar was still up. Turning to the wall, he tapped the wooden panels twice. Tonight, there was only silence from the other side of the wall.

He set his books aside and made a vow to catch up on his studies tomorrow. As Zhi-fu went to extinguish his lamp, an answering double tap finally came from the other side to bid him good night.

Chapter 4

Anlei was jolted awake by someone pounding at her door. At first, she was angry with the fog of sleep still wrapped around her. It was dark in the store room except for a sharp sliver of light that cut through the bottom of the door. It was daylight outside.

She dragged herself up from the floor.

Late again.

Her back ached from sleeping on a bamboo mat laid out on bare dirt, but she fumbled for her clothing and hastily wound the binding cloth over breasts. Throwing on her jacket, she tried her best to smooth out her braided queue before slinging her books over her shoulder. Sunlight flooded the room the moment she opened the door, causing her to squint as she hurried outside.

The warm, fragrant smell of cooking rice filled the courtyard. Her fellow classmates were seated on long benches, spooning thick rice porridge into their mouths. She spotted Zhifu at the dispensary cart, ladling congee into a porcelain bowl. He met her eyes, gave a slight nod. He must have been the one who knocked on her door. Anlei had no idea why he was being so kind to her, but she was grateful. She just had to be careful about getting too close to anyone.

She went to the water pump and splashed water from the communal bowl over her face, drying herself with a sleeve. So much for manners.

Steam spouted from the cart's exhaust port as she approached. A large porridge-filled cauldron was set on top of the dispensary cart. Coal burned in the cabinet underneath, keeping the pot heated. There was just enough rice left inside to scrape together a bowl for herself. She carried her breakfast to a spot on the bench beside Zhi-fu, hoping she wasn't imposing.

She started to thank him for waking her, but he cut her off. "Eat. You have only a few minutes."

The other classmates were already depositing their bowls onto the cart and heading out. Zhi-fu waited as she gulped down her rice.

"You should go," she said, mouth full.

"I'm not worried. My legs are longer than yours," he replied with a grin.

She swallowed the last of the white paste and stacked the bowl onto the top of the precarious tower that had accumulated on the cart. Then she and Zhi-fu both broke into a run. They raced through the streets, weaving around baskets and people and the occasional mule. Zhi-fu's legs were longer than hers, much longer. She remained behind him the entire time, keeping his long, lean shape in sight as he dove through the crowd.

"Come on, Han," he urged over one shoulder. "Late for the first two days and you might get expelled."

She was almost certain he was taunting her, but a sick feeling shot to her stomach. Master Li had told her to turn around and go home if she was late again.

Anlei pushed forward, gulping for air as her legs started to burn. She came up side-by-side with Zhi-fu as they reached the entrance to the Academy. Zhi-fu kept on running, so she did the same. By the time they reached the inner courtyard, she was gasping for breath.

The rest of the students were already gathered in front of the mathematics hall. Some sort of bulletin had been posted outside the door.

"Who's Shi Han?" Someone was saying.

The sound of her name made her want to vomit. Or maybe she had just run too hard. Why were they asking about her?

Zhi-fu pushed to the front of the crowd, or rather the crowd seemed to part for him. Anlei stared up at the posting, reading over his shoulder. It was a list of names. She spotted Kuo Lishen near the top. Zhi-fu's name was there as well, but she didn't see her name until she kept on looking upward.

Hers was the very first name on the list.

Zhi-fu swiveled around to look at her, eyebrows raised.

A wave of euphoria swept through her. She'd scored at the top of the class on the previous day's exam — she hadn't even known it was an exam. Her elation was immediately followed with a feeling of dread as they filed into the hall. Zhi-fu directed her to the bench at the front of the room. Kuo Lishen was already seated there. His gaze had passed over her dismissively the day before, but now it lingered disturbingly.

"Shi Han from Anhui province," Kuo Lishen declared as she found her seat. Thankfully Zhi-fu took the spot between them on the bench, shielding her from scrutiny.

As Master Li began the day's lecture, Anlei forced her attention onto the day's problem set, but it was impossible to ignore. Two upperclassmen had scored second and third below her score and every bench situated behind them could see it.

Her strategy of disappearing into the ranks was a lost cause. She tried to concentrate on the lesson, even though she could feel Jin Zhi-fu's eagle gaze burning into her skin.

The favored sons of the Academy were looking at her with different eyes.

THE LIBRARY at the Academy was located inside a building in the northwest corner of the Academy grounds. Anlei sought it out as soon as the morning lectures were over.

The scholar who had given her directions had called it the Temple and it did indeed look like a sacred place. The red pagoda rose three stories with graceful winged rooftops that curved toward heaven. The eaves were painted with gold.

Her breath caught the moment she stepped inside. Light filtered in from windows on all five sides to pool at the center and every wall was covered with books. This *was* a place of worship, the Tao and the Dharma. She was flooded with a sense of time and knowledge. Here, she was connected to everything.

Would the Academy let her sleep here? She never wanted to leave.

Anlei remembered the first time she'd been allowed into Mistress Wang's studio. A shelf full of books stood behind a polished desk. Anlei had never seen so many books. In her innocent mind, all the knowledge in the world must have been held in those books.

"How many books are in here?" she'd asked.

"Nearly a hundred, Little One."

There were eighty-six total. She had counted them in awe and vowed to read them all, but she never had the chance.

She'd rediscovered that feeling once again here at the Academy. She was a child standing in awe of so much recorded wisdom. All the knowledge in the world. Her chest was ready to burst.

The Directory was actually a set of volumes, each one thick as a tree trunk and heavier than her in weight.

She fished out her journal and turned to the first page where she'd written down a list of titles of mathematical treatises.

She looked up the titles in the Directory. Each of the titles had a number listed beside it. On one wall, there was a large panel set with knobs and buttons. Overhead there was a system of lines and pulleys rigged up. Occasionally, she could hear the click and slide of gears as a book was retrieved from a shelf and deposited onto a slide to be delivered to the waiting recipient.

After locating the first one, she wrote down the number and faced the sorter. It was a control panel set against one wall. A series of knobs etched with numbers were attached to the wall. Apparently, she needed to dial in the location number to retrieve her book. She stared at the panel for a long minute, watching as the levers and gears inside shifted, transferring the turn of the knobs into a cascade of movements.

The machinery proved too much for her. She opted for the stairs instead and started climbing the steps in an upward spiral. The staircase opened up onto the second floor. More books, shelves upon shelves of them. Why would anyone want to rely on the mechanical arms of the sorter? She wanted to run her fingertips along each and every spine.

It took a moment to decipher the location numbers as she wandered along the curve of one wall. The book she needed was on the highest shelf. She stretched up onto her toes to try to reach it, clawing at the spine with her fingertips.

A shadow blocked her view as someone reached over her. An arm brushed against hers as he retrieved her book. Reflexively, she shrank away. Anlei found herself with her back against the shelves, staring up at Jin Zhi-fu.

"This is why the Academy built the sorter," he told her, oblivious to her discomfort. He glanced at the title of the book, tapping his fingers over the cover thoughtfully before holding it out to her. "*The Jade Mirror of the Four Unknowns,*" he read aloud.

Heart pounding, she reached out to take it from him. It took two hands to lift the volume.

He cocked his head, peering at her curiously. "Are you alright, Han?"

"Yes. I'm fine." Hardening her jaw, she pulled her shoulders straight, though she doubted the extra touch of height did anything to close the gap between them. She was shorter than most of the students at the Academy, but with Zhi-fu the difference was more pronounced.

"I've never been able to read it," she explained feebly. The remark was just an excuse to fill the silence.

Zhi-fu raised his eyebrows at that. "It's a canonical text."

"Yes. Required for the examination."

Of course, he knew that already. Anlei had lost control of her mouth. It kept on speaking when she really wanted it to stop.

"Over five hundred years old." She added. Still speaking.

Zhi-fu nodded slowly, wholly uninterested. She hugged the tome to her chest and decided she should go. She was spending entirely too much time in the presence of Jin Zhi-fu. He had a tendency to look closely at her and she needed less people looking at her in any way.

"What are you searching for?" she asked instead, drawn to him despite herself.

"The foreign book collection."

He started towards the stairs. Intrigued, Anlei followed him to a small alcove on the upper floor. The section wasn't well lit and not very extensive, but just knowing that these books were stored here felt like secret knowledge.

"May I?" she asked him as she reached for one.

The corner of his mouth twisted. "You're welcome to. The books aren't mine."

Gingerly, she slid a slim book from the shelf to inspect the cover. It was handwritten with angled characters that flowed together. She couldn't decipher the language.

"What is this?"

"A Western language?" he guessed. "Latin?"

"What a shame that no one's translating these books," she murmured, turning the book over in fascination. It seemed to read backwards.

Zhi-fu only spared her book a cursory glance. He was occupied looking through the upper shelves. Anlei set the book back and slid out another one. This one was definitely a mathematics book. With a little shock of delight, she realized she'd seen the diagrams before.

Euclid's Elements. This one had been translated. She'd read a copy in Mistress Wang's library. The spark of recognition was like the snap of lock to key. Intensely satisfying.

She held the foreign copy a moment longer out of reverence before returning it. When she looked up, Zhi-fu balanced a large bound volume in his hands. He was looking over a diagram for some sort of machine.

"Is that on the examination?" she asked.

He looked up at her question, blinking in surprise as if he'd forgotten she was there. She understood completely. A moment ago, she'd been similarly absorbed in her book.

"Engineering doesn't appear in the exam." He thought about that for a moment. "Too practical," he concluded.

What did he mean by that? Her confusion must have shown on her face, because Zhi-fu continued his explanation. All the while the book with the diagrams remained open between them.

"Engineering is considered a trade. Medicine and the natural sciences are practical pursuits as well. We'll find the books in here, but the examination itself is focused on astronomy and mathematics."

Thankfully those were her strengths. She tried to absorb every word, even considered taking notes. "That's quite a lot as it is."

"And then there are the writings of Master Kong Fuzi," Zhi-fu said absently as he turned the page. His brow furrowed as he reviewed the diagram there.

"Which writings?" she asked, feeling a bit sick at this turn of events. She imagined the hallowed philosopher had written a lot of words in his lifetime of which she had read none.

"*The Analects*." Zhi-fu sounded surprised she'd even ask.

She stared down at the four sections of the *Jade Mirror* she held in her hands. She'd nearly forgotten it, distracted by Zhi-fu and his meanderings. He'd studied for the examinations before and probably had a moment or two that could be diverted. She didn't have that luxury. It would take her a year studying night and day to finish with the mathematical canon she had yet to read let alone *The Analects*.

Anlei started to make her farewell, but Zhi-fu was no longer distracted. Instead, the older student's attention was completely fixed onto her. He was watching her with a hundred questions in his eyes.

"Han, how did you score so well on that exam?"

The alcove suddenly felt very small.

Anlei adjusted her spectacles with a knuckle. "I must be lucky?"

Zhi-fu snorted. "You're a poor liar."

Her heart skipped a beat. Blood rushed to her cheeks at the word 'liar'. He was right that she was bad at lying. She'd had very little practice, and now for her first lie to be such an immense one. The only way she could have told a greater lie was to pretend to be a princess.

"You got every problem right," Zhi-fu pointed out. "And with less time to work than everyone else."

He'd noticed. Other people would notice.

"I just worked through each one methodically," she ventured, fidgeting.

"This is your first year at the Academy. You haven't even read all the books."

She blinked. "Which books?"

Zhi-fu stared back at her in disbelief. "The solutions are from classical texts. Like the one in your hands."

She pulled the enormous volume closer to her chest. She didn't expect anyone would pay any attention to her, a no-name student from nowhere. Especially not someone like Zhi-fu who was well-known at the Academy.

"I dissected each problem until it...reduced," she tried to explain.

"All problems don't reduce."

"But they do," she insisted. "In some fashion."

"The second problem had four unknowns," Zhi-fu protested. "One doesn't just come in and happen upon the answer through trial and error."

She took a breath. "It wasn't trial and error. There's nothing intuitive about understanding Kong Fuzi's Analects or the mechanics of a wheel," she explained, waving a hand at the drawing in the book he held. "But the way numbers fit together is universal. There's a law and a way to mathematics that's innate. It's written in the moon and the stars and the relation-ships of things to each other. We can know these relationships, just by virtue of being creatures of nature. If you take a mathe-matics problem, it's fitted together the way bone is to muscle. It has to be the way it is. It has to solve the way it does."

She'd never been able to put it to words, to anyone. But she was here, face-to-face with a man who was a scholar. Jin Zhi-fu was someone she wanted to be and here he was, treating her as a peer. Listening to her every word while she was surrounded by more books than the eye could see. If heaven existed, could it be any different than this?

Zhi-fu was staring at her curiously and she knew it was dangerous to have him looking so closely at her, but she didn't want him to turn away.

"You're some sort of mathematics prodigy," he concluded finally.

Her skin flushed warm, and she pushed her spectacles up nervously. "Of course not."

Jin Zhi-fu was all seriousness now. "I don't think you're going to be able to deny it. Not any longer."

Chapter 5

Zhi-fu fell into a steady routine over the next two weeks. His strategy this time was to divide his time between the tea house and the Academy. For every night he spent drinking and meeting potential examiners and Academy officials, he spent two nights dedicated to his studies. This had to be his time, this year. If he failed again, it was back to jagged mountains and cold rock of the frontier.

For a hundred years now, the border had been secured by treaties and marriages rather than firepower and cavalry. The banner armies were becoming obsolete. Soon it would be little more than an honorary designation. The Emperor had built his own army outside of the banners. There was no glory in serving a forgotten role in the empire. If Zhi-fu wanted to make a name for himself, he needed to move beyond legacy and tradition.

But not beyond duty. His family had always been entrusted with the protection of the empire. Zhi-fu felt in his gut that black powder and foot soldiers would not be able to protect the empire forever. Not any more effective than the ancient border wall, crumbling to ruin.

He wasn't the only one starting his studies early. Whenever Zhi-fu went to the library, Shi Han was there at the desk in the corner on the last row, taking notes. He appeared to be going through the Computational Canon, book by book. The young scholar must not have owned copies and had to rely on the Academy's collection for study.

Han preferred to keep to himself, which was understandable. The culture of the Academy was one of closely-guarded cliques and rivalries. Han was a first-year and from the provinces. Already an outsider whether he willed it so or not.

Despite the boy's aloofness, it seemed the two of them were becoming friends. Whenever Shi Han happened to see him, they exchanged cordial nods. Han had also approached him in the library a week earlier to ask whether the examinations in the lecture hall had any bearing on the imperial examination results.

The answer was complicated, so Zhi-fu, who'd been in a hurry that day, had merely told him no. Shi Han had proceeded to score neatly in the middle of the pack on the next day's exam, moving his seat into the center of rows.

What Zhi-fu hadn't had time to explain was all of the nuances of the examination — how there was a network of officials who evaluated the results and they were the ones who ultimately recommended that name or this name for consideration. It was all about the exam and not all about the exam and it didn't hurt to curry favor early. Or at least be noticed.

Zhi-fu should have also told Han that his attempt to disappear into anonymity wouldn't work. Han had already attracted the attention of the serious contenders. Zhi-fu for one, and Kuo Lishen for another. Kuo Lishen paid little attention to anybody until they were either a potential ally or rival.

Despite the fact that they were neighbors, Zhi-fu heard very little from the room beside him. He assumed Han was either studying at the library or reading beneath the teahouse lanterns most nights. That was why Zhi-fu was surprised that night when he heard a voice on the other side of the wall.

"*Bèn dàn!*"

The curse was loud enough to cause Zhi-fu to look up from

where he was seated at his desk. He glanced toward the corner of the room nearest to the door.

Another muttered string of curses rose from the corner.

He moved to investigate. It didn't take long to find a hole in the wall down near the floor and large enough to fit a finger through. Zhi-fu crouched to peer into the small opening, seeing only darkness on the other side. He could hear the whispery rasp of a page turning.

"Han?"

There was a long pause before the response came. "Yes?"

"What are you doing down there?" The boy had to be crouched on the floor in his room.

"I'm…ah…borrowing some of your candlelight."

He'd never heard of anything so pitiful. "Come over here."

Zhi-fu stood and opened his door a crack before returning to his desk. By the time Han peeked through, Zhi-fu had picked up his bamboo pen to make notes on a diagram.

"Elder Brother." Han hovered at the doorway with a copy of a book in his hands.

"Did you steal that book from the library?"

Han paled. "I was going to return it!"

He was slight of build and small-boned, making him appear younger than most of the students at the Academy. In the garrisons, he would have been relegated to the role of messenger or runner. Zhi-fu felt naturally protective of Han.

"I'm not going to report you," Zhi-fu assured.

"I did some calculations," Han looked relieved and immediately launched into a breathless explanation, "Of how long it's taken me to go through each book and I concluded there's not enough time unless I sneak into the library at night or sneak the books out. I figured I was more likely to get expelled for sneaking into the library."

Had Zhi-fu ever been that innocent? Or eager?

"So, you have strong opinions about that book," Zhi-fu remarked.

"Oh," Han looked down at the cover ruefully. "The solutions in here are incorrect."

"That text has survived several dynasties. Thousands of scholars, respected and talented, have studied it."

"Mathematical rules don't change with the dynasty," Han replied with a scowl. He ventured further into the room as they spoke.

"It's well-known that the book uses common approximations," Zhi-fu explained.

Apparently, approximation was not one of Shi Han's favorite concepts. "There are also pages and pages of bureaucratic procedure. Certainly, all that can't be on the exam?"

Zhi-fu nodded grimly and Han's expression fell. "It's more history than mathematics," he said glumly.

The imperial examinations were notorious for requiring feats of memorization and there were no shortcuts. He had studied every word in that book as well as the rest of the canon. Some of the methods in the canonical texts were known to be inaccurate which was apparently offensive to Shi Han. This was an area where the boy's innate understanding of mathematics would be a disadvantage.

"You can stay here to study," Zhi-fu offered. "I'm not going to sleep for a while."

Han's face brightened as he pulled the door closed behind him. "I'm saving my candles. Come winter time, the sky will start darkening earlier. I want to make sure I have enough for the end of the term right before the exam."

Han came back toward the desk as he looked about for a place to settle down. "What is that you're working on?"

He was looking at the diagram Zhi-fu had laid out on his desk.

"It's an engine."

"You have a personal interest in engines?"

"One could say."

Even though engineering wasn't part of the imperial exam,

the wreck of the airship had captured his imagination. Shi Han came closer to inspect the drawing. "What is this wheel?"

"It's called a turbine. Do you have any experience with engines?" Zhi-fu asked, surprised by the boy's interest.

"My family runs a paper mill in a remote village. We couldn't afford to employ an engineer and had to keep the machinery working between visits from the mechanic."

They had cargo transports out in the frontier, though his people were horse-riders by blood and preferred the saddle. His knowledge of engineering had come from his time in Peking. "This diagram is copied from a German manuscript."

"The one you were looking at in the library?"

He nodded. "There's a well-known story in Peking. The calendar created by the imperial astronomer had several grave errors so the Kangxi Emperor demanded a public test between Western and Eastern astronomical techniques, to determine which was more accurate."

"I know this story," Han piped up, to his surprise. "The Western astronomer was a missionary and he prevailed in all three of the Emperor's tests. The Kanxi Emperor appointed him Head of the Mathematics Board. And the calendar that year had a month taken off that wasn't necessary, making it more accurate."

Zhi-fu leaned back and regarded Shi Han with new eyes. "There are not many who are interested in Western learning."

"My mis—my master studied astronomy and favored the Western solar calendar."

An ongoing debate to this day. "The Emperor bestowed the name Nan Huairen upon the missionary, who quickly became a favorite in court," Zhi-fu recounted. "It was said that Nan Huairen fashioned a gift for the Emperor. It was a small vehicle that was able to propel itself through the halls of the imperial palace. That vehicle was powered by steam." He tapped the diagram on the desk. "This was the design."

Han looked intrigued as Zhi-fu described what he understood of the engine. It could be powered by any fuel which was ignited and then used to heat water in a separate chamber.

"Very different from a black powder burning engine," Han remarked.

Gunpowder engines were in their infancy, inefficient and prone to becoming clogged with soot.

"I've read accounts of foreign ships that have been spotted by merchants. Fire-wheel boats, they're called. The reports tell of white smoke rising from the vessels and we always assumed they were powered by fire, like our engines. When the Engineering Bureau tried to build larger gunpowder engines, they would catch on fire and occasionally explode."

"You're thinking it wasn't smoke rising from the Western ships, but steam," Han finished for him. "How fascinating."

He hadn't expected to have such a conversation here, with Shi Han from landlocked Anhui province. Living out at the border, with the kingdom of Silla and the Tartar lands nearby, it was natural to come into contact with foreign goods and ideas. His time in Peking and the many advancements of the capital had expanded his interest.

The wreckage Kuo Lishen had shown him was more complex than anything he'd seen in any book. If he extrapolated size from the pistons, the rotor blades — in his mind's eye, the wreck came from a vast hulking airship capable of hiding in the clouds. Could a steam engine generate enough power to drive something that massive? If the West was launching airships, what other machines did they have in their employ?

"Pity there are no courses on this at the Academy," Han added.

"Pity," he agreed. The Academy was focused on the imperial examination which was weighed down by thousands of years of tradition.

The discussion had veered quite a way from the official canon, but Zhi-fu was enjoying it. He'd spent nearly the entirety of his life studying the classics, so much so he'd go to sleep and dream in ancient texts. The taste of them were stale on his tongue after so many years of memorization.

Han remained standing before him. The young scholar shifted his weight from one foot to the other, awkward now that the conversation had come to a lull. Zhi-fu realized he was still searching for a place to sit.

There was only one chair in the room. His apartment was one of the larger rooms in the courtyard, but it wasn't exactly suitable for receiving visitors.

"Go on and use the bed," Zhi-fu suggested.

Han nearly dropped his book, stammering something about imposing. The kang bed was a raised platform built of stone and brick which housed a furnace for the winter months. It was large and level and could easily serve as a desk, but Han ended up settling on the floor, scooting closer to be within the circle of lamplight. Shi Han had relaxed during their conversation, but he was wide-eyed and anxious again, like a frightened bird. Zhi-fu supposed it was because the boy was new to Peking. The Academy could be intimidating.

"Pay particular attention to the Surveyor's Rule," Zhi-fu advised. "It's buried midway through."

Han nodded, balancing the large volume across his knees. Zhi-fu returned his attention to the diagram. He wanted to expand upon the simple model and create a design for a large-scale steam engine. Perhaps he could get one of the workshops to build it.

He'd return to the canon tomorrow and study until his eyes blurred.

Zhi-fu became absorbed in the design, incorporating what he knew of gunpowder engines along with the principles of the steam engine design he'd just discovered. Once he had a preliminary draft complete, he set down the pencil to stretch his arms. Han was still staring at his book. Zhi-fu thought he might have fallen asleep, the boy was sitting so still.

But the young scholar wasn't asleep after all. Han made a sour face at the book before dutifully turning the page.

Zhi-fu was stricken by the differences between them. He spared little thought to the price of candles or oil or the changing of the seasons. Instead he was able to frequent drinking houses, conversing with scholar-officials and making love to courtesans when the mood struck. His infatuation with one particular courtesan had cost him a good part of his second term at the Academy.

Zhi-fu broke the silence, "You can use my books any time."

Han looked up, startled. Zhi-fu imagined if hadn't interrupted, Han would study until morning.

"I have all of those titles on my bookshelf," Zhi-fu continued. "You can borrow them instead of haunting the library."

Han's eyes grew bright. "Thank you, Elder Brother. I'm so humbled. Thank you greatly."

Now this was getting embarrassing. Han thanked him again for making his collection of books available, thanked him for the lamplight.

"It's nothing," Zhi-fu tried to insist.

"It's *everything.*"

Zhi-fu stood and pulled a book from his shelf. "Have you read this one?"

When Han shook his head, Zhi-fu held it out to him. "Return it when you're done."

Shi Han had come here from the provinces expecting to take the imperial science exam when he didn't even know what was on it. He'd never studied the books in the canon, some of which required a year, two years of study in and of themselves. There was no doubt the boy was talented, but no one had properly prepared him.

"Han——" he began as Han reached for the volume.

"Yes?" Han looked like he would have jumped from Mount Tai if Zhi-fu has told him to.

"The imperial exam is very difficult."

"Of course it is."

"Very few candidates pass."

Now Han looked offended. "I'm aware of this."

"Even rarer to pass in your first sitting," Zhi-fu continued. It was best if someone told him now. "If you fail this year, there's always another chance in the next administration period."

Han grew quiet. Slowly he took the book from Zhi-fu's hands, holding onto it reverently as if he could absorb the knowledge through his skin.

"I know how difficult the examination is," he said gravely. "I know someone like me passing would be like—" he paused, searching. "Like capturing the moon."

"I just wanted you to know so you can be prepared," Zhi-fu replied.

"I know. I know very well." Han's reply was soft, slow, with the weight of a thousand stones. "Thank you for your guidance."

Zhi-fu watched as the young scholar stacked the new volume over his stolen copy from the library. As he trudged from the room, the weight of the books seemed to hang heavy in his arms, dragging his shoulders downward.

The door closed and Zhi-fu was left alone, feeling like a bastard. Han was certainly out of his depth in Peking, but he was determined. Zhi-fu imagined him in the next room, holding his book up to a tiny spot of light filtering through the wall. Zhi-fu could hear him on the other side now. The door creaked as Han returned to his room and there was a brief shuffling as he settled into his pallet to sleep.

Shi Han had enough determination for ten scholars. Maybe Zhi-fu was the one who should be taking guidance from him.

Zhi-fu straightened out his desk and prepared for bed. No two candidates could be more apart in circumstance. He had his apartment with a comfortable bed instead of the hard floor. He had a shelf full of expensive books and a lifetime of study. Han had come to Peking with the clothes on his back and a remarkable talent for equations. At the end of the term, they could both be dropped just the same.

Or they could both pass. What a miracle that would be!

The mechanical clock against the wall told him it was well into the first hour, the hour of the industrious Rat. Zhi-fu inspected the diagram he'd spent the night drafting once more before turning down the oil lamp.

An engine was a labyrinth of metal fittings and pistons that wound together in its own set of equations. One where force could be summed and multiplied. If deciphered properly, a hunk of iron parts could generate enough power to fly an airship into the clouds. If his eyes hadn't deceived him, then the Westerners had already done it. An airship like that could cross over deserts and oceans. It would render the frontier defenses his family had guarded for generations obsolete.

Before Zhi-fu could prepare a defense against such inventions, he needed to first pass this cursed exam.

Zhi-fu fell asleep thinking of thousand-year-old approximation methods. And dreamed of steam engines roaring in the skies.

ANLEI WAS STARTING to believe that she and Jin Zhi-fu were attending different academies. Several months had gone by and spring was becoming summer. She spent a lot of time perched just outside her room with the door propped open and her back against the jamb as she read. Not only was it the only way she could get light into her room, it also allowed her to catch an occasional cool breeze.

From there, she would see Zhi-fu leaving his room with a bow slung over his shoulder or dressed for polo in riding attire. Whenever she wasn't at the Academy, she was studying. Her days were filled with lectures, books, more books, and solution sets.

Whenever she did find Zhi-fu's lamp burning, she would venture next door. Tentatively, at first. Zhi-fu had been generous to allow her to join him that first time. Light was an expensive commodity and she couldn't afford to be proud.

Zhi-fu never said anything when she appeared. The door would be unlocked. He was usually at his desk, a deep frown line cutting across his brow as he focused on the page set before him. He presented a striking image; the intensity of that stare. The grim determination in his expression. It would be hard to say whether she was coming over as an excuse to steal a glimpse of him or to study.

Both. She could honestly say the answer was both — though only in silence to herself. The sight of Zhi-fu was much more appealing to her than philosophy. She found herself glancing over at him quite often while studying.

One night, she saw a stool had been set out in the middle of the floor. Zhi-fu was head down in his book as she entered and she had the courtesy not to mention any word of gratitude as she seated herself.

There were times she found her gaze wandering from her page to the chiseled line of his profile. His brow formed a pronounced ridge when he was deep in thought. In the back of her mind remained one warning — she couldn't allow herself to become too familiar with Jin Zhi-fu.

If only she could say she was indifferent to him. At first, she had assumed that it was only happenstance that she had approached him for help that first day, but now she knew that she had been drawn to Zhi-fu the way all people were drawn to him. There was a focus and a sense of purpose about him that exuded confidence. At the Academy, when he spoke, their peers leaned forward to listen. The masters were all nods of approval.

Maybe that was why her insides warmed whenever he turned to her for guidance on a solution. She'd made sure to fall into the middle of the class in rankings, but Zhi-fu seemed to trust her judgment on mathematical matters. She knew the others were starting to talk about them and how often they were seen together. It wasn't uncommon for them to take the morning walk to the Academy side by side or linger in the court-yard between the lecture halls in the afternoons, discussing the day's lessons.

In the middle of class, Zhi-fu would casually pass his note-book over to get her to look over his figures. To Zhi-fu, he was merely getting a colleague's opinion, but her heart beat faster every time he leaned in close.

No one thought it strange — who didn't want to be close to the favored son of an appointed official? For her, such notoriety was dangerous. She needed to be ignored and nobody could ignore Jin Zhi-fu. She certainly couldn't. Something inside her insisted the risk was worth it.

As quick as the turning of a page, Anlei looked up and real-ized they had reached the middle of the term. She and Zhi-fu were now both seated at his desk across from each other, no sound between them but the turning of pages.

On this night, Zhi-fu was absorbed in *The Nine Chapters on the Mathematical Art*, an encyclopedic volume that looked like it could crush a man beneath its weight. Anlei had its counterpart, *The Sea Island Mathematical Manual*, for her night time companion. They read in silence for most of the evening, but she looked up at one point to catch him staring at her.

It must be because she was tapping out a calculation against the desk. "Old habit," she said by way of apology, curling her fingers into her palm to keep them still.

"I've been thinking about what you said before," he said. "What you said has merit."

"What did I say?"

"That we're studying history more than mathematics. Do you know how long the imperial mathematics exam has centered around these same texts?" Zhi-fu continued.

"Five hundred years?" she ventured.

"A *thousand* years." He closed the book with an audible

thump as the pages fell together. "The approaches in them are outdated, inadequate."

"But we need to know them nonetheless," she said, echoing his earlier sentiment.

"It's antiquated."

"Not all of it." She closed her book after carefully placing a silk strip to mark the page. She'd never seen Zhi-fu so animated. Zhi-fu was always composed and uncomplaining, like a stone lion carved out from a larger stone lion.

"Shouldn't the imperial examination include more current developments? Modern approaches and new discoveries. Like science and technology. Western technology."

Light danced in his eyes, luring her over the edge of a cliff. What was it about Jin Zhi-fu that constantly drew her in? He was handsome, strong and beautiful even. But she had never been drawn to beauty.

It was his confidence and sense of purpose. He always seemed to know what to do, what he wanted. There was a quiet power in his presence. He was a force. Where she was intensely focused, his mind seemed to reach out, jumping from one point to another, forming connections.

"The Ministries are resistant to change," she replied.

"Some are resistant to anything that comes from the West."

"My master used to say, 'What does it matter whether it's Chinese or Western? What matters is the usefulness'."

"He sounds wise."

She was. If her mistress were here, she'd remind Anlei that she came to Peking with one purpose. "We should return to our studies," she urged.

But Zhi-fu wasn't finished. "Han," he sighed. "Sometimes I wonder if you're the only one here who can see the truth. The rest of us have been schooled too properly."

She swallowed. Would it be so, so bad if Zhi-fu could see who she truly was? There were times she wondered if he didn't suspect who she really was, at least in some deep part of him.

If he didn't sometimes look at her in the way she looked at him.

But that was just her own secret desire putting dreams into her head.

"What are you planning to do after the exams?" he asked.

He'd caught her off guard. "I…I hadn't thought too much about it."

"Most scholars want an imperial appointment. Perhaps a civil post in an office or bureau in Peking."

She shook her head. "I really hadn't thought beyond the examination."

Part of her had doubted she would ever be allowed in the Academy. She'd wanted to take the exam to honor Mistress Wang and also to prove herself.

Zhi-fu frowned, looking surprised. "You're so focused all the time."

"As are you."

Why was she blushing? Was she so taken with him that just the fact he thought of her as anything but an inconvenience had her stomach in knots?

"Maybe your plan is to go back to your province. Do you have some girl waiting for you back there?"

"Girl?" she asked, throat dry.

"Some girl from a good family you've promised to marry."

It was a foolish question. Of course, she knew what he meant. "There's no one. What about you?"

She tried to sound casual and immediately regretted asking though Zhi-fu didn't seem to mind it.

"No one," he replied dismissively. Then, "You should stay in Peking after the exam, Han. With your skills, there will always be a place for you."

It was a wonderful fantasy. As if she had the freedom of time and money. "I would like to stay," she said cautiously. "There's nothing for me back in Anhui."

Zhi-fu let out a slow exhalation. "I feel the same," he confessed. "There's nothing for me back home."

Something about the way he said it resonated with her. They were from two very different places, only to be brought together by the exams. It was hard not to feel a sense of fate between them. Perhaps they'd remain friends after the term was over.

"What are you hoping for after the exams?" she asked, feeling embarrassed at the direction of her thoughts.

"I want to be appointed to The Ministry of Science," he answered without hesitation.

It was so daring. Not only to have such high aspirations, but to say them aloud without a hint of fear. She admired him for that.

"That's where I'm hoping to be as well then," she concluded. Why not dream? She was already living in the clouds.

Zhi-fu laughed. It seemed he approved.

They spent the rest of the night discussing material that should be in the canon. More recent writings, cleaner methods.

She devoured every word as if she could keep the conversation inside her. These last months had been the happiest of her life, yet there was no one she could ever tell about it. This was her moment, hers alone, and that would have to be enough.

Chapter 6

Zhi-fu lifted his head from the desk. He'd fallen asleep sometime the night before while studying. The only time Zhi-fu had found himself in such a state before was after a night of heavy drinking. Across from him, on the opposite side of the desk, was Shi Han. He was still fast asleep with his head dropped onto one arm.

The market gong clanged from outside in the city.

"Han." His voice was raspy from sleep.

The boy barely stirred. If anything, he seemed to settle into a deeper sleep, burying his head into the crook of his elbow. He was a born scholar, being able to sleep at a desk like that.

"Han!"

Han started awake, straightening his spectacles which had gone crooked over his nose. He blinked around the room in a daze.

The gong sounded again. "We're late."

Han snapped to attention. "The death of me."

"Run."

They gathered their books and shot out the door, like a pair of geese taking flight from a hunter.

"I'm dead! I'm dead!" Han muttered between breaths.

Though Han's legs were shorter than his, Han pulled ahead of him. Zhi-fu watched as the youth darted through the streets, nearly upending the coal seller's wheelbarrow. A cage of chickens squawked when he clipped the corner.

By the time Zhi-fu caught up to him, they were at the gates of the Academy. Sweat poured down both of their faces. They paused in front of the lecture hall to attempt to right themselves.

"How do I look?" Han asked. He ran a frantic hand over his queue, trying to tame the hairs that were sticking out.

The question was so absurd that Zhi-fu laughed. "Like you've been whoring all night."

Han blinked at him, looking genuinely dismayed. Zhi-fu took him by the shoulder and shoved him into the lecture hall.

They tried to take their seats as quietly as possible, picking their way past their classmates who were already seated. At the front of the room, Master Li actually stopped his lecture. He looked like he was about to say something to Han who froze and stared nervously back at the instructor. Master Li noticed Zhi-fu beside him and said nothing.

Zhi-fu had to tug on Han's sleeve for him to sit down. Of course, Kuo Lishen turned to look at them from the front row with a smirk on his face.

"He told me not to come if I was late," Han whispered as he dug for his notebook.

"Never mind that." Zhi-fu already had his attention straight ahead, as if nothing were amiss. Beside him, he could see Han attempting to do the same.

Master Li was reviewing geometrical calculation of the golden section. Zhi-fu glanced down at Han's notebook to see him sketching out a different method, one he'd never seen before.

Near the end of the lecture, Zhi-fu reached over and wrote in the corner of Han's notebook.

Teach me.

Han looked up at him in surprise.

By then their colleagues were rising around them. They stood as well and shuffled out to the aisle.

"Out late whoring?" Kuo Lishen asked, loud enough for everyone to hear.

"Ancient joke," Zhi-fu scoffed, meeting Han's eyes. The boy looked like he was blushing.

"Maybe you won't be too tired to join us tonight. Celebration dinner," Kuo said.

"What celebration?" Han asked.

Kuo looked startled at the question. Han had probably never spoken to him directly before. Zhi-fu could tell it was an act of courage for the boy to do so now.

"Surviving three months. Full moon. Whatever we like," Kuo Lishen replied off-hand before turning his attention back to Zhi-fu. "I'll see both of you there, right? It seems he goes where you do nowadays."

Whatever Kuo Lishen was insinuating, best to ignore it. "Tonight then."

Right after Kuo turned to leave, Shi Han spied something on the ground. He bent to retrieve it and started to call out to Kuo Lishen to return it. Zhi-fu stopped him.

"Burn it," Zhi-fu said.

Han looked at the folded strip of fabric in his hand. It fit easily in his palm and was covered with tiny script, each character no bigger than an ant. They called it fly-head script — writing small enough to fit on a fly's head.

"I think Kuo dropped it—"

Zhi-fu cut him off and took the strip away, crumpling it inside his closed fist. They stepped aside as Master Li moved down the aisle, bowing respectfully. The cloth burned in his palm.

"What is it?" Han whispered. At least he had caught on that it wasn't something to be mentioned aloud.

"Nothing you have any need for," Zhi-fu replied.

He went out to the courtyard and straight to the reflective

pond. Making sure no one was watching, he wrapped the cloth around a stone and dropped it into the water. Thankfully it disappeared beneath the dark surface.

"Kuo—"

"I didn't see who it belonged to," Zhi-fu said. Thankfully it was true. If he had, he had a duty to report it.

He stared at Han, waiting for his reply.

"I...I didn't see either," Han said.

It was well-known that candidates cheated in the exams. The Academy was very strict about the conduct of its students. Its reputation depended on it. If any of them were caught, they'd be immediately expelled. Perhaps barred from ever taking the exam. If an official passed and it was later discovered he'd cheated, his rank would be stripped in disgrace and his result stricken from the record.

"It's not worth the risk to be dishonest," he told Han. "You're talented enough to pass on your own merit."

Han nodded at that, though he looked pale. They were lucky that Master Li hadn't caught them with the cheat sheet in hand. Zhi-fu's name might hold enough influence to get the Academy to look the other way when he was late to a class, but it certainly wasn't enough to protect him from a cheating accusation.

"Let's go," he said and Han fell into step beside him. "What was that method you were using in there?"

The young scholar launched into an explanation, confident now that he was speaking about mathematical concepts. Kuo Lishen taunted him for the time he was spending with Shi Han, but their time together certainly felt more productive than the wasted hours of bragging and foolishness he seemed to engage in as a requirement with Kuo.

THERE WAS a light glowing in Zhi-fu's room that night. Anlei stacked her arms full of books — half of which she had borrowed from him in the first place — and headed next door. Zhi-fu appeared before she could knock.

"It's time to go," he said, prying the books from her hands. He disappeared inside and the light was snuffed out before he re-emerged, hands empty. She started to protest.

"Kuo Lishen invited you too, remember?" he replied.

"He was only being polite."

Anlei had always meant to ignore Kuo Lishen's invitation. He was a bully and a braggart and she didn't trust the perpetual sneer on his face. Going against Jin Zhi-fu was much more difficult for her.

Zhi-fu shook his head at her remark. "Kuo Lishen will take the opportunity to act slighted if you don't come. And I need someone to talk to."

Which was untrue. Zhi-fu didn't have any shortage of friends, but his words sent a thrill down her spine nonetheless.

"I really need to study," she insisted, re-gaining some sense, but Zhi-fu was already striding toward the gate.

"We studied all night last night." He held the gate open for her.

At that point, it was impolite not to follow.

While she hurried to catch up, Anlei tried to figure out whether it would appear odd to *not* come out with her classmates at least one time. The drinking houses were considered the night time lecture halls. This was an integral part of the examination experience, if the frequency of verses about wine was any indicator.

"This is good," Zhi-fu said when they finally matched strides. "I'll make some introductions for you."

"Thank you, Elder Brother. Maybe you can take the exam for me as well."

Zhi-fu looked at her, eyes narrowed, before breaking out in laughter and she knew she had responded correctly. It had taken these three months for her to figure out humble apologies and effusive thank-yous were embarrassing for all involved. Insults were the preferred currency.

Peking in the early evening hours was one of the liveliest times. They traveled through crowded streets over to a neighboring hutong. The destination was a two-storied building with a signboard gilded with gold paint and rosy lanterns swaying by the entrance. The host greeted them with an enthusiastic bow and enough "my lords" that a few fell on her as well.

The interior opened up into a sumptuous hall adorned with dark wood panels that gleamed with a lacquered finish. Square tables were laid out in a chessboard of diners. An opera stage was laid out at the back of the hall and there was a show in progress with a trio of costumed performers. The piercing melody of the erhu rose above the general din of the crowd. Elegant lanterns with red tassels swung from the ceiling, lighting up the place as if it were still daytime. A staircase led up to the second level where there was more. Impossibly more.

Anlei was intimidated enough to want to turn immediately around. The largest eatery she'd experienced was the tea house on the corner of their street which specialized in steamed buns and braised pig knuckles.

"Here they are," Zhi-fu said, and she was surprised he was able to discern anything through the crowd. Her eyes continued to adjust as she followed behind him to a cluster of tables that had been pushed together. About fifteen of their fellow classmates had gathered there. They sat in a rough circle, a murder of crows in their black scholars' jackets.

Kuo Lishen stood and waved them over, his fox-eyes narrowing for the barest second on her before fixing on Zhi-fu. "Good, now everyone is here."

In the greetings and shuffling for seats, she was separated from Zhi-fu. He was ushered to the far side of the tables while she ended up beside Kuo Lishen who clapped a hand over her shoulder hard enough to jolt her from her seat.

"First time, eh?" He set a cup between her fingers and

started pouring. "A cause for celebration!" he announced to the group at large. "The elusive Shi Han has finally honored us with his presence."

She wasn't particularly happy with the attention, but enduring a bit of mockery also seemed to be part of the experience. She raised her cup in response to Kuo Lishen's gesture and took a drink, the sweetness of the wine coating her tongue before warmth spread down her throat.

Kuo Lishen glanced at the remaining wine. "Tradition says the first cup is an indicator of how many attempts it will take to conquer the exams."

It was probably a lie, but the classmates nearby had picked up on the jibe and began taunting her about it. Anlei shot Lishen a side-eye as she downed the rest of the cup. Heat pooled in her belly. So this was how expensive wine behaved.

Kuo Lishen was quick with the second pour. "Now a penalty drink," he said crookedly. "For arriving late."

Across the table, Zhi-fu met her gaze, raising his cup for his own penalty. The moment of connection lifted her and she downed the wine in one swallow, steeling herself against the rush of warmth. Across the table, Zhi-fu gestured to get her attention again, then made a show of turning his cup to place it upside-down on the table. Elder Brother indeed. She followed his lead and did the same.

With that ritual complete, the attention eased away from her and onto the drinking in general. The tables were already laden with plates of food; platters of roasted dark meat accompanied by plates of thinly sliced cucumbers and pickled radishes.

She picked up a slice of meat with bamboo chopsticks.

"Duck," Lishen supplied, correctly guessing from her pause that she was unfamiliar with the dish.

The first bite seduced her as crisp skin gave way to succulent meat and a flood of spices. She'd eaten duck before but apparently, she'd never *tasted* duck before. Meat for her meant feet and tongues and necks — not this richness in her mouth.

"It's good, right?"

Kuo Lishen leaned toward her as he spoke and something about his manner raised the hairs on the back of her neck. His tone was too soft, too smooth. She could feel his breath against her cheek and when she turned, his gaze locked onto hers. She adjusted her spectacles and immediately regretted it. It was an obvious nervous gesture and she'd unwittingly found herself in a male contest of wills.

He stared at her, his face closer than he had a right to be. His mouth was still locked in a smile, but his eyes had gone cold and all she could do was tell herself: do not, do not, do not look away first.

And she didn't. She managed to keep her eyes fixed onto him, saying nothing. She held the stare as she took another bite of duck which at first seemed to work. When Kuo Lishen relinquished his claim, his gaze didn't so much turn away as it wandered, slowly tracing the line of her face in a lazy arc before sliding his focus away.

"Zhi-fu," he called out, raising his voice above the chatter.

Every instinct in her screamed at her to flee. All around the table, their classmates quieted.

"I have a wager for you, friend."

Zhi-fu, in the midst of drinking his wine, nodded gamely. He sat with his shoulders back and relaxed.

"Whichever one of us achieves first rank, the other hosts a banquet in their honor in this very hall."

"Done." Zhi-fu didn't even take a breath to consider.

The others laughed in approval and Anlei relaxed now that the attention was once again off of her. Then Zhi-fu spoke again.

"You know Shi Han might just as well win first rank." Zhi-fu looked to her, his expression serious. "He has the best mind for mathematics here."

She could feel each beat of her heart like the clang of a

gong. Kuo looked appraisingly at her. "He just might," he replied slowly.

By now her face was burning. What battle were these two fighting and why was she in the middle of it? The gap of silence had become strange and awkward.

"It could be any of us here," she murmured, staring into her cup.

"What, none of these simpletons!" Kuo Lishen taunted, which appropriately broke the tension. The others jeered at him, called him a turtle's egg, a eunuch. Someone threw a sesame bun.

With that, peaceful disorder was restored, but Anlei couldn't free herself from the sense of unease that gathered over the base of her neck. With Kuo Lishen, she felt like a chicken selected for slaughter.

Fortunately, the performance drowned out most conversation for the rest of the meal, but that wasn't the end of it. After dinner, they were off to the eight alleys of Bada Hutong. From the way her colleagues spoke of it, wide-eyed and grinning, Bada Hutong sounded like somewhere notorious she was supposed to know. And indeed, it was. Bada was the pleasure district which was apparent from the moment she set foot onto the main avenue.

The area was laid out like a centipede with eight alleyways that cut across the main road. Colorful ladies came forward to beckon at them as their entourage strode by. Zhi-fu was at the head of the pack and Kuo Lishen had attached himself to Zhi-fu's side as if claiming ownership. That left Anlei among a group of first and second-year candidates, which suited her fine. She didn't need Jin Zhi-fu to protect her and he didn't need another leech clinging to him. He appeared to have a parasite already.

"These alleys here are the seedier brothels," one of her classmates informed her.

"Chen speaks from experience!" another chimed in with a snort.

Anlei glanced at the colorful lanterns hanging from the doorways. Many of them were painted with prostitute names, like Precious Pearl and Fragrant Jade.

"The green houses are at this end here," Chen said.

Which was where they seemed to be headed.

"The girls here are more refined. They've trained at the conservatory."

The moment their group passed through the beaded curtain at the entranceway, they were surrounded by an army of courtesans who swirled around them in colorful silk dresses like a bed of flowers. Young, lonely scholars from wealthy families — Anlei imagined their lot would be quite popular in Bada Hutong, whether it be at a low-class brothel or one of the higher end green houses.

The girls seemed to know most of them by name. Promptly, their members started pairing off to disappear to the far corners of the pleasure house. Divide and conquer.

"Which one are you?" the courtesan wearing a green qipao asked. She had a peach-shaped face and a voice as smooth as silk.

"The poor one," Anlei replied humorlessly.

For a moment, the courtesan's pleasant expression remained unchanged, hanging from her face. Then either Anlei's poverty or lack of charm convinced the courtesan this scholar wasn't worth the trouble. The girl floated away, as effortless as smoke.

Anlei wandered toward the salon where one of the hostesses had disappeared with Zhi-fu. She found him seated beside a nobleman who appeared about twenty years his senior. The two were engaged in conversation while two hostesses stood behind them, kneading their shoulders with long, elegant fingers.

Kuo Lishen was situated on a wide settee. A girl in a tight-fitting blue cheongsam hung over his arm. The casual intimacy of her pose in such a public setting was jarring. Anlei almost regretted sending the peach-faced girl away. Imagine feeling out of place because she didn't have a courtesan on her arm.

Kuo beckoned Anlei over the moment he saw her and Anlei considered ignoring his invitation since he'd been such a demon to her at the restaurant earlier. Unfortunately, there was no other place to sit in the small salon and the rest of the house was even more intimidating. Zhi-fu remained deep in his discussion with the elderly gentleman and barely glanced up as she sat.

"This is Shi Han of Anhui province," Kuo Lishen introduced her to the girl in his lap.

"Shi *Gongzhu*." The courtesan addressed her with a honeyed look and an honorific befitting a gentleman.

"Be nice to him, Little Pearl." Kuo Lishen grinned crookedly at Anlei. "He has the best mind for mathematics in this whole place."

Anlei shot him a poisoned look. Unperturbed, Kuo Lishen shifted over to make room on the settee, pushing Pearl to the far end.

"Is it your first time here, Young Lord Shi?" Pearl asked, looking her over curiously.

Anlei stiffened under the courtesan's assessing gaze. She hadn't considered how another woman might easily see through her disguise.

"I-I've been studying," she stammered.

"How diligent of you." Pearl's eyelashes fluttered like two butterflies. If the courtesan noticed anything amiss, she said nothing.

A string of unintelligible words came from the other side of the sitting area. Anlei turned at the sound of Zhi-fu's voice, but he was speaking to the gentleman in an unfamiliar dialect.

"Manchu," Kuo Lishen provided. "The dialect of the inner palace. Another one of Jin Zhi-fu's advantages — as if he needed any."

Kuo handed her a cup and picked up one for himself. Pearl

was quick to fill them. One sip told Anlei what they were drinking here was a lot stronger than the wine at the restaurant.

"Zhi-fu is Manchurian?" Anlei asked.

Kuo Lishen nodded while tossing back his drink. "Manners, Han," he nagged, gesturing toward her cup which was still full. "Pearl, tell Shi *Gongzhu* it's the house rule."

"It's the house rule," Pearl echoed, laughter dancing in her pretty eyes.

Anlei finished the cup in one swallow, grimacing as the liquid burnt a fiery trail down to her belly. "Zhi-fu is Manchurian?" she repeated.

She was eager to get back to talking about Zhi-fu, not this other nonsense.

"He's not just Manchurian. His family flies the bordered red banner."

Jin Zhi-fu was a bannerman? He had told her his family mounted the defenses along the northwestern frontier. She hadn't realized that meant he was part of the Emperor's long-time army. Zhi-fu wasn't merely wealthy. He came from one of the most powerful clans in the empire. The thought stole her breath. The two of them could not be any further apart.

She took the next drink of her own accord, welcoming the sharp burn followed by the dull haze. "Who's that with him?"

"Liu Yentai. Chief Engineer of the Ministry of Science."

"Ministry of Science," she repeated listlessly. She blinked, but it did little to clear her head.

Kuo Lishen laughed, poured. "Chief Liu is important. He's also rumored to be one of the examiners this year."

"Steam?" the engineer said in disbelief, this time in the more common Peking dialect.

"In the fire-wheel boats, what if what witnesses saw wasn't smoke, but steam?" Zhi-fu continued.

"Hmm." Liu considered it. "Would that power anything more than a copper kettle?"

"What is that all about?" Kuo Lishen's query broke her concentration.

She looked back at him, annoyed. "Steam engines," she replied brusquely.

He frowned.

"It's an ob—obsession of his," she said with a wave that ended up being a lot more expansive than she anticipated. Zhi-fu and the Chief Engineer paused in their conversation to look over at her and she realized her voice was also much louder than she thought. Her cheeks flushed hot with embarrassment. She needed to be careful.

"So is it true?"

She turned back to Kuo Lishen. "Is what true?"

He sipped at his drink, took his time. "Zhi-fu tells me you're entirely self-taught."

"Zhi-fu talks about me?"

Kuo Lishen smiled at that, thoroughly entertained. He reclined against the back of the settee while Pearl was practically curled in his lap. Anlei marveled at how the women had inserted themselves, even circumstantially, into the conversations of men. Over at the chairs, the pretty girl with the red lips was pouring drinks for Zhi-fu and the Manchu official. She leaned over to say something into Zhi-fu's ear. He shook his head, reaching a hand up to touch her sleeve. The intimacy of the gesture made Anlei's throat tighten.

"Zhi-fu talks about you all the time. He thinks your talent is immeasurable. That you're some sort of prodigy."

But Zhi-fu would never, never think of her as a woman. Because that would be the end of everything.

She had to look away from the scene at the center of the room. "I attended a school in Anhui province," she replied absently. "We studied mathematics and astronomy."

Pearl leaned forward to pour more spirits into her cup. Anlei didn't remember drinking the last one.

"What's in this?" she asked, her words slurring together.

"Our house specialty," Pearl replied. "Rice liquor infused with ginseng."

"Good for...stamina," Kuo Lishen added, slanting a sly look at Pearl.

She planted a hand on his chest and leaned in to kiss him, but Lishen ducked away. Surprisingly, he seemed more interested in continuing his conversation with Anlei.

"You said your school had a headmistress?" he asked.

When had she said that? "No, that was the headmaster's wife."

The lie tumbled awkwardly over her lips. A fog hovered in her head, refusing to clear. This was too dangerous. "I should go home."

"It's early, Han."

"I need to. Study."

Kuo Lishen laughed, the sound piercing through her skull. Zhi-fu happened to find something funny at the same moment. He laughed as well and it seemed they were both laughing at her.

"You'll never find your way back, Han. We'll all go together after," Kuo said.

He was right. She had no idea how to get back to her room from the eight alleys of Bada Hutong. It felt as if in one night she'd gone a long, long way from the safe and familiar pathway she'd carved out.

Chapter 7

B y the time they left the pleasure house, their number had dwindled to five. Many of her classmates had chosen to stay on with their perfumed companions. Maybe they would stay the night or leave after a few more hours once their money ran out.

Zhi-fu was with Kuo Lishen and the others. They walked in a group, laughing and talking loudly while Anlei trudged a few steps behind. Out in the fresh air, her head began to clear. She was considering finding her way back on her own when Zhi-fu hung back and fell into step with her.

He hooked a rough arm around her shoulders. "Good duck, eh?"

The duck? They hadn't spoken since the beginning of the evening and the first thing he had to say to her was a comment about the food.

"Maybe I should write a poem about that duck," she said dryly.

"It's been done," he said with a laugh.

His arm remained around her, trapping her against his large frame, and the effect was devastating. Solid was the first word that came to mind. She was pressed against a wall of hard, heated muscle. She could certainly compose a poem about that. The warmth of being anchored against him. The confusing storm of thoughts warring inside her head. How relieved she was that Zhi-fu hadn't opted to stay at the pleasure house, in the soft arms of Lady Fragrant Spring or whatever her name was.

"I saw you and Kuo Lishen staring each other down at the restaurant," he said, lowering his voice.

So that was why he mentioned the duck. His mind was all the way back there.

"I wouldn't say we were staring each other down."

"Like two battering rams," he said with a laugh.

She laughed in return. His deep voice surrounded her, warming her skin. Why did this feel so good right now? Good enough to chase away the worst parts of the evening: how bad she was at keeping her composure around Zhi-fu. And how Kuo Lishen seemed to jump on her every weakness.

"I wish you wouldn't use me like that," she said.

"How am I using you?"

"To provoke Kuo Lishen."

He made an annoyed sound. "You can't back down against that sort. You have to stand tall against him."

"Well, some of us naturally stand taller than others."

She glanced pointedly up at him. The street lanterns framed his silhouette in strong, stark lines as he looked down on her. He was so handsome. And thoughtful and generous and over-whelming. His mere presence did that to her. That was the moment she knew she was losing herself, wooed by the full force of Zhi-fu's attention after being abandoned all evening.

Kuo Lishen led them deeper into the narrow alleyways of Bada Hutong. To a darkened corner with an unmarked door. Anlei followed the rest of them. Zhi-fu's arm was no longer around her, but she was being pulled by him nonetheless. The confidence in his stride lulled her into believing nothing was amiss. No harm would ever come to her while he was there.

Inside was a single room, lit with a few flickering oil lamps that provided isolated points of light in blackness. A pungent, sweet smoke curled around her. Her eyes had become accustomed to darkness and she was able to make out several low, wide beds arranged against the walls.

They were in an opium den.

Two shadowy attendants approached and Kuo Lishen spoke with them in a low tone, working out the transaction. Anlei had heard of opium dens and the dangers of smoking. Opium had been banned in Peking for decades, yet it was still everywhere.

Zhi-fu had settled onto one of the wooden beds and Anlei felt the gentle hand of one of the attendants tugging at her sleeve, directing her to the side opposite him. An objection hovered on her tongue, but instead all she said was that she'd never smoked before.

"It's easy," Zhi-fu assured. "Just breathe deep. It'll help clear your mind."

She wasn't so sure of that. Nervous fear clawed at her skin and her heart pounded frantically. But Zhi-fu was calm as he reclined back against the pillows on the bed. Again, she was pulled by the invisible tether between them. She leaned back against the headrest, wanting to appear just as composed, just as confident as he was. Kuo Lishen and the others must have also settled in, but she couldn't see them in the darkness. All she was aware of was Zhi-fu lying beside her and the attendant who stood over them, preparing a long pipe.

The attendant held a taper to an oil lamp and used the tip to light the pipe. A heavy smoke rose from the bowl, smelling of burnt resin and incense. Like a dark temple.

The attendant offered the pipe to Zhi-fu and he inhaled, holding in the smoke as he laid back, eyes closed. As he breathed out a plume of smoke, the muscles of his face relaxed as if in sleep. Every muscle in his body seemed to melt into the bed.

It was her turn. The attendant brought the pipe to her, holding it to her lips. Zhi-fu opened his eyes and turned to watch her. In the darkness his pupils were dark pools of blackness. She could still leave, but, then again, she couldn't.

She tried to copy Zhi-fu's movements, but the moment she inhaled, a cloud of sickly sweet smoke rushed into her lungs and she coughed violently. The attendant held the pipe out to her once more and her instinct was to push it away, but instead she breathed in once more, tasting smoke and a subtle perfume. Flowers on the back of her tongue.

With each breath, the world faded. Like a gentle breeze against rocks, flowing over sharp edges and gradually wearing them away. The attendant presented the pipe to Zhi-fu once more and he raised onto his elbows to take it. She didn't know how much time passed before the pipe was brought back to her.

How much was too much? After inhaling the smoke once more, she stopped worrying about that. She stopped worrying about anything, the exams, her disguise, what Zhi-fu thought of her. The lies.

"See?" Zhi-fu asked thickly, his eyes half-lidded.

They had rolled on the bed to face one another. Vaguely she considered answering him, but what was there to say? His face was so close, she wanted to reach out to touch his cheek, but even that took too much effort. Her muscles loosened and she lay boneless, like a skein of yarn unraveled all at once.

The rest of the den faded away and there was only Zhi-fu and her, stranded on the bed together. Her thoughts slipped by, refusing to solidify into any meaning. Soon even Zhi-fu seemed to drift far away. She reached out to him, searching for some anchor, but her hand only stretched out toward emptiness. He remained a presence in the space just beyond, no longer a thing of substance but of dreams.

Once in a while, the pipe would come to her and she took it willingly. The smoke took away the heaviness of her body and the weight of her mind. For the first time in her life, there was a quiet space inside of her. There was peace in nothingness. It was so very easy to lose herself in it.

SUNLIGHT FILTERED in slivers through the curtain when Anlei finally awoke. Groggily, she pushed herself up from the bed and glanced over her shoulder. Zhi-fu was stretched from one end of the bed to the other, still asleep. She recognized a few more of her colleagues huddled in the corner. Disconcertingly, there were also a number of reclined sleepers she didn't recognize.

One of her slippers had fallen from the bed and she bent to retrieve it and shove it onto her foot. Then she ventured outside.

Kuo Lishen was waiting there, leaning against the stone wall of the alleyway, arms folded in front of him.

"This is good for someone like Zhi-fu," he began. "He's under so much pressure: family honor, serve the empire, save every stray dog that comes along. Sometimes he needs to forget for a few hours."

"And you're so kind as to provide it to him." She hadn't missed the jibe about taking in strays, but her brain was just emerging from the fog. Her mouth was full of cobwebs.

Kuo Lishen straightened, his sharp jaw hardening. "You know he'll never notice."

She was afraid to ask what he meant. Kuo, however, was more than ready to elaborate. "Zhi-fu is too preoccupied with his own ambitions to trouble himself in the everyday affairs of men...or women."

His smug look told her everything. Her stomach dropped, sickened. She must have slipped and said something, done something last night.

Anlei glanced over her shoulder to make sure there was no one on the other side of the curtain. She edged them away from the entrance toward the end of the alleyway.

"Are you going to make trouble for me?" she demanded through her teeth.

"Of course not," Kuo Lishen said, acting as if it were the farthest thing from his mind when she knew it wasn't.

"What are you plotting, Kuo Lishen?"

As Zhi-fu told her, one had to stand tall against a bastard like Kuo. He had been baiting her all night.

"I have to say that was a clever trick last night, that bit in the alleyway." He cupped his hand in front of his crotch, mimicking a spraying motion.

She had been surrounded by men long enough not to be mortified. "Seriously, Lishen," she muttered.

"What would I gain from ruining your chances? I want my friends to do well."

She narrowed her eyes at him. "Friends?"

"You and Zhi-fu have talent, while I only know enough to know I have none."

"But you consistently get high marks—"

"Why do you think that could be?" he challenged, eyebrows raised. "Do you think I'm generous because of a kind and giving nature?"

Anlei was surprised he'd admit or even hint at any misconduct. He could be expelled.

"My only talent is making friends," he went on. "See, I've just told you something private and personal about me." He leaned in close and her first instinct was to back away, but it set her against the wall. "And I know something private and personal about you. That makes us friends, am I right?"

At that moment, Zhi-fu emerged from the opium den. His broad shoulders filled the narrow alleyway as he blinked against the morning sun.

"Teahouse?" he suggested in a voice still rough with sleep.

Kuo Lishen fell back and Anlei quickly peeled herself off the wall. Zhi-fu looked slowly from her to Kuo Lishen. The two of them nodded enthusiastically in agreement. Yes, teahouse.

As Zhi-fu engaged Kuo Lishen in conversation, Anlei let herself fall a step behind them. Kuo Lishen was right. Zhi-fu was too absorbed to notice who she really was. She should be grateful for that, shouldn't she?

She wasn't sure how she felt about it.

The noises of the street surrounded her. As she was swallowed by Peking once more, invisible and insignificant, she missed the soft, complete silence of the night before for just a moment. When she had lain beside Zhi-fu, face to face. The hours had seemed to stretch out forever and she had been free of fear.

But now, in the harsh morning light, all her fears came rushing back tenfold. Someone knew her secret. She had given Kuo Lishen the power to tear her dreams apart. And it was all due to her own carelessness.

Chapter 8

Zhi-fu sat back to watch as the courtesan tilted the flask of wine with a practiced hand, wrist gracefully exposed. One paid dearly for his drink to be poured so prettily.

"Where's your friend?" Kuo asked from the seat opposite him.

"Studying."

The answer was an easy one. Han was always studying.

Kuo raised an eyebrow as he sipped his wine. "He's very determined."

The girl hanging on Kuo's arm went by the name of Little Plum. She dutifully peeled the thin shell from a lychee and placed the pale fruit into his mouth. Kuo had paid little attention to her over the last hour as she doted on him.

Zhi-fu waved away the lychee offered by his attendant. With a pout, she placed the fruit into her own mouth, deliberately drawing attention to her red lips. He was being a bad customer.

"Do you think he really has a chance of passing?" Kuo went on.

"Do any of us?" Zhi-fu replied with a shrug.

"Come now, Zhi-fu." Kuo straightened, leaning forward. "You two are like a pair of ducks in the same pond."

It was an odd choice of phrase—the symbolism of ducks insinuated a friendship that was more than close. Kuo watched him intently as he waited for a response.

Keeping his expression blank, Zhi-fu leaned back and folded his hands in front of him, fingers intertwined methodically. Their hostesses detected the change in the atmosphere at once.

Both girls exchanged a quick glance and Lotus quietly sank back from the tray, lest she cause an undue distraction. Plum relinquished her hold on Kuo's arm, only resting lightly onto him. Their attempts at playful conversation ceased.

"Are you afraid he'll replace you?" Zhi-fu asked, eyebrow raised.

Kuo scowled. "He is better at equations than I am."

"But it's not all equations, is it?"

"Talking about your studies again," Lotus said with a pout.

Just as the two girls had read the tension in their room, they also sensed Zhi-fu's attempt to smooth over troubled waters. As always, they played along. It was what they were paid to do.

"Penalty drink," Little Plum declared.

Zhi-fu ignored her. "Luck, connections, then talent—right?"

"Never forget we got here together," Kuo said, raising his glass soberly. "Through the years, brother."

Zhi-fu frowned. Something had gotten into him. Kuo Lishen, born into wealth and privilege and afraid of no one, was envious of a poor scholar from the southern provinces. Maybe he was realizing his bribes weren't as all-powerful as he'd assumed.

"Just because Shi Han might pass doesn't mean our chances are diminished," Zhi-fu told him.

Kuo snorted. He drank his wine, mood darkening with each swallow.

"I heard there was a petition to the Ministry of Rites to incorporate technology and modern sciences into the exam," Zhi-fu said, changing the subject.

"And why would we find this exciting?"

"Engineering, alchemy, *Western* sciences," Zhi-fu pointed out. "Finally, things are changing."

"Western studies?" Kuo Lishen scoffed. "It will never happen."

"What does it matter if it's Western or Chinese? What counts is its usefulness."

"I have nothing to learn from foreign devils."

As Zhi-fu echoed Han's argument, he couldn't help but note how much more interesting this conversation would be with Han. At least the young scholar was open to new ideas.

"There are so many areas of study we've completely ignored, at least in the exam. Which means the Academy ignores it," Zhi-fu argued. "The course of study isn't practical."

"You're asking to invalidate a thousand years of tradition."

Zhi-fu shrugged. "I'm not asking for anything. It's just interesting that this petition would come now, upon the heels of your discovery."

"It *was* my discovery," Kuo declared. "As if anyone remembers."

Kuo set his cup down onto the table with some force. Little Plum moved to rub his shoulders, but he waved her away as if swatting a gnat. "We don't need to incorporate Western technology into the exam. The Ministry is going to need people who understand war machines, firepower—"

He had veered into entirely different territory, and Zhi-fu finally understood it wasn't Han that Kuo Lishen felt threatened by.

Zhi-fu straightened. "It's late," he said quietly.

Kuo met his eyes, his gaze sharpened for battle. "Mark my words, the next head of the Ministry will be someone from the military."

"But the Ministry doesn't need a soldier," Kuo pressed on. "It needs someone who can manage the politics of the court."

"You're getting ahead of yourself, Kuo." Zhi-fu stood to go.

Kuo Lishen had positioned himself alternatively as rival and ally over the years Zhi-fu had known him. He had always known that Kuo considered everyone part of an elaborate game—a battlefield of chess pieces.

The truth was his fellow scholar was no strategist or master manipulator. He simply feared anyone who didn't need anything from him.

Zhi-fu had wasted too much time thinking Kuo Lishen, with his wealth and his illusions of influence, was the one with all the answers.

He didn't make any more effort at a cordial farewell. The moment he set foot outside the drinking house a weight lifted from his shoulders.

Shi Han didn't pretend to know the answers to anything more than what he knew. And he worked hard over each problem, preferring the difficult ones to the easy ones.

A warm breeze stirred the evening air. The drinking houses continued to hum with activity, but he was done for the night. He walked back to the tenement, opening the gate to let himself in. The courtyard was silent though light glowed in many of the windows. They were in the summer now and the studying would become more intense as the term continued on.

He started toward his room, but the next stir of the evening breeze brought the bitter smell of smoke. It wasn't the scent of incense or an opium pipe.

Han's door was closed which meant he had either gone out to steal candlelight from the tea houses, or was shut in and asleep. Zhi-fu walked past the narrow area to look into the other half of the courtyard. That was when a billow of smoke surrounded him.

Fire. There was a fire in the room next to Han's.

Zhi-fu ran to the gate to ring the bell. "Wake up! Fire!"

Doors started to open. Startled eyes stared out at him. Zhi-fu ignored their questions to rush to the burning room. The door flew open and one of his classmates stumbled out. His sleeve had caught fire and he was frantically trying to stamp it out.

Zhi-fu ran to assist him, smothering the sleeve against the dirt. When he looked up, he could see the other residents spilling out into the courtyard, but Han's door remained closed. His friend was caught inside, sleeping while the building filled with smoke.

ANLEI STARTED AWAKE. She was surrounded in darkness and someone was pounding on the door.

"Han!"

Zhi-fu. The insistent banging continued. "Han, wake up!"

Groggily, she fumbled around the edge of her pallet, feeling for her jacket. The night had been warm and she'd removed her bindings before falling asleep. She was wearing only a thin tunic over a pair of trousers.

Panic struck her as the pounding on the door grew stronger. Suddenly the door flew open. A stream of lantern light filtered in and she could see the outline of her jacket laid over a crate. She reached for it, scrambling on hands and knees.

Zhi-fu stormed into the enclosure. "There's fire."

When his hand closed around her arm, Anlei bit her lip to keep from crying out.

"Come on!" he growled, yanking her up.

She stumbled. Off-balance, she fell into him. Zhi-fu caught her out of reflex, and she wished with all her being that he hadn't.

As Zhi-fu's hands closed around her shoulders, he went as still as a statue in the darkness. Her breasts were flush against his chest and she could feel the halted rise and fall of his breathing. Her heart beat frantically against him. She had stilled as well and the next moment passed in complete silence.

Then the next. She could hardly breathe.

The shouting from the courtyard startled her into action. Anlei pushed past Zhi-fu and stumbled toward the door.

Once outside, she forced herself to breathe. Under the glow of the lanterns, she saw that the entire building had poured out into the courtyard. She shook her head to try to clear it.

It had been just a moment. Just a moment in complete darkness. Maybe Zhi-fu hadn't noticed anything. *Please let him not know.*

With her heart in her throat, she turned around to see Zhi-fu emerging from her doorway. Smoke billowed around him, coming from the room just to the left of hers. Orange flames danced inside the open door, crackling and spitting as it ate at the walls.

Without meeting her eyes, Zhi-fu jumped into the action, moving to join a crew gathered at the water pump. They filled buckets as quickly as they could and ran to throw water into the room.

Zhi-fu threw off his jacket and rolled up his sleeves as he worked. Sweat poured down his face. She could still feel his hard chest pressed against her and the way he'd stiffened at the touch, his hands tightening briefly over her shoulders before abruptly releasing.

It was dark, she insisted. He couldn't suspect. He couldn't have figured anything out.

Zhi-fu had taken the lead, barking commands to the others to form a line. Should she join them?

Anlei gathered the front of her tunic in her fist and instead watched in mute silence. She considered running back inside her sleeping space to retrieve her belongings. Her books, the calculating device, and her clothes were her only possessions in the world. The plumes of black smoke kept her away as well as the fear of attracting any notice.

She kept her eyes trained intently on Zhi-fu. He fought the fire in earnest, his jaw set and determined. Never once did he look her way.

She was afraid to move and afraid not to move.

Gradually the fire died away, leaving charred wood and a

burnt hollow of what used to be a bed chamber. The landlord held his lantern up and waddled inside to inspect the damage.

"Oil lamp," someone murmured.

Zhao Hong, the student who had knocked over the offending lamp, dragged his feet as he ventured back into the ruins. The rest of the crowd began to scatter, returning to their own chambers.

"Ay," she called out to Zhi-fu as he moved past.

He stopped, angling his head just slightly. She was presented only with the hard line of his profile. His mouth remained pressed tight.

"Lucky that—" her voice scraped against her throat. She coughed to clear it. "Lucky that you caught it early. Before the fire went too far."

Zhi-fu nodded once, refusing to meet her gaze, before disappearing into his room. The door swung shut firmly behind him.

Anlei's heart pounded like thunder. He knew. He knew.

He knew.

ZHI-FU ROSE EARLY the next morning. He made sure to rise early. He made sure to step quietly past the door beside his room as he headed out into the street.

His clothes still smelled of smoke, reminding him of the night before. He hadn't yet figured out what to think of last night. He'd fallen asleep in turmoil and woken up in much the same state.

Shi Han was…not who he thought. Or Zhi-fu could be sorely mistaken. He didn't even want to think of that moment. Of what happened last night. He wished his head had been fogged with drink.

The gates of the Academy were still closed when he arrived so he wandered to a nearby tea house. Ordered a pot of tea that he let go cold, and then dragged his feet when it was time to go to the first lecture.

Han was one of the last to arrive, as usual, and Zhi-fu took pains to only glance quickly, out of the corner of his eye.

And he knew then, without a doubt, that he wasn't wrong.

For the next hour, Zhi-fu fixed his eyes onto the front of the room where Master Lu drew chalk lines representing the trajectory of a projectile. When the lecture was done, he gathered his books to leave, charting a determined trajectory of his own.

He heard his name called out and ignored it, though his stomach sank at the sound of Han's voice.

Once classes were done, Zhi-fu avoided the library. He knew Han would typically stay there until nightfall. Instead of returning to the residence, he wandered the hutongs until his feet were sore.

It was late in the evening when Zhi-fu finally returned to his chamber. By that time, the scholar residents were walled in for night with lamps burning in every window. He dipped a wick into the lantern in the courtyard before slipping into his room. The thin paper glowed orange in the darkness as he walked the few steps to his desk.

He touched the wick to the dish of the oil lamp and a yellow glow illuminated the room. Almost immediately, a knock came at the door.

He ignored it, instead bending to open his notebook. Thumbing through the pages one by one, he turned to the notes from the morning's lecture when the knock came again.

Zhi-fu forced out a breath and braced his hands against the desk, head bowed. Of course, Han would be awake, waiting, no matter how late the hour. Studious Han, or whatever Han's real name was.

His stomach churned as he walked toward the door and cracked it open.

"Zhi-fu." Han stood in the muted lantern light of the courtyard, staring squarely at him.

"Yes," he replied curtly.

A troubled look flickered across the young scholar's face. "Let me explain—"

"There's nothing to explain."

It was so obvious to Zhi-fu now that he knew. The delicate features, the slight frame. What he'd overlooked for youth or frailty was neither.

Softly curved cheeks, delicate mouth. It was a woman's face, unmistakable. The fog over his eyes had lifted and he could see Han with sharp clarity.

"Please, if I may come in." Han started toward him, but Zhi-fu stood firm, blocking the doorway like a stone sentinel.

"You shouldn't be here," he replied coldly.

"Do you want this to happen out here then?"

Her gaze swept over the courtyard in a silent challenge. Though the central space lay vacant, the tenement was very much awake.

With gritted teeth, Zhi-fu stepped aside to let the impostor slip into the chamber.

He closed the door firmly before swinging around. "You cannot come here. If anyone finds out who you are, you'll be expelled." He turned away, staring at the desk as heat rose up the back of his neck. "And I'll be expelled along with you."

"Nothing would ever happen to you. No one would dare— one of the favored sons of the entire Academy."

Her words pricked at him like sharp needles. "Everyone knows you and I are associated."

Women were not allowed to sit for the imperial exams, nor were they admitted into the academies. If it was discovered that she had deceived the academy, she'd be forced to leave and he would face ruin for hiding the truth.

"I—I'm sorry for not being truthful to you," she began haltingly. "And I understand that…that things can't continue as they were. But please don't tell anyone."

It was more difficult turned away like this, when he couldn't see her. She sounded like Han, but Han had never asked him for anything. "You're asking me to lie for you."

"If you were ever a friend. Just let me pass or fail on my own strength."

He turned slowly. She would bring up their friendship now? When she had betrayed it.

"The risk is too great," he replied coldly.

"No one will ever find out! We've studied together every night. You were closer to me than anyone, and you never suspected until—"

She looked away, blushing.

His chest tightened as her words knifed through him. He'd thought of Han as a colleague, as a brother even. Someone who he could trust.

"You don't belong here," he spat.

Her eyes flashed with anger. "I *do* belong here.

This wasn't the Han he knew at all. This was a deceitful woman, who threatened everything he had worked for.

"You're not even who I thought you were," he accused. "What do I call you—your name isn't Han, is it?"

"It's Anlei. Shi Anlei." She sounded broken. "And I've been truer to you than I have ever been to anyone."

He made a harsh sound. "Despite the lies?"

"The silence was the lie."

Anlei was certainly brash in a way that Han never was. It was impossible for him to look at her. He could only see the deception.

He could have nothing more to do with her and turn a blind eye, but it was well-known he'd taken Han under his guidance.

"Does anyone else know?"

She was silent and his stomach dropped.

"Who else knows?"

"Kuo Lishen."

The admission hung heavy in the air between them.

"Kuo," he echoed hollowly. Their one colleague who reveled

in manipulation and blackmail. There was no way this secret could remain hidden.

"You should go now," he said quietly.

"Zhi-fu, please——"

He shook his head, his gaze cutting. There was nothing more to discuss.

Anlei let herself out, slipping quietly through the door. For a long time, he stared at the spot where she had been. Then he moved to his desk and tried to resume his studies, but it was pointless.

Instead, he ground out a supply of fresh ink and took out a sheet of rice paper. With a heavy heart, he dipped his brush and began to write.

HE LEFT his room the next morning before the sun had risen, closing the door quietly behind him. A knot tightened in his chest. It didn't loosen once he'd exited the courtyard to enter the streets.

The letter he'd stayed up half the night writing was tucked securely into the pocket of his jacket. It had taken him seven drafts—he'd worked meticulously over each word.

It has come to my attention that a student has been admitted to the Academy under false pretenses.

He avoided any discussion of merit. Any hint of wrongdo-ing. Anlei just did not belong there. Women were forbidden to take the imperial exams. It didn't matter if she excelled at math-ematics. Or worked night and day. This wasn't her place and by allowing her to stay, he was complicit.

This had to be done. He had no choice.

The walk to the Academy was both long and short. Long in how each step was taken with difficulty, short in how he found himself too soon before the front gates. The sky had begun to lighten, yet he had no recollection of how time had passed. He was still thinking of Anlei, looking at him with Han's face, begging to be allowed to fail on her own.

When he reached the Headmaster's office, he found the building doors locked. It was still too early. He was forced to return to the streets where he wandered in a listless circle. An elderly man stood at one corner selling steamed buns. Zhi-fu bought one and bit into it, pondering his situation. The bread tasted like sand in his mouth.

The letter in his pocket would mean the end of Anlei's enrollment at the Academy. The end of any future for her. Was he doing this out of respect for the rules of the Academy, or simply to protect himself?

He tossed the half-eaten bun to a stray dog in the street and returned to the Academy. The Headmaster's door was finally open and a clerk sat at the desk in front. The young man nodded respectfully as Zhi-fu approached.

"I have an urgent matter for Master Sun," Zhi-fu began. He fished the letter from his pocket, holding it delicately between his fingers like a scorpion by the tail.

"The Headmaster has not yet arrived, but this servant will give him your message. The Master can send for you then."

Zhi-fu hesitated. The folded paper hovered just above the clerk's outstretched hand.

The clerk shot him a curious look.

Taking a deep breath, Zhi-fu surrendered the letter. He watched as the clerk laid it on top of a stack of notices and communications piled on top of a bamboo tray.

Zhi-fu had thought it would lighten the weight on his shoulders. What's done was done — but the pressure bearing down on him increased ten-fold.

When he turned to leave, his feet felt as if they had become lead. His heart pounded as he retreated down the corridor.

This wasn't his fault. Women were not allowed at the Academy. Anlei may be talented, but this wasn't the proper place for her. The problem was, there wasn't a proper place for someone with Anlei's abilities.

His palms were damp as he re-entered the main courtyard. By then, he could barely hear his own thoughts. Blood rushed loudly through his skull.

Pass or fail, on her own. Anlei had begged him.

Zhi-fu turned on his heel and ran all the way back to Master Sun's office. By the time he reached the clerk's desk, he was breathing hard.

"I would prefer to bring up this matter directly," Zhi-fu said. "If I could have the letter back."

"Of course, sir."

The clerk retrieved the paper from the top of the stack. Zhi-fu stuffed it into his pocket and exited the office once again, this time walking even faster.

At the courtyard, he ducked into the Temple of Knowledge. Surrounded by a haze of incense, Zhi-fu took the letter from his pocket and tore it to pieces, feeding them into the brazier that stood before the altar. He watched the pieces blacken and curl, burning away until there was nothing but ash. Only when he was certain the letter was completely destroyed did he turn to leave.

Chapter 9

Over the next few days, she and Zhi-fu avoided one another. It wasn't through any conscious effort on her part. She left her room after he was up, happened to return long before he did. When they did encounter each other at the Academy, they would wander towards seats at opposite ends of the lecture hall.

At night, she was forced to bundle herself up with every shirt she owned beneath her jacket before venturing out to the tea houses. Summer had come to an end and the coming autumn had brought a chill to the night air. It had also made the proprietors a little less tolerant. After an hour nursing her single cup of cold tea, she would get dirty looks.

Anlei was burning quickly through her supply of candles. The light they produced was meager compared to the oil lamp Zhi-fu employed, but it was what she had. Zhi-fu wasn't even returning to his room early enough for her to steal any light through the hole in the wall.

Still, by some fate, she ran into him while hurrying toward the laboratory one afternoon. Her books and papers fell onto the floor and she ended up on her hands and knees gathering them up. Zhi-fu stood silently by, uncertain of what to do.

She had nearly gathered all of her notes, but there was a page right at his feet. She glanced at it, mentally calculating how likely it was that she needed that particular piece of paper.

After a pause, Zhi-fu bent to retrieve the paper. She shot to her feet just as he straightened and they were face to face for the first time in a week.

"My apologies," he said.

"It's nothing."

She waited for him to return her notes, but he held onto the page. He seemed to be lost in thought, on the verge of saying something.

As the moment stretched on, their colleagues passed by, flowing around them.

"I was on my way to the alchemy practicum," she explained.

"Yes," he replied, without a glimmer of interest. There were dark circles beneath his eyes and she knew that he'd been returning to his room well after midnight.

Anlei stared at the paper, waiting. As Zhi-fu extended his hand to return it, she had one last chance to say something to him. She could ask about fast-burning versus slow-burning black powder formulas. Or maybe demand whether he was intent on setting fire to his own fleet?

Instead she mumbled her thanks and clamped the page back beneath the cover of her notebook. She hurried into the practicum, expecting Zhi-fu to eventually come inside as well. She kept looking to the door over the next hour during the alchemical practicum, but Zhi-fu never appeared. It left a hollow feeling inside of her, a place where she'd had something taken from her so quickly, she couldn't be certain what it was she had lost.

IT WAS late and Zhi-fu was drunk.

Not drunk in the way of poets and philosophers. He was

drunk in the way of louts who drank too much and too fast and was now too far gone to enjoy the jokes his companions tossed out at his expense.

"I'm going," Zhi-fu said, standing up and knocking over an ewer of wine that suddenly appeared at his elbow. Warm wine splashed over his arm, soaking into the sleeve. *On his father's grave.* He was a disaster.

Laughter erupted throughout the room. He was surrounded by fellow scholars from the Academy who'd gathered at the one table as the night wore on.

"I'm going," he said again, smoothing a hand over the front of his jacket in an attempt to appear dignified.

"You're paying for this round. A penalty round," Kuo Lishen declared to a chorus of cheering.

There might have been some rule established earlier about that. He didn't remember and he didn't care. Zhi-fu turned to exit the establishment, his world tilting precariously as he hit the street.

Damn, he was drunker than he meant to be. A month ago, he'd been determined. He and Han had studied every night, a plan of attack in place. And now...

Now it hardly seemed worth it.

The last times he'd failed, his father had demanded Zhi-fu give an accounting of where he'd gone wrong. Was it wine? Women? This year the answer would be easy, wouldn't it? Zhi-fu barked out loud with laughter. The sound echoed off the stone-lined streets.

"Very funny, indeed." Kuo was suddenly beside him, propping him up beneath the shoulder. "Looking as sorry as you do, you're likely to get robbed and tossed into the canal. We'll all laugh long and loud then."

"I'm fine," Zhi-fu muttered. "Just going to get some sleep."

"You can't even find your way home."

Zhi-fu looked at the buildings surrounding them. He had to

admit, they looked wholly unfamiliar. He kept his mouth shut as Kuo dragged him down a lane.

"Where has your friend Han been lately? Lost track of your shadow?" Kuo asked.

"Go die already." Zhi-fu shook free of his hold. He could walk on his own. "He's not my shadow. He—we're nothing alike."

He'd believed in Han. Thought that he'd been a good judge of character, for once.

"*Hmm.*" Kuo made a knowing, clucking noise with his tongue which was a thousand times more irritating than any words could ever be.

Zhi-fu shoved past Kuo, not caring that he didn't know exactly where he was. As he staggered forward, he could hear Kuo's footsteps following at a slow and steady pace.

"I have to say, I have never seen you quite like this before." Kuo's tone remained light, but Zhi-fu knew he must be planning something.

Zhi-fu had been out too late the night before. And the night before that. For what? Because Han—-because Anlei would be back at her room? Because he'd have to walk past her door propped open with candlelight burning inside and be reminded of how he'd been deceived.

"You know it doesn't matter what we do," Zhi-fu said. "We'll bribe who there is to bribe. Our names will be noted or not noted. And then, come spring, we'll pass or not pass."

"That is true and not true," Kuo replied matter-of-factly. "Bow your head down if you feel like vomiting."

Kuo took hold of his arm again, slinging it over his shoulder. Given how calm his colleague was, Zhi-fu wondered if Kuo had much to drink that night at all.

"This is our year, Jin Zhi-fu," Kuo continued. "Ours to win or lose, but going on like this you're going to be back next term."

"Wrong, *friend.*" Why was it taking so long to get back to the residence? His feet dragged over the stones. "Fate is speaking to me. I'm meant to fill some barren post in the frontier. Do you know it takes no learning to fire a cannon? You don't have to know a dog's ass about trajectory to do it."

He'd first come to Peking looking to serve the empire. He would meet distinguished scholars, learn from the greatest minds. Instead Zhi-fu had hit the high, thick wall of tradition. A wall that wouldn't crumble fast enough. The Ministry of Science cared more about politics than the advancement of knowledge.

Kuo snorted. "If I didn't know better, I'd say you're acting heart-broken."

"I have no heart left. It's been broken by this bastard, turtle-egg dropping, dead dog of a soul-killing *system*."

Peking was a place for someone cynical and calculating, like Kuo Lishen. It wasn't for him.

He was starting to sink, his weight dragging him downward. When he hit the ground, he decided Zhi-fu was going to stay there awhile. Kuo thwarted his plans with a hard tug, pulling him upright.

"Come on, Zhi-fu. If you weren't too drunk to perform, I'd take you to Jade Lily. She might improve your mood a bit."

Just when he thought Kuo Lishen was being helpful. "I don't need a woman, bastard."

"You need something."

The most frustrating thing about this night was that selfish and opportunistic Kuo was being so damned...reasonable.

The gates of the courtyard house were ahead of them now. He recognized the jade green lantern that hung from it. Inside, the more serious scholars would be studying. Anlei would be there.

Zhi-fu had made the decision to remain loyal to Anlei, even though he was honor-bound to uphold the laws of the Emperor, the palace, the Academy.

If anyone deserved to be there, it was Anlei. Even though

she so clearly did not belong. And there was no way for him to reconcile the two. No amount of drink. No amount of avoidance.

That's how Zhi-fu knew from the moment the sun went down that he was sliding toward disaster.

"Han isn't going to pass," he said. "Sh—he doesn't stand a chance."

Kuo lugged Zhi-fu forward. "You might be correct. But Han is at least making a valiant attempt."

"It didn't matter what I decided. I could help her—help him or not help him. Han wasn't going to pass anyway. Why should I grind my teeth about it?"

"Right."

Damn Kuo. Being reasonable.

"I can walk by myself." Zhi-fu tried to shove free as they cleared the gates, but Kuo held onto him, guiding him across the courtyard.

Zhi-fu remained quiet as they neared his chamber. Anlei's door was propped open as expected. The inside was dark except for the single glow of a candle.

"Help me out here," Kuo said, speaking off to the side.

"Again," came Anlei's quiet rebuke. He couldn't see her, but he knew she was there. He always knew.

He'd never mistake her voice for a man's voice again. Zhi-fu didn't know how he'd ever thought so in the first place. There was an underlying softness to the tone that touched his spine.

"Again," Kuo concurred with a sigh.

Zhi-fu saw his door, and then the ground. Another pair of hands joined Kuo's to take hold of him. The darkness of his chamber surrounded him and he was tossed onto the platform of his kang bed. He lay there, grateful to no longer be moving.

"If only there was a drinking section in the examination," Kuo quipped as the door closed, leaving him in darkness.

He was unable to discern Anlei's reply beyond the muffled

sounds of conversation. He envied Kuo's ability to speak to her as if nothing had changed.

If only he could go back. If only he could pretend that it didn't matter, and they could still be friends.

He'd wanted very much for Shi Han to succeed. The young scholar he'd taken under his care — he was a better person when he believed in something.

Now I'm just a fool, he thought as he drifted off to sleep. And very much acting the part.

ZHI-FU VOWED to visit death upon whoever had just thrown his door open. The morning sun slashed across room, searing his eyes. He squeezed them shut and tried to bury his face into the crook of his arm. His head was still ringing from the night before and his mouth tasted like the gutter.

"Donkey-headed, white-eyed fool."

The voice that spoke was most certainly Anlei's and not Han's.

Cautiously, he opened one eye to see her moving through the room, retrieving papers from the floor and shoving books back into place on his shelves. He dragged himself up to sitting position on the bed, feeling as if he was being besieged.

"You've wasted two weeks," she railed.

A book thudded against his chest. He really *was* under attack.

"Han—" It was hard to think of her as anything else. In one moment, he'd lost his friend to a stranger. There was no logic to it, but it became easy to let go of everything after that.

Anlei wasn't giving him any time to get philosophical about it. "Were you going to drink the rest of the term away?"

"No. Just these two weeks." He glared at her pointedly, fully awake now. "Don't throw any more of my books. They're expensive."

Anlei glared right back at him. Why was she angry? She should be grateful he hadn't reported her. Humbled. And sorry, at least.

Instead Anlei was as single-minded as she'd ever been about studying.

"Open it," she commanded.

He threw her one final cross look before scrubbing a hand across his face, as if he could wipe away the cobwebs. The book had fallen to his lap. He righted it and turned to the first page.

Anlei continued to move about as he read, pushing the window panels open, organizing the books on his desk. Zhi-fu kept his eyes on the page, though he failed to absorb any of the content. When he turned the page, it was a pantomime.

"You were kinder to me when you were in disguise," he said gruffly.

"It was all pretense."

Zhi-fu didn't believe her. Despite the sudden break in their friendship, despite his doubts, she was still here.

He heard the clink of porcelain as he stared at the book. Anlei had cleared his desk so there was a place to set the tray of tea she'd brought. She poured two cups and carried one over to him.

"You don't have to—"

Serve him? Tend to him? Han wouldn't have done so.

She gave him a cold look while he gnashed over his words. When he was unable to figure out anything intelligible to say, she plunked the cup into his hands. He sipped at the tea, welcoming the familiar bitterness.

Anlei set her own cup at the edge of his desk and sat on the stool where she'd spent many an evening studying. She opened her journal and made a show of reviewing her notes. The familiar routine only emphasized the fact that it would never feel familiar again. They were only locked in this ritual because they didn't know how to be around each other otherwise.

"It's hard to keep your secret." He continued to stare down

at the page as he spoke. "What I mean is, it's hard to be around you for fear of slipping."

"It's not hard." Her voice was tight. "Just say nothing. We spent a lot of time together and you didn't suspect anything."

"You know it's different now."

She turned the page. He turned the page.

"I'll go if you want."

His head shot up. "From the Academy?"

She met him with a withering look. "From this room."

Anlei fell silent after that, but the next turn of her page cracked the air like a whip.

"The exam—" She stopped short, biting her tongue.

He could feel the anger radiating off of her. It seemed Anlei was too accustomed to biting her tongue.

"The exam is everything to me. I'm not giving it up for you or for anyone," she said fiercely. "And you shouldn't either."

"Even if it means sacrificing your honor?" he asked quietly.

He didn't ask this to accuse her. It was something he wondered himself, more and more.

"Zhi-fu." She spoke his name as a sigh. "It's easy to talk of honor when every door is open to you. For the rest of us—"

She didn't finish.

In the end, Zhi-fu didn't ask her to stay, but he didn't ask her to go either. He kept on reading and drinking tea.

And she did the same.

When night came, he didn't escape to the drinking houses. He stayed in his room and lit the oil lamp to study.

Chapter 10

Summer passed and the pace of the Academy intensified as the air cooled and the trees became barren. Anlei could feel the change in the tension that thickened over the scholar's quarter. The taverns and brothels were more sparsely attended. Instead students stayed in, studying late into the night.

Zhi-fu continued to allow her to study by the light in his room, but he remained distant even when they were on either side of the desk. They rarely spoke except when she had a question for him about the Analects. Similarly, he would occasionally ask a question about a mathematics principle. The exchanges were stiff and coldly factual, but she came to accept that this was the way they were now. It was how they always should have been. The temporary connection she'd had to Zhi-fu had been an anomaly, a peculiar convergence of events. They had been like brothers, as odd as it sounded now.

To her surprise, Zhi-fu did start walking beside her to the Academy again. Anlei assumed it was only to keep up appearances. He would make the trip in silence. At the Academy, they would sometimes sit together in the lecture hall, sometimes apart, but always with the same stifling veil of silence.

When the rankings from the latest classroom examination were posted, Anlei deliberately scored in the middle of their class as she always did. But she was alarmed to see that Zhi-fu had placed down there as well.

"What happened with your exam this week?" she asked the next day as they started toward the Academy. Her words formed puffs of smoke in the cold air as she spoke.

"I misinterpreted one of the questions," he said, irritated. "Anyone can make that mistake."

"You can't let yourself get distracted. Not now," she urged, which only irritated him more.

"I'm not distracted. The Academy becomes more competitive as the exam period nears."

He lengthened his stride as if to get rid of her, but she quickened her pace to catch him.

"Is it me?" she asked, lowering her voice. She trembled, waiting for the answer. Or maybe it was just the cold autumn air making her shiver.

His only answer was a scowl and he continued to charge through the streets. Fine. Zhi-fu didn't want to talk about it, she wouldn't talk about it.

Anlei had to push herself into a jog to keep up with Zhi-fu, but at least it helped keep her warm. He slowed as they came in sight of the Academy gates. A harsh breeze swept past them, carrying a hint of ice with it. Anlei breathed into her cupped hands to warm her fingers. She'd bartered away some candles for a few strips of wool cloth from a laundress, and had wrapped them around her hands to shield them from the cold. Unfortunately, there wasn't enough material to cover her fingertips.

"You don't have gloves," Zhi-fu observed, his tone flat.

"I didn't realize Peking would get this cold."

Anhui province remained relatively warm even in wintertime. Zhi-fu was much better prepared. Unlike her, he had a change of wardrobe to suit the seasons. The jacket he wore now was lined with a lustrous collar of fox fur while she still wore the same jacket she'd had the day they met. It was her only jacket.

Wordlessly, he started pulling off his gloves.

"Stop," she chided. "We're almost at the Academy."

Zhi-fu's gloves would look ridiculous on her, and such gallantry would be out of place between colleagues. Shi Han would want to save face and Zhi-fu should strive to preserve Han's dignity. The sum of it was, she was meant to suffer cold hands and they weren't supposed to talk about it.

She was looking forward to the lecture hall with its ground heating system that transmitted heat from an external fire pit through air flow channels.

Later that evening, Zhi-fu asked her to come over and review cubic equations. She recognized it as a gesture of peace, but it felt good to be speaking to Zhi-fu again. Even if it was about nothing more than equations.

They drilled through cubics and quadratics until Anlei could no longer hold back her yawning.

"I didn't sleep well last night," she confessed. Her room was meant for storage and wasn't heated like the bed chambers. The chill had come without warning—though those who were accustomed to living in Peking told her it was common.

Zhi-fu's attention was focused on putting away his ink brushes. "You should stay here tonight."

His invitation made her face go hot. She was glad he was looking away. "I can't."

"Don't be hard-headed about it. It's only going to get colder."

The admonishment was the closest Zhi-fu had come to sounding like Zhi-fu of old talking to Han. A tiny flutter swirled in her chest as she went to retrieve her bed things. There was nothing unusual about it really. Nothing scandalous at all. It was common for several students to crowd into a room.

Anlei folded her quilt and rolled up the bamboo sleeping

mat, tucking it under one arm as she returned next door. Zhi-fu grabbed the mat from her as soon as she entered and carried it to the kang bed arranged against the wall. With a flick of his wrists, he unrolled the mat and laid it on the right side of the platform.

"The floor will be good enough," she protested.

The heat from the kang bed warmed the entire room. She could huddle at the foot of the platform and it would feel like summer compared to the dirt floor of the store room.

"Nonsense." Zhi-fu turned, his expression unyielding. "Stop worrying so much. I don't think of you in that way," he said impatiently.

Her throat went dry and she swallowed with difficulty. "In what way?"

His scowl deepened. "You're bright enough, Anlei. You know what I mean."

He turned his back to her to prepare for bed and she meekly climbed onto one side of the platform, pulling her blanket over her head like a cocoon. She willed herself to disappear and for morning to come quickly. Thankfully, she was exhausted. She fell into sleep before Zhi-fu even climbed into bed.

ANLEI STEPPED ASIDE at the foot up the stairs that led up to the observation deck. Zhi-fu took the lead, holding his lantern high to illuminate the steps.

"I hope this is worth it," he said. "I could be studying Liu Hui's algorithm for calculating *pi*."

A cold wind batted against them as they climbed to the top of the Observatory.

"It's just one night," Anlei insisted.

She was never one to say such things. The examination was only five months away and she had spent nearly every night at the books since arriving in Peking. The only exception had been that one night out drinking and going to the opium den — something she'd made a vow never to repeat. She didn't like that feeling of losing herself to something formless and invisible.

The wind blew stronger on top of the tower. Anlei shivered despite the layers of clothing she'd wrapped herself in. The brass instruments atop the platform cast intriguing shadows in the lantern light. They crouched beside the stone enclosure at the foot of the globe-like armillary sphere for shelter.

"You were able to get permission so quickly." Anlei tilted her head up to gaze into the night. The sky was clear as glass above, dusted with a field of stars.

"I sent a petition to the Bureau of Astronomy," he said, as simple as drawing breath. "Apparently the family name is good for something."

She wouldn't have known what to do or even considered it a possibility to climb to the top of the Observatory. Yet the night patrolman had waved them up with a courteous bow.

"It's not your family, Jin Zhi-fu. It's you. You know how to talk to people."

He leaned against the stone structure, head back exposing the long line of his neck and the shape of his jaw. He was like the carefully crafted instruments around them: precise, well-defined. Stark and spare in their beauty.

"So, we're supposed to see the stars fall tonight," he said.

"I've seen it once before. Mistress Wang recorded the dates in her astronomical journal over several years. It happens on the same days every year, but only if you use the Western calendar. One of the reasons she was a proponent of it."

She joined him on the wall. Shoulder to shoulder, they watched the sky.

"When is it supposed to happen?"

"You have to be patient."

She could hear Zhi-fu's steady breathing beside her. They stared up at the stars together, searching for movement.

"How long did you study with your mistress?" he asked.

"Five years. She came to my father's mill one day to purchase paper when I was thirteen, maybe fourteen years old. And she saw me. I was writing in my father's ledger book, making number patterns."

"That's what you did for amusement," he observed dryly.

She made a face at him. "It was a very small village."

He grinned. Then a thoughtful expression crossed his face. "How old are you now?"

"Nineteen."

"Hmm. Thought you were younger."

"Well, you were wrong about a lot of things."

"Brat."

The breeze picked up and she hugged her arms around herself to try to stay warm. Zhi-fu, as usual, seemed impervious to the cold. Even when he wasn't wrapped in wool and fur, he appeared to weather the cold better than the rest of them. Certainly, better than her.

"You need to get some warmer clothing," he said. "Peking is going to get colder in the coming months."

Her teeth chattered. "This was the thickest jacket I could find at the pawn shop," she said ruefully. "The foxes were hiding. I couldn't hunt down an entire den to wear like you. Poor things."

"A den of foxes." Chuckling, he plucked the fur-lined cap off his head and planted it on top of hers. It was still warm from him.

"But you'll be cold," she protested, though she really didn't want to give the hat back just yet.

"Don't worry about me. It gets much colder where I'm from. Do you know fox hunting doesn't start until the coldest part of the winter? That's when their coat is thickest."

"It snows a lot in the winter where you're from?"

"Every year. Jilin has a long, long winter. There's snow on the ground for months and the trees become completely covered in ice. They look like they're made of glass."

The Manchu people originally came from the northeast before they descended down to defeat the Ming Emperor. She didn't know much more except that the Emperor and his elite court were Manchurian. Many Han subjects still considered the Manchu to be barbarians and invaders.

She huddled closer to Zhi-fu, warmed by the story as much as his nearness. They'd rarely spoken about such personal things. She'd always been curious, but she was afraid if she asked anything about him, he might turn around and ask about her when she'd been intent on remaining hidden.

"Was it difficult at first, coming to Peking?" she asked.

He shifted to look down at her in confusion. "Why would it be?"

"Coming to such a big city from the frontier."

An odd look flickered across his face. Then he burst out laughing, the deep sound resonating atop the empty tower. "We're not all hunters living in mud huts. Jilin is a thriving city."

Her face heated with embarrassment. "You're the one always talking about the 'barrenness of the rocky frontier'," she glowered.

"I was being dramatic."

His eyes flashed with amusement which only caused her face to burn hotter. It was an honest mistake. She probably knew about as much about Manchuria as he did about paper-making.

Hunching over like a turtle retreating into its shell, she started re-wrapping the wool around her hands. She still hadn't managed to find gloves, but she did get thicker strips of wool.

"You look like a leper all wrapped up like that," Zhi-fu remarked.

She shot him a foul look. "That's an awful thing to say."

"That won't do. Here—"

She tried to shove his hand away, quite cross with him now despite her warm feelings just moments ago.

"I know how to deal with cold weather," he insisted.

He took hold of both of her hands and tucked them inside

his coat, pressing down to trap them there. The movement pulled her nearly up against him, though he acted as if there was nothing untoward about it at all.

There were so many times in the last weeks when he'd treat her with the same casual familiarity as before. As he had when she was Shi Han.

"You could lose fingers if you're not careful," he said.

She was almost certain it wasn't *that* cold, but she had her hands pressed to his chest. She could feel the beating of his heart against her fingertips. Her own pulse quickened in reply.

Anlei was at a loss for words, and Zhi-fu seemed to be as well. He just held onto her in that awkward position, his eyes fixed onto her as if waiting for something. His heart beat out a fast rhythm as if he were running, but she'd never seen him so still.

I do think of you in that way, she wanted to tell him, but no power on earth could make her lips move.

Then a movement over his shoulder caught her eye. She made a small sound of delight as a white streak moved across the sky like the quick stroke of an ink brush. Zhi-fu turned to look, but missed it.

Suddenly there was another. "There," she said.

Zhi-fu caught it this time. He loosened his hold on her and she slipped her hands out of his jacket. They were more than warm enough now.

She had nearly forgotten why they'd come up there in the first place. They resumed their initial position, shoulder to shoulder, to search across the sky. Each time a star fell, Anlei's spirits lifted knowing she was witnessing it along with Zhi-fu. A scattering of tiny moments that connected them together.

Then the stars started to fall like rain. She held her breath as her heart soared. Zhi-fu's hand brushed against hers inadvertently as he shifted to watch the shower of lights. He didn't move away for a long time.

On high over the great city of Peking, with the vast sky above, it was like being on top of the clouds. She was sad when they had to climb down from the heavens, to return to the earth down below.

Chapter 11

Classes at the Academy came to a halt as the weather got colder. Students were left to continue their studies on their own over the winter season. The midnight outings and parties ceased and the drinking houses emptied out as the imperial exam date drew nearer.

By the eleventh month, a layer of ice formed over the wash basin in the mornings and Anlei's makeshift room became uninhabitable. She had no choice but to join Zhi-fu in his room.

They would start the night on opposite sides of the platform bed, backs turned. At some point, while lost in sleep, they would inevitably move toward the center of the bed, seeking the heat that radiated from underneath. Anlei woke up tangled in Zhi-fu's blanket more than once. When it happened, they would separate without a word and rise to resume studying.

She imagined Zhi-fu must have been relieved when the weather warmed enough for her to return to her room.

Finally, the day of the examinations arrived. It was early in the spring. She couldn't believe it had been a year since she'd first set foot in Peking. So much had happened.

Anlei barely slept the night before. She was plagued by dreams and a jumble of restless thoughts. Among them the startling realization that she was so close along with the fear that she could still be discovered.

She rose early to pack a supply of rice, salt fish, and pickled vegetables in her bag. Anlei had laid out her other supplies the night before: a lamp with a vial of oil, her remaining candles, brushes, and ink sticks. She even folded her quilt and tied it over her back. The examination would take three days during which they were prohibited from leaving the examination hall. Candidates were expected to bring all of the essentials themselves.

When Anlei stepped outside, she saw Zhi-fu emerging at the same time. It was as if their minds had become entwined after so many nights studying together.

Zhi-fu appeared calm and completely well-rested as he acknowledged her with a courteous nod. He was neatly groomed with his hair braided in its queue and every crease in place on his silk jacket. In contrast, Anlei was certain the dark pits beneath her eyes were deep enough to bury bodies.

They gathered in the courtyard with the rest of their class-mates and ate in silence. All the while, Anlei's stomach churned inside her. She was hours away now. Only hours from the impossible.

Zhi-fu finished his rice, drank his tea, and rose. Steady as ever. How could he be so calm? She had only finished half of her meal, but stood nonetheless. Her stomach was too nervous to eat as it was.

Zhi-fu also had his supplies slung over his shoulder. They began their walk to the examination hall, joined on all sides by others undertaking the same task.

A procession had formed on the main avenue as the candi-dates funneled themselves towards the examination hall. The beat of drums accompanied them as she and Zhi-fu were swal-lowed by the throng. There she could see not only some of her classmates, but a mass of new faces, young and old, who were also assembling to sit for the exams. Not all the candidates had the privilege of studying at the Imperial Academy. She was one of the few. Her chest swelled at the thought.

The start of the imperial exam was a celebration in the capital. Onlookers gathered on either side of the street to cheer them on. Shyly, Anlei waved back to a little boy who sat perched on his father's shoulders. She looked over to Zhi-fu who stood tall above the crowd. His shoulders were squared and straight. He could have been marching unwavering into battle, jaw set and determined.

As if sensing her eyes on him, he looked over to her. The line of his mouth lifted for just a moment. A small warmth bloomed in her chest. She'd thought she'd be going at this alone, hiding her deep secret. She hadn't realized how much it would mean to have someone by her side. Someone who understood what she'd been through.

The procession slowed to a halt as the candidates pooled before the examination hall. There were easily a thousand bodies gathered there. She could sense the nervous energy humming in the air.

"Do you have enough food?" Zhi-fu asked as they stood waiting.

She nodded. "Though I doubt I'll be able to eat anything, as nervous as I am."

"You need to keep up your strength. What about ink?"

"I have some." She pulled the compressed black rods out of her bag to show him.

"That might not be enough."

He fished through his supplies, ignoring her protests, and produced a handful of his own ink sticks to give to her. His were stamped with a gold insignia, much fancier than hers.

"One year, a candidate ran out of ink on the last day and was unable to finish," he warned. "The guards are notably unsympathetic if you exhaust your supplies."

"But what if you don't have enough?"

"I'll be fine."

Zhi-fu was still Zhi-fu. She took the sticks from him and put them away in her bag, touched by his thoughtfulness.

The line was starting to move. Anlei started trudging forward with the rest of the crowd.

"Han—"

It had been a long time since he'd called her that.

"One other thing." Zhi-fu held out a large round token made of bronze. "For you."

He looked nervous as she reached out to take it. It was warm to the touch, as if he'd been holding it all this time. She turned it over and over in her palm. The token had been cast with an image of a man with horns standing on a turtle.

"It's Kuixing," he explained. "The god of the examinations. It's a good luck charm. My family gave it to me the first time I took the exam."

"When you didn't pass?"

His face fell and Anlei wished she could take back her words. It was obvious the charm meant a lot to him. Though Zhi-fu had been more than generous to her, this was the first time he had given her something that wasn't a necessity. It was a gift.

"Thank you," she said, folding her fingers carefully over the charm. A simple thanks felt insufficient. "Thank you — for everything."

He didn't say anything and she couldn't be sure he had even heard her. The crowd surged, pushing them forward. Several candidates had wedged in between them, eager to get started.

At the steps of the examination hall, the proctors marked off their names and sorted them out into the rows of cells. Their belongings were inspected for any hidden notes or crib sheets. Anlei stiffened when the guard reached out to feel along her sleeves and inside her pockets.

Panic gripped her. Looking back over her shoulder, she tried to search for Zhi-fu but she couldn't find him. There were so many candidates surrounding her and waiting for their turn.

Zhi-fu had warned her they would search for anything that

might be used to cheat. She breathed deep and forced herself to remain calm, at least outwardly.

The search was completed and the proctor wrote her compartment number on a slip of paper to pass to her. Tentatively, she stepped inside, feeling the rush of centuries of tradition flowing into her. So many hopes, from so many families across the dynasties had hung their hopes on this practice.

The building was separated into corridors with rows of compartments on each side. She would be enclosed inside a small closet with a bench and a wooden plank laid across the compartment to serve as a desk. A curtain closed over the space giving her a modicum of privacy.

She lowered herself onto her bench and set her sack onto the desk. All around her, hundreds of other bodies were doing the same; settling into their spaces and laying out their supplies. She took her time arranging her candles.

It really was a prison. There were stories of candidates dying in the course of the examination only to have their bodies tossed unceremoniously outside so as to not disrupt the proceedings.

The examination booklet was set out before her. Her heart skipped as she looked at the blue-gray cover. It looked so harmless - just a stack of paper bound together with glue, but it held all the promise in the world.

She'd waited for this moment for so long. Mistress Wang had dreamed of it.

Anlei set out her brushes and calculator. Then, pulse pounding, she opened the cover and started on the first problem knowing that somewhere, in the honeycomb of cells, Zhi-fu would be doing the same.

ZHI-FU STOOD BACK and watched as the guards searched through Anlei's things. He tensed when the guard reached out to search her clothing. Only when she was waved on did he let out a breath and move to rejoin the queue.

What could he have done if she had been stopped? Nothing he could think of — but he still couldn't abandon her until he was certain she was through.

And now she was.

He didn't think of her in that way, he'd told her the first night she'd shared his bed.

Then why was his heart pounding so hard, watching the place where she had been as if the air held some memory of her?

Why did even the thought of her sharing his bed make his palms sweat?

He gave his name to the proctor who put a mark beside it in his ledger. The guards gave only a cursory glance over his belongings before he was waved through.

Inside, Anlei had already disappeared inside her cell. He went to his assigned spot and settled in, methodically laying out his brushes and ink stone. The place smelled the same from year to year. It was the smell of sweat and tears.

He had studied harder this year than any other time. Partially because it meant he could stay by Anlei's side from the moment he woke up to the moment he fell asleep. And also, because Anlei expected him to do well.

She'd thrown a book at him to impress that upon him, hadn't she? She would accept no excuses for failure. Certainly not his own apathy.

He didn't think of her in that way, because what had grown inside him from that moment, the moment she insisted he could be better than what he was, had very little to do with thinking and everything to do with emotion.

He'd lain awake nearly every winter's night, his skin too aware that Anlei was lying beside him, almost close enough to touch. But he didn't touch her. He stayed awake just to make sure he didn't reach for her in his sleep. Anlei needed a place to sleep and he couldn't think of her that way, if he wanted to preserve the tenuous arrangement they had.

He looked at the exam booklet. How much time had passed already while he philosophized about unwelcome emotions?

Anlei would likely throw something even heavier at him if he didn't pass. Zhi-fu prepared his ink and bent to begin reading.

He wanted to be better. For her.

———

THE PORTER CAME by with tea periodically and to check the chamber pot. Other than that, she was left alone. She didn't know what time it was when her eyelids started to droop. Her back was aching and the characters blurred before her.

The wooden slat of the desk became her bunk and she climbed on top of it, curling her knees up to her chest to catch a few moments of sleep. At least she was accustomed to small quarters, living in a storage closet. There were small sounds of movement on the other side of the wall. She imagined it was Zhi-fu there, his brow furrowed in concentration.

Maybe he wasn't beside her, but he was somewhere inside the examination hall, sharing the same moments. When she closed her eyes, she could feel his presence beside her. Was he permanently imprinted there?

Would she still be able to feel him so close when this was all over?

Oh Anlei, now was certainly not the time to get sentimental. At least about anything but mathematics.

By the time she reached the last page, the characters looked like black spiders crawling before her. She completed the final problem set and flipped back through the other sections, checking her answers. She had started dozing off when the clang of a gong rang through the hall.

With a jolt, she started awake as the gong sounded four

more times, reverberating through the cells. It was the Dragon Hour. All around her, she could hear the sound of shuffling and scraping as the candidates started gathering their belongings. The examination period was finally over. She was done.

Outside of her cell, a long line had formed in the corridor. Her fellow candidates were trudging step by step toward the exit, looking half-alive with their limbs hanging from their bones. Everyone had dark circles under their eyes. In contrast, she could barely stand still. She glanced one last time at her examination booklet before flipping the pages closed and setting it onto the proctor's desk at the door.

Finally, she was outside with the sun shining too brightly overhead. No one spoke around her. The other scholars shuffled off through the streets like automatons. Anlei searched for Zhi-fu among the scholars, but it was futile. Everyone looked alike in their dark jackets and caps.

She pushed free of the crowd and broke into a run, flying free with her heart pounding and the air rushing between her fingertips. She rushed back to their residence and burst through the gate. The problems from the examination swirled through her mind's eye.

Anlei was the first to reach the residence. She grabbed hold of the basin and drew water from the well before ducking inside her closet.

Everything was as she'd left it, but different somehow. She'd done what she had come here to do. Everything she had worked for, all the nights of study, the promises to her mentor had all been fulfilled. The results wouldn't be announced until the end of the week, but for now a feeling of accomplishment washed over her. She was triumphant.

And she was filthy.

She set the basin down on her stool and stripped off her clothes. It had been days since she bathed and she was covered in ink stains and soot and sweat. She scrubbed the yellow cake of soapbean over her skin and washed and rinsed her hair before running a hasty comb through it. She heard Zhi-fu's door open and close as she was re-braiding her queue.

Anlei wound the binding cloth around her breasts and dressed quickly in her gray tunic and trousers. The rest would have to be laundered, but she would worry about such incidentals later. She rushed outside, happy to see Zhi-fu's door was ajar. She slipped inside with only a cursory knock.

Zhi-fu was seated at his desk. He appeared to be methodically cleaning his ink brushes and placing them back into their proper locations.

"Anlei," he greeted while she tore past him to search the bookcase.

"What did you think?" she asked. "More difficult than last year?"

"How much did you sleep?"

"Maybe an hour, here and there." She could feel his gaze on her as she rifled through the books, searching for the copy of *Jade Mirror*. When she turned back around, Zhi-fu was leaning back into his chair, watching her.

"I must have been blind," he mused, his gaze lingering on her face for longer than she'd ever remembered.

Her heart pounded. She hugged the book to her chest, unable for the life of her to remember what she had wanted to look up inside it.

His hair was also wet and despite the hollowness beneath his eyes, his skin glowed from the bath house and there was a slight flush to his cheeks. Heat crept up the back of her neck.

"The...the imperial exam is finally over," she managed.

His lips curved faintly. "It did seem like a lifetime, didn't it?"

"We can finally get some rest."

His eyes never left hers. "If that's what you want."

She swallowed past the dryness in her throat. "I should go."

She had somehow lost her breath. The words came out barely a whisper. She moved quickly, desperate to flee.

"If that's what you want."

His voice was suddenly there, right beside her ear as she reached the door. His hand rested against the frame just above hers, not stopping her. Just there, the way he was there. The way he'd always been for months now. His large, solid presence.

She turned to face him, pressing her shoulder blades back against the wood. He filled her vision, surrounding her. What she wished was not to go, not to have to leave him and the only place where she was known and seen.

Her heart leapt as he reached for her, but his fingers closed gently over the book still clutched in her hands. The mathematical text she was holding onto like a shield. Zhi-fu worked the pages loose from her fingers while she could do nothing but watch him, dizzy with his closeness.

They didn't have the examination looming between them anymore. The figures, the calculations. There was nothing between them but the short draw of one breath. He bent his head toward her. At the same moment she reached out, her fingertips just grazing against the buttons of his jacket.

When their mouths touched there was the final quiet of knowing. Two halves of an equation finally locking into place.

It was obvious to her Zhi-fu had done this before—and that she most certainly had not. His lips pressed against hers, seeking, while she was lost in more ways than one. In all ways.

She took a breath, taking in more of him. The scent of his skin and the touch of his mouth. She dug her hands into the front of his coat, fingers twining with the cloth to pull him closer.

The next moments were a swirl of colors—the first burst of flame after a spark. She raised onto her toes to reach him. Zhi-fu's arms closed around her. Their kiss broke for a moment which made her want to weep, but then they found each other again, clinging harder. She could taste him. Black tea and cloves.

Zhi-fu made quick work of the fastenings of her jacket. With head bent, he pressed his mouth to her chin, her throat. The graze of teeth against her shoulder made her jump, but then she sank into him like warmed wax, every inch of her skin alive and yearning. How long had she been yearning for this moment without even realizing?

His hands were moving beneath her jacket now, large, warm and searching. She realized he was looking for the end of her bindings. She shrugged the garment from her shoulders, letting it fall to the floor as she reached down to help him. Her gaze settled on him as he unwound the tightly wrapped linen. His head was bent and his brow furrowed in concentration and there was no sound left but the deep draw of their breaths. A strand of his damp hair touched against her skin. There was something raw about this moment and the unbidden need for less between them. Less words, less meaning. Less clothes.

This time when their mouths met, her tongue touched his in a moment so foreign and delicious her bones dissolved within her. She tugged at Zhi-fu's clothes even as he urged her toward the bed and eased her onto it with his steady hands at her back. She could smell his skin in the blankets.

He hovered over her, the weight of him supported on his elbows and the rest of it against her as she tugged his jacket away. He himself tore away his tunic in a single impatient move-ment and all the sudden there was skin before her. Bronze skin and the dark, endless depths of his eyes fixed on hers. She had to touch and keep touching, her hands exploring every inch. Heaven and earth, he was warm. Warm and gloriously heavy.

Zhi-fu watched her as they removed the rest of their clothes, working together in awkward silence. Then they were finally skin to skin, arm in arm. His mouth closed over hers again. It was impossible to think that just moments earlier they had not so much as embraced. Now she had given Zhi-fu her first kiss and she was ready for so much more. For everything.

"I don't know how—" she began, halting when she realized she didn't have the words. She'd never seen them, read them, heard them out loud.

"Nature will do what it must," her mother had told her in a hushed tone the night before she'd left home. It was meant to be instruction for her wedding night.

Zhi-fu nodded, his expression so grave and serious that she wanted to crush him in her arms. He fell silent as his hand moved between their bodies, feeling his way gently along the curve of her hip. He continued to watch her face as his hand moved lower, the tips of his fingers questing over her thigh. Anlei bit down on her lip, afraid to look away from him. His gaze was focused, intent. Darker than she had ever seen. She would drown in those depths.

She squeezed her eyes shut the moment before he touched intimately against her. It was just a touch, but the lightning of it swept through her body. A shock of pleasure and fear. And a deep longing beneath it all.

Without realizing it, she had stopped breathing and her chest constricted. The beating of her heart was nearly painful as he stroked reverently. She would have forgotten to breathe if not for the gasp that escaped her lips.

Still Zhi-fu said nothing, told her nothing. Just touched, drawing liquid sensation from her until there was nothing left but his weight anchoring her to the bed, his fingers telling her all her secrets.

She didn't know how long they went on, only that she wanted it never to stop. She was almost afraid if she moved, if she spoke, if she cried out like she so desperately needed, this wonderful torment would end.

Suddenly something changed and Zhi-fu shifted over her. She felt the heavy weight of his organ resting against her. She blinked her eyes open, but saw nothing but a blur of shadow and color. Zhi-fu's shape rose above her. His breath rasped inside his throat as he parted her below. The hard, smooth weight of him pressed against her.

Again, the fear and curiosity and longing. She'd never been so afraid and elated at once.

This was so confusing, she thought through the haze of the moment.

And then Zhi-fu was inside her and she was yielding as he pushed deeper. He pressed his face against her shoulder, his breath ragged as his body pressed closer still. The sensation of being stretched seemed to go on forever.

Then he was still. She was still.

"Are you hurt?" he said, the words whispered against her neck.

"No. It's just…new."

Her voice felt ridiculously small.

She couldn't imagine why she felt the need to give a better accounting. It was the first moment she'd been able to catch up with her thoughts. The pleasure had receded to a new sensation. Pressure, almost pain, but still there was some promise with each shift of Zhi-fu's strong body over her.

Zhi-fu moved above her and she exhaled in surprise. Then he gathered her closer in his arms, pulling her hard against his chest and thrust again, a slow, shallow move that brought back a hint of that promise. She pressed her lips to his shoulder because it was all she could reach of him. Sweat beaded on his skin, and he groaned as she touched her tongue against his neck. He tasted of salt.

"Anlei." It wasn't pretty how he said her name at that moment. It was raw and hard and had a tinge of the gutter to it as he continued to move. Each thrust sent a streak of wildness into her.

No wonder. No wonder there was no way to explain. Zhi-fu thrust faster, making her yearn for something she couldn't explain. She could do nothing but cling to him, arms around him, legs wrapped around his hips.

He found a rhythm that seemed to call to him and began to move harder faster, almost desperate in its pace. All the while, the promise of that first discovery of pleasure.

The expression in his eyes was just as lost.

Then suddenly Zhi-fu's strong body stilled over her, every muscle rigid and locked tight. Then he collapsed as if his bones had fallen away. After a long pause, he seemed to remember she was still there and rolled onto his side to keep from crushing her beneath him. Slowly, almost drunkenly he kissed her mouth, her breasts, before sinking down exhausted with his head beside hers.

"You look thoughtful," he said. His voice sounded deep, raspy. Different. Everything seemed different.

"It's all very confusing," she admitted. Parts of her sore in ways she hadn't known.

He merely nodded and rose to retrieve a damp wash cloth which he pressed intimately to her.

Moments later, Zhi-fu's breathing deepened and she thought he had fallen asleep, but he pulled close once again, cradling her by his side. His hand slipped between her legs where her flesh was swollen and tender. He moved slower this time, stroking in lazy circles with his fingers first and then, after lowering himself, his tongue.

Things became even more confusing then — before everything became startlingly clear. She did let out a cry, biting the flesh of her palm to keep from screaming.

It was dark outside before Zhi-fu's arms were back around her. His hair hung about his face, having fallen loose from its knot. She tugged at one of the strands drowsily, appreciating the sharp planes of his jaw.

"There will be scandal," she murmured. There had always been talk about how much time they spent with each other. There would be more talk now.

Zhi-fu glanced toward the window, listening to the sounds of their peers out in the courtyard. He stroked his fingers over her bare shoulder.

"We wouldn't be the first," he said, unconcerned.

Chapter 12

Anlei woke up tangled in the covers. Zhi-fu's arm was draped over her, uncomfortably heavy. Sensing she was awake, he shifted. Turned. Then he opened his eyes slowly to look at her.

"Anlei."

"Zhi-fu."

For a long, unbroken moment, they simply lay facing one another. There was all the time in the world now that the exam was done.

His eyes were almost golden in the falling afternoon, rich brown touched with lighter flecks. As much time as they'd spent together, she'd never seen him this close.

Zhi-fu was handsome. She'd never thought she cared for such things, but he was. And he was hers, at least a part of him.

"You're smiling," he said.

She shifted to rest her cheek against the crook of her arm. "I'm happy."

"I can see. And I went so long without seeing you." His gaze roamed over her and Anlei was reminded that they were still naked beneath the blankets.

They quieted as someone moved past the open window.

Outside, they could hear the sound of footsteps and muffled conversations. Their fellow students were starting to recover from the examination as well. There was already talk about celebrations that evening.

"What happens now?" she asked.

"It will take at least three days for the palace to review the exams. When all scores are done, we'll be called to the palace, to the square beside The Meridian Gate. Then we pray that our names are called out."

The thought that she might have passed stole her breath. She knew there was only a small chance, but perhaps…perhaps.

"Do you think you've done enough?" she asked. "Was this exam more or less difficult than previous years?"

He regarded her without answering, his expression unreadable, and Anlei regretted asking the question. It was the sort of question that would frustrate her to no end — it had no answer.

"It feels different this time," he said finally. His gaze lingered on her. "Very different."

Her heart beat faster. She wanted it to be different for him this time. She wanted with her very soul for Zhi-fu to succeed. It wasn't just that he was determined and that he'd worked so hard. They'd all worked hard, hadn't they? But Zhi-fu had been kind to her, when he could have ignored her or seen her as a rival. He'd been open and generous and accepting.

"I have a good feeling about it," she said.

His jaw tensed. "Let's not talk about the exam. My entire life is the exam," Zhi-fu said.

Kuo Lishen had mentioned something outside the opium den—that Zhi-fu needed the release. Though he rarely spoke of it, Zhi-fu was under constant pressure to uphold his family honor, but there was more than that.

Zhi-fu was unfailingly loyal to anyone he called a friend. She'd seen it with Kuo Lishen. Despite their differences, Zhi-fu felt on honest kinship with Lishen. And she'd seen it with her, how he'd kept her secret. The weight of maintaining such a strict sense of duty and loyalty weighed on him.

She reached out to trace her fingertips over the line of his collarbone then down his chest. It was a pleasure just to look at him. Firm muscle. Well-defined shapes and enticing shadows.

He breathed deep and exhaled slowly. She could feel him relax beneath her touch.

"This is the best time," Zhi-fu said. "For a moment, what's done is done. You're allowed to hope and dream that you've succeeded. All things are possible until those names are read."

"What will we do with our newfound freedom?"

Zhi-fu's answer was to gather her into his arms. "I don't plan to leave this room."

She laughed, muffling the sound against his shoulder. The scent of his skin surrounded her, warm and earthy. His breathing deepened as he pulled her tighter against him.

"I thought of this every night. Every night you were here and even when you weren't."

He touched his lips to her cheek, to her throat. Her back arched at the scrape of his teeth over the sensitive skin of her neck.

"I thought of it too," she admitted shyly.

"I couldn't sleep."

She loved hearing him talk like this. Zhi-fu was usually so reserved and focused. Now he tugged impatiently at the blanket between them. She helped him, squirming and pulling to toss it aside so they were skin to skin. She pulled him down to her, seeking his mouth with hers.

The second time was a vast improvement — they were both dedicated students, after all.

By the time they fell back against the bed, the sky outside had grown much darker. Zhi-fu rose to light the oil lamp before returning to the bed.

They came together once more, curling into one another.

"We need to stay here for the rest of the month," she said. *Or forever.*

The moment she allowed herself to think it, it was as if cold water had been thrown over her.

Zhi-fu sensed the change in her. "Anlei?"

She shook off his concern and curled in closer. "It's nothing. I was thinking about the exam."

It was obvious Zhi-fu didn't believe her. He was too observant and intuitive to be fooled, but he played along.

"I'm hungry," she said, stomach rumbling.

They only had to poke their heads outside to hail down a traveling vendor passing by on a pedicab. Every food seller in the city knew this was the day they'd find starving students. This one offered baskets of fried turnip cakes and noodle bowls. Hot soup dispensed from the heated canister attached at the back of the pedicab.

Zhi-fu paid the seller and they ducked back into the room to eat among the books and brushes. Then laughing, they lit the remaining candles until the room was dotted with the flames.

As warm light flooded the room, Anlei felt unaccountably wealthy. How many nights had they sat opposite one another, squinting over a single pool of light?

Zhi-fu pulled her into his arms again. So, this was the way of new lovers. Hungry and shameless. She liked him this way.

"Gently, this time," she whispered into his ear.

And he was. So gentle with her it nearly brought tears to her eyes.

Afterward, Zhi-fu extinguished the candles as she started to doze off. Then he climbed back onto the bed and pulled her back to cradle her against him. Exhaustion had finally caught up to them.

Anlei closed her eyes, listening to the rhythm of Zhi-fu's breathing as she had done so many times. They sank into sleep, hoping and dreaming together.

EVERY SEAT WAS OCCUPIED at the drinking house. The number of scholars in Peking had thinned after examination week as their classmates took the opportunity to return home or travel during the short break. There were always enough scholars staying to keep the quarter busy.

"Four more days," Kuo Lishen recited as Zhi-fu wove his way into the opposite seat. "I hear the examiners are being especially tough this year."

"You've heard nothing of the sort," Zhi-fu countered as Kuo waved the server over to call for more wine.

The ministers who scored the exams were forbidden from leaving the palace until the entire lot was done. It was a measure to prevent corruption.

He recognized Kuo's bravado for what it was now. An attempt to mask his fear and insecurity.

"Well, do you know Peking has dispatched observers to the port cities?" Kuo reported. "The Ministry is in a fever over our engine. They want more information about Western machines."

"Now it's 'our' engine?" Zhi-fu said with a chuckle. "I thought you would have claimed it entirely as your discovery."

Kuo Lishen looked annoyed. "Didn't it strike you as curious? The focus on physics on the exam? The questions on navigation? They're recruiting a wartime ministry. Maybe that's good news for you and your shadow. Where is the infamous 'Shi Han'?"

"Probably at the library." Zhi-fu craned his neck to look around the common room. Anlei was supposed to meet him here, but if she'd arrived early, he couldn't see her. "She—he seems to be the only scholar with his nose still in a book."

He shot Zhi-fu a look that indicated no one was the fool there. "Even after the exams? A true believer. The Ministry must be very impressed."

Kuo was in some mood. Zhi-fu attempted to retrace the

conversation. "Why would a wartime ministry be favorable for me?"

Kuo sneered. "You're the son of a military official and Han —well, he, or rather she, benefits simply by association."

Kuo's sharp tone set him on guard. Zhi-fu realized Kuo had never learned Anlei's name, even though he'd discovered her secret.

"Shi Han is more qualified than you and I combined."

"Of course." Kuo tapped his cup against the table with more force than necessary. "Honorable Jin Zhi-fu wouldn't make some rash decision based on *brotherly* affection, would he? Not when he and I have cultivated over five years' worth of experiences together."

Kuo's expression darkened and became more serious than Zhi-fu had ever seen it.

"These carefree days at the Academy. These are the bonds that one will remember always," Kuo said. "But consider very carefully who you bring along with you. That future is not so carefree."

"I'm not in a position to bring anyone—"

"This is your time, Zhi-fu." Kuo interrupted bitterly, draining his wine cup. "You might as well already have that degree in your hands. It's time to start thinking of the next part."

"What's the next part?"

Zhi-fu looked up to see Anlei standing at their table. She had her satchel slung over her shoulder and appeared flushed, as if coming from a long walk.

"Those who pass the exam can petition for an appointment," Zhi-fu explained.

"And the rest go crawling away in defeat," Kuo finished for him.

"A feeling we know well," Zhi-fu added, trying to lighten the mood.

"You and I, we tend to rise or fall together, do we not?" Kuo Lishen's remark held a hint of warning.

Anlei looked from one to the other, puzzled.

"Take this seat here." Kuo cracked a cold smile and stood. "Apparently it's already been marked for you."

She watched Kuo Lishen warily as he retreated into the crowd. "What was he talking about?"

Zhi-fu shook his head. "Kuo is never content to solve the problem right in front of him. He has to make up new ones."

He looked down to see a black stain on her hands. "What's that there?"

"Just some engine grease." She rubbed at the stain on her palm though it did nothing to remove the dark smudge.

"Engine grease? How?"

"I've been doing work at a repair shop. Just here and there, when I can," she said, looking embarrassed.

"Since when?"

"Since autumn, before the exam."

He was surprised. "I always thought you were going to the library."

Anlei made a face at him. "You don't know much about me at all."

Her words stung. Anlei had a habit of disappearing around mid-morning and sometimes wouldn't return until sundown. Thinking back, this had started in the autumn.

"There's a repair shop near Dashilan market," she explained. "The rickshaws and street vendors go there for maintenance. Mostly they sell spare parts."

An odd feeling grew in the pit of his stomach. "Anlei, do you need money?"

Her face flushed pink as she looked away. "Let's not talk about this." Then, in the next breath. "Everybody needs money, Zhi-fu."

She told him this as if he was a simpleton, but maybe in this matter he was. Anlei lived in a storage closet and burned each candle down to the stub, yet he assumed her funds, humble as they were, came from some distant benefactor. Just as his money came from his family.

He hadn't ever considered that Anlei was out earning money coin by coin while he played polo and drank.

"Well, have you eaten yet?" he asked.

It was a reasonable question and one he would have asked on any day, but today Anlei flashed him a narrowed look. "I'm not hungry."

Which he knew to be a lie. Anlei was always hungry, no matter what time of day it was — which was something he had also overlooked.

She walked slightly in front of him the entire way to the temple. He followed, reading the stiffness in her spine clearer than any book, while searching for conversation. He tried to convince himself that it was Kuo Lishen who had put her in a dark mood, but he knew it was him.

They reached the Temple of Knowledge located near the Imperial Academy. The temple wasn't dedicated to any deity, but rather to the great philosopher Kong Fuzi. They entered the main hall to burn joss sticks and pray to the soul of the venerable Master Kong for a favorable result on the exam.

A thick cloud of incense smoke filled the chamber. They were far from the first students to have visited that day.

When they returned to the courtyard, Anlei skirted around the towering cypress that grew near the steps. The tree was over five hundred years old with a thick trunk and branches that twisted every which way.

In a past dynasty, a palace official had walked by the tree, and one the branches had knocked off his headdress. The man proved to be treacherous and corrupt, giving rise to the superstition that the tree could detect evil. Since learning the story, Anlei always made a point to stay far away.

"We should give the cypress an offering," he suggested.

Anlei shook her head, looking at him as if he were mad.

"It's just a tree," he placed a hand against the rough wood. "And you have nothing to fear anymore. There are only four days left until the calling of the names."

Reluctantly, Anlei procured another stick of incense and lit it before kneeling down to bow once at the foot of the tree. She planted the incense beside the roots, leaving the stick to burn down to ash.

She touched a hand to her cap as she rose, but the cypress left her alone.

They ended up in a public park, eating steam buns from a street vendor while sitting on top of the moon bridge. By then, a quiet peace had settled between them. Zhi-fu would have to accept that as improvement.

"What are you going do after the exam?" he asked.

Anlei was looking into the water with her neck curved gracefully downward like a swan's. "I'm going to pass with impressively high marks and become Chief Mathematician." She lifted her head to reveal a grin, but it was forced.

She had told him before that she intended to remain in Peking, but that was before he knew her secret.

"If you stay here, you'd have to maintain your disguise."

"That's my intention."

"You'd continue to live life as a man…forever?"

She didn't even blink.

"Oh, come now," she chided when he regarded her in disbelief. "There's no need for that fatalistic look. What else am I going to do?"

"Doesn't your family expect you to…I don't know…"

"Get married?" she finished for him. "I was never going to get married anyway, Zhi-fu. Why do you think I was left with these big feet?" she wriggled her foot at him as it dangled over the side the bridge. "These are feet resigned to a life of drudgery. Why shouldn't I want use my mind instead?"

"But to pretend for the rest of your life."

"I had you fooled, didn't I?"

But she hadn't. Not for long.

"Are you afraid I'll drag you down too?" she asked growing serious. "Is that what that turtle's egg Kuo Lishen was talking about?"

He straightened abruptly. "No. It's not that at all."

You aren't unremarkable, he wanted to shout at her. The more time he spent with Anlei, the more convinced he became that her secret would be discovered sooner or later.

"Good," she replied finally.

She broke off a piece of the steamed bun, but instead of throwing it down to the carp circling below, she threw it at him. It bounced off his chest. He took it as a peace offering.

He watched as Anlei leaned back, hands planted onto the stone bridge, with her face upturned. It felt like the two of them were balanced on the center of the earth atop this arch.

The silence was the lie, she'd told him. If the girl she'd been before was hiding Anlei's true self, then Shi Han had only partially revealed it. It was the Anlei he'd met after her disguise had failed that he'd fallen for. A person somehow truer than yin or yang for having been both.

And he was still falling.

———

ANLEI WOKE at the sound of the market gong from Zhi-fu's bed. He was asleep on his stomach. Snoring. It was precious knowledge — knowing that Jin Zhi-fu snored like that.

She rose to dress and prepare for the long walk to Dashilan Market, but paused as she picked up her shoes.

Zhi-fu had knelt on one knee before her last night to remove her slippers, with careful hands.

"I like your feet," he confessed, the candlelight dancing in his eyes.

"Big, ugly feet," she pronounced, her toes wriggling against his palms.

He planted one kiss and then another, gently on top of each foot before rising to take her into his arms. They sank into bed, side by side, and spent the next hours trying to fill in the gaps and empty spaces where they had fallen apart. It was only possible there, sheltered from the loud voices of the city, when they could speak in a way that words could not.

She reached out to place her hand on Zhi-fu's back, resting between his shoulder blades. He didn't stir and she rode the rise and fall of his breathing for just a moment before climbing from the bed. She made sure the door shut soundlessly behind her as she left.

Three more days.

The entire quarter was counting down.

Her feet were tired by the time she reached the repair shop. The back lot was already crowded with carts and sedans. Beside each vehicle stood an impatient owner, waiting to be tended to. The hutongs were so thick with street vendors that the mechanics and fix-it men of Hu's shop were always busy.

Though the term Fix-it "man" wasn't entirely correct. Mingming, the owner's daughter, came to give Anlei instructions. Unlike Anlei, Mingming's feet were bound into the traditional tiny "lotuses" which gave her a short, tottering gait. Somehow, the girl still managed to maneuver around the shop and take on repair jobs the same as the rest of them.

"There's a steam cart and a passenger carriage toward the back of the lot," Mingming directed.

Anlei nodded, wondering, as always, if Mingming ever suspected Anlei wasn't what she claimed. If she did, Mingming showed no signs of it. The young woman went to greet the owner of mechanical pedicab who had just arrived, moving slowly on her bound feet, but with purpose.

The steam cart was an easy fix. It looked like the external pipework had been damaged, perhaps in a collision. It wasn't uncommon for vehicles to get banged around in the bustle of Peking's streets.

The motorized carriage was a different matter entirely. Anlei stopped short as she approached. The vehicle was fashioned out of copper and steel polished to a gleam. There was not a single dent or visible trace of soot on it, not even around the exhaust pipes. Whoever the owner was kept it pristine, which immediately signaled wealth. Only vanity and the hands of servants could keep such a machine so clean.

She was itching to find out what sort of engine ran inside. Zhi-fu would have been seduced by it if he were there.

Anlei moved in closer to begin her inspection and found a book had been left in the passenger seat. She climbed up into the carriage to retrieve it and was surprised to find it was a manuscript on astronomy. She opened the book to a description of a lunar eclipse.

A shadow fell over her and Anlei looked up, startled. An elegantly-dressed lady stood before her holding a painted bamboo parasol. She looked to be forty years of age or so.

The woman smiled. "Young sir, I hear it told that you are a scholar."

"I am," Anlei replied warily.

The sound of the woman's voice sent a pang of longing through her. Anlei was reminded of her mother, though the woman looked nothing like her.

Anlei never did send any letters to her family. She'd occasionally write a letter whenever the feeling of loneliness became too much, but then she'd fold the letter and tuck it away. She hadn't communicated with her parents for over a year now and she might never again.

"You're Shi Han from Anhui province?" she continued.

Anlei froze, her hands going numb. That name wasn't known anywhere but at the Academy.

The woman looked delighted. "You're Wang Zhenyi's student, aren't you?"

Anlei's jaw dropped. "How could you possibly know?"

The lady glanced slyly at her, and then at the manuscript in her hands. How had Anlei not recognized it? It was her mistress' handwriting. Mistress Wang had sent her manuscripts to a friend when she knew she was dying...

"We've heard so much about you," the woman said, delighted. And then, "Are the exams as difficult as they say?"

They stayed there for the next hour, head-to-head beneath the parasol. The lady's name was Madame Yi. She was the wife of a minor official and wanted to know everything. What was the library like? Were the lectures at the Academy difficult to understand? How many questions were on the imperial exam?

Anlei learned from Madame Yi that there were enclaves of women dedicated to the study of poetry, astronomy, mathematics, history. They met in studios and private dens throughout Peking, exchanging books and ideas. The women corresponded with groups in other cities, forming an intricate tapestry throughout the empire.

They'd heard rumors of her before she ever arrived.

"May you meet with success in the exams," Madame Yi said finally as she rose to go. "We're all very excited for you."

Anlei nodded weakly, taking in a deep breath.

"What's the matter?"

She was too frightened to say it aloud. "I hope I don't disappoint you. All of you."

She had never met these women, but already felt she owed them something. There were so many people watching over her and wishing her well.

"You won't disappoint us," Madame Yi assured. "None of us can make this journey alone. Your mistress could only go so far, but she passed on what she knew to you. And you've carried us a few steps further. Can you imagine who will take us through the next steps?"

When Madame Yi bowed to take her leave, she placed a silver ingot into Anlei's palm, closing her fingers gently over it.

"For your time, young sir." Her eyes shined bright.

Madame Yi's servant appeared to wind the crank, and the

gunpowder engine started up with a soft whir like the beat of a hummingbird's wing. Madame Yi climbed into the carriage and placed Mistress Wang's manuscript carefully in her lap. She gave a final wave as the transport pulled away from the lot.

Anlei's chest swelled with emotion as she looked at the silver in her hand. It wasn't the amount of money that overwhelmed her.

Her secret had never been completely secret, and she'd never been completely alone.

Chapter 13

Two more days.

It was a familiar scene the next morning. Zhi-fu was sitting at his desk, focused on a thin book. Anlei was reclined on the kang bed, reading through a book of strange tales she'd found on Zhi-fu's shelf. Before the exam, she'd never allowed herself to read anything so fanciful.

"The young scholar actually falls in love with the fox spirit in this one," she marveled. She'd always seen *huli jing* depicted as dangerous creatures.

When there was no reply, Anlei looked up to see Zhi-fu absorbed with his reading.

"That must be an interesting book."

Still nothing. Zhi-fu's eyes remained fixed on the page. His left arm rested on the desk, cradling the side of the book and forming a barrier. What was it that had him so entranced? She knew every book on his shelf, but she didn't recognize this one.

He finally looked up, startled, when she approached.

"What is that?" she asked. "A new book on engines?"

"Just a book of poems." He stood so quickly that he nearly knocked the chair over. "I picked it up from a cart in Dashilan."

"Oh, let me see." Casually she reached for it, but Zhi-fu

swung it around to his other side. She made a face at him. "What's the matter? What's in that book?"

"Nothing—" He swung around again, presenting his back to her to block her view.

She tunneled under his arm to snatch the book, and Zhi-fu sank back against the wall, arms folded over his chest and head thrown back in resignation as she read the characters on the cover.

"Secrets of the Jade Chamber."

Zhi-fu squeezed his eyes shut.

"Jade stem…yang essence…is this a sex book?" she asked.

Her question was met with a long-suffering sigh.

She peered at the characters scribbled in the margins, her lips twitching as she forced back a giggle. "You're taking notes."

"*Brat.*" With a surprising amount of composure, Zhi-fu reached out a long arm to pluck the book out of her hands.

"Was that an entire page on feet?"

Zhi-fu looked like he was about to rush and tackle her, but they were interrupted by a knock on the door. With a look of relief, he went to answer it, pausing momentarily to toss the book aside. It landed squarely in the center of kang bed.

A messenger stood outside, searching for candidate Shi Han.

"That's me," Anlei acknowledged. Moments earlier, she had been laughing with Zhi-fu and feeling warm and secure. All of that drained away in an instant.

The messenger handed her a letter and promptly departed.

"What is it?" Zhi-fu's shadow fell over her.

She stared at the Academy seal, and her palms beginning to sweat. It couldn't be her examination score. The passing scores were to be announced tomorrow at the Meridian Gate.

She opened the letter, tearing through the fine paper in her nervousness.

"It's a summons," she said flatly, reading and re-reading. "To Master Sun's office."

"That's…unusual." Zhi-fu was trying to remain calm. She wasn't sure if it was for his sake or hers.

Her heart was racing. "I'm supposed to go now."

"Then you should go."

Of course, she had to go. Her stomach sank, as if filled with stones.

"Why would the headmaster want to see me?"

"I don't know." Zhi-fu regarded her with a grave expression. She knew he was thinking the same thing. The thing they didn't dare to say out loud.

Anlei slowly rose to her feet and started toward the gate before stopping herself. She'd forgotten her jacket.

"Do you want me to go with you?" Zhi-fu asked when she emerged from her room with her scholar's cap on and jacket properly buttoned.

"No." Her throat constricted. "Why would you?"

He held her gaze for a long time, his look unfathomable. She had to go before fear paralyzed her.

She didn't know what this was. It could be nothing. Well, it certainly wasn't nothing, but perhaps it wasn't anything bad.

She left through the gate with feet of lead, walking through the streets like an automaton. Everything looked strange. By the time she reached the Academy, her heart was pounding.

The main courtyard was empty. The term had ended and there were no lectures or classes. She wound her way past the halls to the headmaster's office.

It was the first time she'd been back to his office since her arrival at the Academy. Anlei was just as frightened as she'd been that first day. The summons was crumpled in her hand and she fought to keep her knees steady as she entered.

Headmaster Sun was seated at his desk just as he'd been for her first audience. A wild thought came to her that perhaps he was perpetually set there, a permanent fixture at the Academy like a temple statue.

He looked up at her approach. Her stomach dropped when

she saw the examination book set before him. It was closed and there was no way to be certain—but somehow, she knew it was hers.

"Candidate Shi Han."

"Headmaster," she dipped her head in deference.

"There is no need to prolong this. It has come to my attention that there are some irregularities with your situation."

She frowned. "Irregularities?"

His black gaze fixed on to her. "You know of what I speak."

Her heart thumped against her ribcage. *Admit nothing.* "With the utmost respect, I do not."

"The Academy cannot accept your examination," he proclaimed in clipped tones.

Half of her wanted to flee, the other half was desperate to sink into the ground and disappear. She had risked her future for the Academy and this examination. She couldn't run away now.

Swallowing past a lump in her throat, Anlei finally managed the question. "Why?"

"The details are not important—"

"I beg of you! The Academy is everything to me. More than food and water."

Master Sun regarded her for a long time, his expression unreadable. "This office received notice that the exam is invalid," he said finally. "For there is no young man named Shi Han enrolled at the Academy."

Her cheeks burned. It really was over. Her long journey, her disguise, the elaborate deception. She felt nothing, but emptiness.

"Who told you this?"

The headmaster's gaze darkened, the last light draining from his eyes. "You are also hereby dismissed from the Academy. It is best that this matter be handled quietly."

Which is why they'd waited until the exam was done. That way, she could just disappear and never return.

In his way, Master Sun was trying to be courteous. He didn't address her great deception directly. He continued to address her as a candidate, albeit a tarnished one. It was so they both could save face and leave without confrontation, but she was beyond saving face.

"Was my examination scored?" she asked.

"It would be pointless."

"Of course, Master Sun. Because what if I had passed?" she replied quietly. "What then?"

It was her last act of defiance. She took one final look at her exam booklet before leaving.

Anlei fought tears as she hurried back across the courtyard. All the mornings she'd run through the grounds, rushing to make it to the first lecture on time. All the times she and Zhi-fu had lingered by the steps to discuss the day's lesson.

This is the last time, her soul wept. When she saw Zhi-fu standing just beyond the gates, she nearly collapsed.

A sob built up in her throat.

"Anlei—" Zhi-fu took one look at her face and reached for her.

She shook her head furiously. Didn't he realize his reputation was still in danger?

"It's done," she muttered, pushing past him. She needed to put distance between herself and the Academy.

"What happened?"

He followed behind her as she veered into an alleyway. Only then did she turn to face him.

"Someone reported me."

"Who?"

She shook her head. "Maybe it was Kuo Lishen. He was the only other person who knew, unless someone else suspected. Master Sun said he received a notice—"

Zhi-fu suddenly looked as if the breath had been knocked out of him, and she knew. Her entire being went cold.

"It was you."

She could see the answer in his eyes.

"I took the letter back before anyone saw it," he said in disbelief. "I tore it up—"

Her eyes flooded until Zhi-fu faded into nothing but a blur. She shoved past him. When Zhi-fu called after her, she broke into a run, as far away from the Academy as she could go. Far away from this place of broken dreams.

———

ZHI-FU SEARCHED the streets for hours. He even ventured out to Dashilan and searched for repair shops in the area hoping to find Anlei. He wandered from corner to corner, but she had disappeared. The entire time, he was wracked with guilt. He retraced his steps from that fateful day over and over. He'd handed his report to the clerk, then hurried back to retrieve it.

In that short amount of time, just a short walk away, had the clerk opened his note? Of course, he had. The Academy knew who he was, recognized that he came from a distinguished family. If he was someone else, they wouldn't have paid any attention to him at all.

Anlei wouldn't have been expelled.

The worst of it was — as bad as he felt for Anlei — he was also worried about his future. The Academy knew he was aware of Anlei's secret. They could very well call his conduct into question and expel him as well.

When Zhi-fu finally gave up and returned to his quarters, the sun had gone down. Anlei's door was shut and there was no sign of her. He waited in his room, listening to the sounds in the courtyard. It was a long time before he heard footsteps outside and the opening and closing of the door to the room beside his.

He hurried to the hole in the wall that connected their two rooms.

"Anlei," he began. What could he possibly say? "I was angry.

I felt betrayed—I know why you had to do it now, but back then I was trying to set things right."

Silence.

"For me," he amended, feeling sick to his stomach. "I was trying to set things right for me. I thought I was being honorable and honest, but it was to protect myself. But I was wrong. You were the one who needed protection."

Still silence.

"Anlei, can you hear me?" He placed his fingertips against the wood, desperately imagining Anlei on the other side. Hoping she still cared about what he had to say.

"It was only for a moment." That didn't matter to her. "I tried to take the report back." But failed.

"We're in this together, Anlei," he said to the wall, to the darkness beyond. "I'll try to set things right, I promise."

He left the lantern burning that night so she could see the light through the wall and know that it was for her. Though it was hardly enough to show her what he felt for her. Merely a pinpoint of light in the darkness.

THE NEXT MORNING, he saw Anlei at her door as she was leaving. He'd timed his exit and he imagined from the cold look in her eyes that she knew that had been his plan.

"There was no mention of you. Your standing isn't in danger," she assured him. "We aren't in this together."

He started to protest, but Anlei cut him off, her tone knife-sharp. "Don't worry. There is nothing for you to set right."

Chapter 14

The final days moved like a slow drip of water. Or the slow seep of a wound that refused to heal. Even though she had nothing left to hope for, she waited with the rest of the scholars in the quarter. She had earned it after all, this waiting.

She remained in her room with the door firmly shut the morning the candidates went to assemble for the reading of the names. Their voices outside were tense, hopeful. She waited until the footsteps died away before stepping out.

And found Zhi-fu standing before her door, waiting for her.

Her breath caught as she pulled to a halt. He wasn't more than two steps away, closer than she could bear. Why did the sight of him cause so much pain? She used to be happy for every glimpse of him.

"I've been trying to find you," he said.

And I've been avoiding you.

"I've found something," he began haltingly. "If you plan on remaining in Peking."

He waited for some acknowledgment from her, but she didn't have any to give. Her future, if she had a future, was uncertain.

"The Bureau of Engineering is about to start a major development. A project sponsored by the Ministry. I learned of it from Chief Engineer Liu. He was there that night when—"

She closed her eyes. "I remember the night, Zhi-fu."

The night when she'd lost herself trying to chase him.

"They're going to try to recreate it: an engine. An airship. The forges in the city will be fired up, the builder's workshops expanded. They'll need everyone: mechanics, metalworkers."

"Mathematicians," she finished for him.

He brightened. "I can get you in. There will be prototypes drawn up. Built. They'll have need of calculations and measurements. You'd be quite capable—"

The flat look in her eyes stopped him short.

"More than capable," he amended sheepishly. "The work would be for Shi Han, of course—

She didn't think it was possible for her stare to grow any colder.

He wanted so much for her to absolve him, perhaps even thank him for his kindness. Offer him some peace of mind. She could see it in his eyes. Zhi-fu may not have believed it seeing her coldness toward him, but she wanted something else beside this emptiness between them as well. Maybe as much as he did.

But even wanting it, she couldn't summon up anything more to give to him. Her disappointment was still too raw.

"There is another option," he went on in a quieter tone. "Maybe it's too far of a reach. Knowing you as I do, I know you'd never choose this path over the first one." His hands clenched and unclenched and he looked away to gather himself before meeting her eyes. "You can become my wife."

Everything was so easy for Zhi-fu, wasn't it? Offer this. Offer that. He'd always held the world in his hands, without even realizing it.

Zhi-fu looked genuinely distressed as he waited for her answer.

"So, I can continue pretending to be someone I'm not working for the Engineering Bureau," she recounted slowly. "Or I can do the exact same thing and pretend to be content to be your wife."

Zhi-fu flinched, but he took the blow standing.

"You won't be offended if I take some time to consider your proposals?"

He nodded before turning stiffly to leave the courtyard.

She gave him a generous lead before heading out in the same direction.

The streets were empty of any scholars. They were all assembled in by the Meridian Gate by now. It was the first time she had gone to the palace. She wasn't allowed inside, but she gathered with the crowds in the public plaza outside. The announcements from inside would be relayed by crier out to the populace.

Though her view was blocked by a wall, she could imagine the scene so clearly. Rows upon rows of scholars, standing at attention in dark silk jackets and woven caps. She'd worn her scholar's outfit as well. Anlei may have been expelled, but she'd earned her place here. She'd completed a term at the Academy and sat for the imperial exam.

Jin Zhi-fu would be standing at the front. Kuo Lishen as well. If she'd been there, would she have dared to stand there with them, those favored sons?

She stilled as the crier began relaying the names. They would only name those who had passed and would be rewarded a degree. With each name, her heart lurched. It would never be her. It would never be her.

She recognized the names of a few of her classmates. She heard Kuo Lishen's name announced in the early ranks, but she was waiting for one. The crier had moved onto the highest degrees.

"*Zhuangyuan* Jin Zhi-fu!" he announced jubilantly. The final name. The highest ranked.

She turned to walk away from the plaza, not wanting to be seen lurking when the scholars came out.

At least she could happy for Zhi-fu, she told herself.

This was never her dream to dream in the first place, she told herself. She was always reaching too high, too far.

She didn't know how much time had passed before she found herself at the top of the moon bridge where she'd sat just two days ago with Zhi-fu. She stared into the still, black water below and could just make out her reflection. The image of a darker self.

She had sworn that she would not fail. And she had failed.

Students were known to throw themselves to their deaths after failing to pass the exams. She could understand it — after so many sleepless nights, to have the bone-deep desire to succeed met with crushing disappointment. There were legacies to fulfill that would not be fulfilled. Family reputations to uphold.

She had no family. She'd left hers behind to follow this dream.

What would she do now?

Zhi-fu had dangled two options before her. Marriage or employment, offered as penance. She didn't need either bestowed upon her.

There was a time, could have it only been days ago, when they had been lovers, colleagues. Equals. She would rather starve in the alleys of Peking than accept Zhi-fu as a benefactor now.

In Zhi-fu's world there were those who deserved to rise and those who did not. That fate had been determined at birth.

Now Zhi-fu was first ranked, the top student, and she was expelled. Fate hadn't been wrong, had it?

A tear rolled down her cheek and splashed into the water. She wiped away the next one with a harsher motion than needed, as if she could scrub away the despair as well.

The rippling surface gradually quieted. In the dark,

distorted reflection, she could see other faces. Scholars who had fallen into despair after failing the exams. She'd put so much hope into the promise of the hard work and study at the Academy. It had been dangled before her like the moon.

If she could have done things differently, what could she have done? She reached into the pocket of her jacket. She still had the brass charm Zhi-fu had given her. She also had the silver ingot. It was enough money to take her home, back to the paper mill in disgrace.

But she had come too far to go back.

None of us make this journey alone, Madame Yi had told her.

The next girl. The next girl would make it one step further, but that didn't mean Anlei's journey was over.

She wiped her eyes with the back of her hand. Slowly this time, deliberately, she turned away from the water and descended from the moon bridge. Anlei had found the answer to her question.

If she could have done things differently, she wouldn't have held back. She wouldn't have dropped down to the middle of the class and pretended to be average. She would have continued to score at the very top, where she belonged.

PLEASE COME.

The characters were in Zhi-fu's hand, weighted slightly on the down stroke. Strange how she knew his brushwork almost as intimately as she knew his touch on her skin.

The invitation also listed the location of the banquet and a starting time with no end. A celebration to last until no one was left conscious.

She could have stayed in her dark room with its dirt floor and bamboo mat, angry and sullen, but she was hungry.

The best thing about offered wine is it usually came with offered food.

The banquet was at the same restaurant with the crispy roasted duck where Zhi-fu and Kuo Lishen had made their wager. All the lanterns had been lit, casting the building in a rosy glow. From the music and singing coming from the interior, it was clear the celebration was already underway.

Inside, she found Kuo Lishen immediately. He was at the center of a throng of admirers, candidates who had passed and most who had not passed. All were there to either rejoice or drink away their sorrows. It was a rite of passage. One that she'd earned as well.

She searched the crowd for Zhi-fu, but it was Kuo Lishen who called out to her

"Han!" he pushed through the crowd to come to her, which was a surprise. Kuo always wanted the rank and file to come to him, as subjects to a king.

"Congratulations, Kuo Lishen," she said, and she meant it.

"Ninety-fifth rank," he exalted, lifting his cup in triumph. She shook her head when he offered it to her. "You should be here," he added soberly.

It was the first time she'd ever seen any hint of kindness from him. "On to the next battle," she murmured.

He nodded, then sighed. "You are looking for Zhi-fu." Without waiting for an answer, he gestured towards the stairway. "He's moping upstairs. Wasting a perfectly good opportunity to bask in a victory."

She thanked Lishen and headed for the steps. They wound around a central pillar to lead up to the second floor.

Anlei had expected to see a raucous party like the one on the ground floor, but it was quiet upstairs. All of the tables were empty except for one where Zhi-fu sat looking out the window. He turned as she ascended the final step, his chest filling.

"We had a bet," he said in answer to her questioning glance around the empty floor.

"I remember. I was there. This is a poor showing for a victory banquet," she observed.

"I only sent one invitation."

He rose, waiting, but she didn't come any closer.

"I want books," she demanded. "Shelves and shelves of books."

His expression brightened. "A hundred," he promised.

"A thousand."

"Anything."

"And our children will be educated, sons and daughters," she insisted.

He moved toward her, but she held back.

"Promise," she insisted, holding his gaze.

"I swear."

And the next part was the most important part of all. "There is no such person as Shi Han from Anhui province. I'm going to go the Chief Engineer with no name but my own, and he'll take me as I am. Or not at all."

Zhi-fu stared at her, stunned. Her time at the Academy had made her fearless and she needed to know if Jin Zhi-fu was fearless as well.

He caught her in his arms. "There will be scandal," he said, quite serious. "But it won't be the first."

Anlei closed her eyes and sank into him, breathing in the warm scent of his skin. All of the anger had drained from her on the bridge. Mistress Wang had never gotten angry. It took too much energy. Instead she had read books, written them, and mapped out the stars. And she had found the next generation of students to teach.

"You know your family will object," she said.

"I'm first-ranked, I can be obnoxious about it. I learned that from Kuo Lishen." Zhi-fu pressed his lips against her hair. "Everything else, I learned from you."

It had only been days since they'd last been this close, but it felt like a lifetime.

"They've probably already matched you with some duke's daughter."

"I don't want some duke's daughter."

"What if she's particularly gifted with cubic equations—"

Suddenly she was crushed against him. "I couldn't have done this without you, Anlei."

They had come a long way side by side. So many books. All the nights. Nothing could take that from her.

Zhi-fu's hand remained wrapped around hers as he poured the wine. They drank in the moment together.

"Luck, influence, talent," he said, circling his arms around her once more. "I met all three on the road that first day when I met you."

They looked out the window upon the winding hutongs and courtyards of Peking. Glowing lanterns dotted the cityscape— each orb of light a promise and an opportunity. Anlei had stolen candlelight from so many tea stands until she had found a hole in the wall leading her to Zhi-fu.

Some commotion from downstairs interrupted their reverie. A moment later, the entourage came up the stairs with Kuo Lishen at the lead, loud and boisterous, and looking for more drink. Zhi-fu chased them immediately downstairs before returning to her, where they started mapping out their future.

It wasn't so very different than a series of equations. Ones that formed intricate patterns, yet somehow fit together. As lovers and numbers do.

TALES of the Gunpowder Chronicles features novellas from the steampunk world of the Gunpowder Chronicles series, introduced in Gunpowder Alchemy—Book 1. Sign-up for Jeannie Lin's mailing list to receive updates on new releases, appearances, and special giveaways.

Author's Note
LOVE IN THE TIME OF ENGINES

Here's a bit of trivia: Every book mentioned in *Love in the Time of Engines* is an actual book, including the manuscript describing lunar eclipses by Wang Zhenyi, the German book containing descriptions of an early steam engine car, and the sex manual Zhi-fu is caught reading.

Out of all the stories in the collection, *Love in the Time of Engines*, is the one that plays out more like a historical than hardcore steampunk. It serves as a prequel to lay out how Jin Soling's parents met as well as the "first contact", so to speak, that the Qing Empire had with a western-style steam engine.

This story takes place more than twenty years before the start of *Gunpowder Alchemy*. Thus the gadget-y gadgets weren't as developed as they are later in the series.

The hero and heroine are Jin Soling's parents, whose backstory is hinted at in *Gunpowder Alchemy*. This was a chance to give them their happiness.

It's a tribute to book nerdiness and historical science geekdom and right in line with my original vision for the *Gunpowder Chronicles*: a geektastic series where scientists and engineers are the heroes.

On that note, here's some fun historical and scientific facts:

Anlei's teacher is identified as Wang Zhenyi, a self-taught mathematician and astronomer. Wang Zhenyi did exist and was one of the most notable female scientists of the Qing Dynasty. I took the largest liberty with the timeline of Wang Zhenyi's life. The recorded date of her birth and death (1768-1797) would have made it impossible for her to be actually Anlei's teacher. So I shifted dates around.

Peking never "changed" its name to Beijing. They are the same name. In Chinese, the two characters for both Peking and Beijing are: 北京. The difference is due to two different systems of romanization. Peking is used in the Gunpowder Chronicles as a throwback to common nineteenth century romanization for Chinese place names.

The students do indeed feast on Peking roast duck on their night out. *Bianyifang*, the restaurant where they meet, is an actual restaurant that was founded in the 16th century and still serves duck to this day, nearly 600 years later. But beware! After *Bianyifang* was mentioned in a poem as being famous for duck, restaurants named *Bianyifang* sprang up all over Peking.

The hutongs (alleyways) mentioned in the story still exist in modern day Beijing.

Anhui Province was well-known for being the origin of many notable mathematicians, including the Mei clan (a whole family of math geniuses) which included Mei Wending. The mathematicians of Anhui were known for commenting on and incorporating Western math and science in their work.

Nan Huairen is also known by the Dutch name, Ferdinand Verbiest. He was appointed the Head of the Mathematical Board and Director of the Observatory by the Kanxi Emperor. He was one of several Westerners appointed to prominent positions within the imperial court.

Verbiest lays claim (unverified) to being the inventor of the first self-propelled automobile (1670). Diagrams indicate it ran on a steam engine.

Euclid's *Elements* was indeed translated into Chinese.

The Computational Canon for mathematics does exist and the Qing Dynasty was the first and only dynasty that offered specialized examinations in subjects such as mathematics and science.

The trope of a woman masquerading as a male scholar is a VERY popular one in Chinese culture (and very popular in Jeannie-land). So much so that this author is convinced that it must have happened.

An interesting note: The main story of Gunpowder Chronicles revolves around events of the Taiping Rebellion. When the Taiping Rebellion formed a splinter government within the Chinese empire, they enacted their own exam system and allowed women to take them. The top graduate was a woman and she went on to become an administrator in the Taiping government centered in Nanjing (aka Nanking).

A final footnote: mathematical and scientific duels and challenges were apparently a THING in both Western and Eastern academic culture. They were high stakes and dramatic, leading to glory for the victor and ruin for the loser. If I could have figured out a way to depict such a showdown dramatically on the page, I would have!

Alas, that is a story for another time.

For more information about the Gunpowder Chronicles, sign-up for Jeannie Lin's mailing list to receive updates on new releases, appearances, and special giveaways.

Also by Jeannie Lin

The Gunpowder Chronicles Series

Gunpowder Alchemy - Book 1

Clockwork Samurai - Book 2

Tales from the Gunpowder Chronicles

Steampunk short stories:

The Warlord and the Nightingale

The Lotus Palace Mystery series

The Lotus Palace - Book 1

The Jade Temptress - Book 2

The Liar's Dice - novella

The Princess Shanyin series

Historical erotica published under Liliana Lee

The Obsession

The Enslavement

The Fulfillment

The Complete Princess Shanyin Saga

From Gunpowder Alchemy - Book 1

PROLOGUE

Q ing Dynasty China, 1842 A.D.

The Emperor waited on his golden throne.

The Hall of Supreme Harmony was a place of grand ceremony and state occasion, too ostentatious for an audience of one, yet Chief Engineer Jin found himself alone before the Son of Heaven. In accordance, he had worn his best court attire: a silk robe embroidered with the bordered red banner of his ancestral line.

The Forbidden City was closed at night to all but the royal family and the Emperor's closest attendants: the palace eunuchs, the imperial guard, the harem of concubines and consorts. Despite the ordinance, Jin Zhi-fu had been summoned in this late hour to appear before his sovereign.

Jin lowered himself to his knees and placed both hands before him, pressing his forehead to the tiled floor once, then again. Three times three. Nine times for the proper kowtow. When he was done, he waited with his head lowered, staring at his hands laid flat on the ground before him. His left arm from the elbow down was fashioned from steel bones and copper muscle. Gold-tipped acupuncture needles connected the contraption to his nerve endings, allowing metal to take the place of what was once flesh. A small price to pay in service to the empire.

He was not allowed to rise or speak until addressed directly. The silence went on, and his heartbeat grew louder in the absence of sound, pounding with great force until the cadence of it filled his ears.

The Emperor's voice rang through the assembly hall like a clap of thunder. "Do we not outnumber the foreign ships?"

"Yes. Imperial Majesty."

"A hundred men for their ten."

"Yes."

Jin closed his eyes and breathed slowly. He counted each throb within his chest. Each one had become painfully significant. It was said the heart could continue pulsing for a full minute even once the soul had fled.

"Why was the Western fleet not destroyed?" the Emperor demanded.

The imperial commissioner had guaranteed success. Each of the senior ministers had assured the same, as well as the grand admirals of the imperial navy. Yet here he was, the humble chief engineer, to deliver failure.

"The cannons held Wusong for days." Jin tried to project as clearly as he could with his head bowed. "But the Western gunships—"

The Emperor cut him off with an impatient noise. He didn't want an explanation, and from that moment, Jin knew he had only been summoned for one reason.

The Ministry of Engineering had heard rumors of powerful weapons from the West. His men had worked to secure the ports. They had outfitted the forts with cannons and an arsenal of gunpowder and explosives. The nautical division had developed superior sails so the war junks could maneuver without equal through wind and water.

Yingguo, or England as the foreigners called their land, had countered with something his engineers had never seen before.

Iron-clad devil ships had roared into the harbor to tear through the war junks as if they were made of paper. The Middle Kingdom had been defeated by a fleet of steam and iron.

The Son of Heaven was perfect and infallible. If the empire had failed, then someone else, someone mortal and imperfect, was to blame.

The chief engineer could protest his innocence. He could blame the greater men who had come before him who had underestimated the English threat, but he, too, had remained silent for the sake of pride. A thousand years of pride. He had allowed the imperial navy to sail against the superior Western fleet to be destroyed and, even worse, humiliated.

"The failure lies with this unworthy servant," Jin conceded.

A sound of rage bubbled from the Emperor's throat. "Remove this man from the Emperor's sight."

The Forbidden Guard appeared from the recesses of the hall to take him. Jin's mechanical arm froze as their rough grip displaced the control needles. They dragged him from the hall with his feet scraping helplessly over the tile.

Perhaps his death would be enough. The engineers who served him could be spared. And his family—He prayed his family would remain unharmed. His wife had watched him with haunted eyes through their final embrace. Soling, his ten-year-old daughter, had curled her slender fingers tight over his as she'd walked with him to the front gate.

She was growing so tall now. He'd somehow missed that part, with the war with the foreigners taking up all his time. He would only be able to watch over her now in spirit.

Jin Zhi-fu emerged from the hall to the towering shapes of the Forbidden City and the stark night sky above. He was nothing more than dead weight now, a burden, a thing as the sentinels pulled him further into the hidden depths. His body grew slack and his knees refused to hold his weight.

He was afraid to die after all.

The war was already over, though no formal surrender had

yet been issued. Jin had known it since Canton fell a year earlier. More strongholds followed: Tinghai, Ningpo, Wusong, Shanghai. A slow death sentence of a thousand cuts, slice after relentless slice. It was ill omen to speak of failure, so no one had said anything. They had all of them remained so very quiet.

Chapter 1

Q ing Dynasty China, 1850 A.D.—*Eight years later*

I felt heat rising up the back of my neck as I walked past the center of the market area. Past all the places where any respectable young woman would be found. Everyone knew what lay at the end of the alleyway. We liked to think that because it was at the edge of our village, that dark little room was hidden. A secret thing. If no one spoke of it, it didn't exist.

By the same rule, everyone knew there was only one reason anyone went out there.

Though there were no eyes on me, I could feel them all the same. Linhua was small enough that there were no secrets. It was small enough that people didn't even pretend not to know.

The back door was buried deep at the end of the lane. As far as I knew, no one ever used the front entrance. I knocked twice and stepped back. After a pause, the door slid open, the corner grating against the dirt floor. The man who stood behind it gave me a wide grin. "Ah, Miss Jin Soling."

A sickly sweet smell wafted into the alleyway. Though faint, the pungent floral notes were unmistakable. Our village wasn't large enough to have a grain store, yet we had an opium den.

"Shang," I greeted.

Cui Shang was thin, long in the face. I knew he was ten years older than me and his father was a widower. Once, a generation before, their family had worked a plot of farmland, but now the Cui family had no other trade besides opium.

"Are you here to try a pipe with me, Miss Jin? It will take away all your burdens; remove that worry line always hanging over your brow. You might even be pretty without it."

I held out my palm to display the two copper coins, half of my earnings from Physician Lo that day.

"I have this week's payment."

"That's not enough," he said.

"This is how much it always costs."

Shang scratched the side of his neck with one bony finger. "Don't you know? The runners have raised their prices. News is there was a fire in the docks in Canton. Several large shipments of opium were destroyed."

"I haven't heard anything of it."

He shrugged. "It's the truth."

I kept my face a mask. He was trying to play me like an old fishwife in the market. "This is all you'll receive."

Shang tried to stare me down, his lip curling into a scowl. Straightening my shoulders, I stared right back even though my pulse was racing. I was taller than most of the other girls in the village, but at my full height he was still half a head taller. Though constant opium use left him gaunt in appearance, he was still stronger than me.

I had my needle gun in my pocket, a spring-loaded weapon I kept with me when I had to travel on the lonely roads that surrounded the village to tend to patients. If Shang tried anything, all it would take was a single dart in his neck or torso to immobilize him, but I couldn't draw with him so close.

With a shrug, he disappeared into the den while I shifted my weight from one foot to the other. It had been a long day. Old Lo had sent me far out to the edge of the rice fields for the monthly visit to farming huts. Now it was late and my family would be holding our evening meal to wait for me.

Ten minutes passed by and he had not yet reappeared. I loathed to go inside, but I was prepared to do so when he finally emerged.

"I had to give you a smaller amount," he announced with even less of an attempt at politeness than before. "You can't expect any special treatment, acting so superior all the time."

Without argument, I held out the cash, which he took after thrusting the packet into my hand. Inside was a pressed cake of black opium. I slipped it into the pocket of my jacket and didn't bother to say farewell before turning to leave.

"*Manchu witch.*"

He spat on the ground behind me. My face burned at the insult, but I didn't stop. I hated knowing that in a week I would be back.

By the time I reached our home, I was still livid. We lived in a small village, and the walk wasn't nearly long or strenuous enough for me to forget.

My family lived in three small rooms surrounding a patch of dirt where we attempted to grow vegetables. I hesitated to call it a courtyard. The moment I set foot inside the front gate, the scent of cooking rice floated from the kitchen. I also heard a wail coming from one of the sleeping chambers: "*Soling, Soling, Soling…*"

Each call of my name pierced into me a little bit less. I went to the kitchen even though the cries grew louder.

Our maidservant Nan was at the stove, stirring a pot of congee for our evening meal. My eight-year-old brother Tian had his head bent over a notebook at the table. The flicker of an oil lamp illuminated the pages.

"I am sorry I'm late," I told them.

"No, no need to be sorry," Nan soothed. "Everything is still hot. Come sit."

The old maidservant had been with us in Peking. She'd

stayed with Mother and me when we'd relocated to Hunan province. There had been other servants with us then, though they had gradually drifted away. We could no longer support other servants besides Nan. By now, she was family.

Tian closed his notebook and laid it onto his lap as soon as I sat down. The third chair remained empty.

"How was school today?"

"Good," Tian mumbled.

From the sleeping chamber came another cry. "Soling!"

I pushed on. "What did you study?"

"We practiced calligraphy."

Tian played along admirably, though he kept his head down as he spoke. Nan ladled rice porridge into two clay bowls and set them before us. I picked up my spoon but set it down when I heard my name again, this time accompanied by a low moan.

"Go to her," I said quietly.

Nan nodded and I slipped the cake of opium from my pocket into her hands before she left.

THE ADVENTURE BEGINS in *Gunpowder Alchemy* - Book 1 of the *Gunpowder Chronicles*

CPSIA information can be obtained
at www.ICGtesting.com
Printed in the USA
LVHW080022090422
715627LV00011B/864

9 780990 946267